THE SEESAW SYNDROME

THE SEESAW SYNDROME

Michael Madden

DURBAN HOUSE PUBLISHING

Library of Congress Cataloging-in-Publication Data
Madden, Michael, 1949-

The Seesaw Syndrome/ by Michael Madden

Library of Congress Catalog Card Number: 2003105049

p. cm.

ISBN 1-930754-42-6

First Edition

10 9 8 7 6 5 4 3 2 1

Visit our Web site at
http://www.durbanhouse.com

ACKNOWLEDGEMENTS

I would like to thank John Lewis, Publisher at Durban House, for both his unmitigated enthusiasm and his advocacy. I am also indebted to my editor, Bob Middlemiss, for his insight, hard work and editorial suggestions. Similarly, I benefited from the discerning eyes of Jerry Gross, Peter Murphy, M.D. and the attention to detail demonstrated by my copy editor, Jennifer Adkins. And I also would like to thank my former literary agent, Tony Seidl, for his efforts on my behalf.

In addition, I'd be remiss if I didn't express my gratitude to the many people who shared their knowledge and wisdom in teaching me the art and science of surgery. I would particularly like to credit my parents: My father, John L. Madden, M.D., combined exceptional technical skill and wisdom with genuine empathy for his patients. He was the compleat surgeon, an individual who had the courage of his convictions to challenge medical dicta and by doing so, improved the care of countless people. And my mother, Bertha Madden, who encouraged us all and provided the nurturing environment that allowed my father, my siblings and myself to pursue our individual goals.

Secondly, Frank Miller, M.D., Emeritus Professor of Pathology at

George Washington University School of Medicine and Health Sciences, who imbued in me an appreciation for the role of literature in the practice of medicine.

And G. Tom Shires, M.D., the former Chairman of Surgery at The New York Hospital-Cornell Medical Center, who along with his surgical faculty exemplifed the ideals of the medical profession on a daily basis.

I am grateful to my colleagues, surgical residents, members of both the burn and trauma teams, and the many other dedicated health care professionals who I have had the privilege of knowing. And I thank my patients for the honor of caring for them and for providing me with insight into the human condition.

I would like to acknowledge the friendship and support I have received from my firefighter friends particularly Jimmy Curran, his wife Marilyn and the other members of the New York Firefighters Burn Center Foundation. Their volunteer efforts have benefited thousands of New Yorkers afflicted with burn injury.

Finally, I want to express my gratitude for the reassurance given to me by my stepson, Jon, a talented journalist whose writing skills far exceed mine. And most of all I am grateful to my wife, Susan, my first editor, who married a surgeon but ended up with a struggling writer. Her love and encouragement allowed me to pursue my neglected passion for writing and fulfill a delayed aspiration.

For Susan
and
In memory of my parents

If good men don't speak up, evil will triumph.

— *Edmund Burke*

Everyone dies alone, but some die more alone than others. Dr. Nikki Moriarty nodded to the nurse, signaling it was time to end Mrs. Lamb's suffering. The patient had no friends or family, no one to speak for her, no one who could have cautioned her about the side effects of the experimental drug. Now she was about to die, and her living will was her only voice. It directed Nikki, the health care proxy, to stop her treatment. But terminating life went against her training. The process reminded her of the sacrifice of a laboratory mouse at the end of a study—the patient's response to the drug had been documented, and now it was time for her to die, but, of course, with dignity.

After Nikki gave the order to discontinue treatment, the nurse removed the ventilator, leaving the unattached endotracheal tube protruding from the patient's mouth.

"I'm just going to suction you," the nurse said. She aspirated mucus from Mrs. Lamb's trachea, which slurped its way up the catheter into a plastic cannister. The patient's body bucked in response to the stimulation.

The nurse removed the tape that harnessed the endotracheal tube to the patient's cheeks. Mrs. Lamb's lips, distorted from the pull of the adhesive, reverted to their customary position. Next, she deflated the balloon that anchored the tube to the wall of the trachea by withdrawing five cc's of air from its port with a syringe, and the patient hiccupped as the foot-long tube was withdrawn from her throat. A feeding tube, her only source of nutrition, had been threaded into her stomach through her right nostril, and was secured to the bridge of her nose with paper tape which the nurse peeled off, leaving a sticky residue. She forewarned the patient that she was going to remove the feeding tube. The tip of the tube, coated with yellowish bile, flailed as it exited her nostril. It trailed its contents and an acrid odor onto the patient's bedding. The nurse smiled in acknowledgement of the spillage and squelched the wiggling tube in an emesis basin. Mrs. Lamb's eyes remained closed and her face motionless, comatose from metastatic breast cancer.

A remnant of bile mixed with mucus tracked from Mrs. Lamb's right nostril onto her upper lip, and the nurse pinched it with a gauze pad. After her top sheet, stained with bodily fluids, had been changed, the parish priest was allowed to enter and annoint her with holy oil, rubbing it with his thumb on her forehead, lips and hands. He murmured prayers of absolution, while Nikki observed the prolonged interval between respirations, each breath shallower than the last. Even after the technical support had been discontinued, her body clung to life—a corporeal mutiny to maintain an existence she no longer wanted. Several minutes passed, and the beat of her heart slowed, mirroring the decreasing level of oxygen in her blood. When her heart rate was less than forty beats per minute, the wave form on the monitor became undisciplined, flickering till all undulations ceased. Mrs. Lamb gave a last gasp—a sigh of relief—and was pronounced dead.

The nurse removed the patient's urethral and intravenous catheters, and unsnapped the cardiac leads from her chest. She then folded Mrs. Lamb's wrists over her abdomen, securing them together with a roll of gauze. The top sheet was pulled over her head, and Nikki left the room, disappointed that Mrs. Lamb's last wish had been only partially honored. She had died unattached to life support in acccordance with her living will, but she never should have been intubated. If the on-duty resident had only listened to the nurse, she would have died in peace three days ago. He claimed that he wasn't informed on sign out rounds that the patient was not to be resuscitated, and he didn't want to be responsible for a patient dying prematurely—especially a study patient of Dr. Cogswell.

The absence of life support machinery was supposed to assure death with dignity, but Nikki didn't think that Mrs. Lamb's death was dignified. Dying alone in an institution, without the presence of family or friends, was not what she would wish for herself. An organic death was a better description—no antibiotics, no growth factors, no industrial strength cardiac drugs to squeeze her heart and forestall death—but not a dignified one.

The funeral service was held two days later, and Nikki decided to attend, not only out of obligation as the health care proxy, but also because she wanted to pay her respects. She glanced at her watch and realized that she had ten minutes to find a taxi and get to the church for the 9:00 a.m. service. After stepping off the curb on First Avenue, she scanned southward, looking to cull a cab from the approaching herd of vehicles. A palpable haze mugged her face, and droplets of sweat beaded down her cheek. She intercepted them with a flick of her index finger. A taxi blinked its high beams, acknowledging her inadvertent hand signal, and swerved across three lanes of traffic, braking with a screech at her feet. She squirmed into the back, wedging her legs into the space compressed by the driver's seat and its attached plastic bulkhead. A series of perforations breeched the divider. She leaned towards the openings, declaring her destination:

"Eighty-ninth between Park and Madison."

The stench of body odor, unabated by the scented amulet dangling from the rearview miror, forced her towards the open window. The cab lurched forward, creating a breeze, a desert wind, as refreshing as if her ex-boyfriend was blowing in her face. While she nuzzled the shoulder of her blouse to determine if the fug had permeated her clothes, the driver observed her through the rearview mirror, awaiting an opportune time to talk.

"You a nurse?"

"No, a surgical resident."

"Not a nurse, a surgeon?"

"That's right, a surgeon."

"A woman surgeon." He shook his head.

"It happens," Nikki said, and flipped him the finger behind his back.

The cab arrived in front of the church just as the meter clicked $3.20. She stuffed $4.00 into the money exchange drawer and looked over her shoulder for oncoming cars before opening the door.

"Get out at the curb, Doc."

She extricated her legs and wriggled towards the opposite side, exiting the taxi as directed, and walked up the stairs to the open doors. Even though she had not been inside a church in over twelve years, she still considered herself Roman Catholic—a "cafeteria catholic," the pope's eponym for followers who picked and chose what they wanted to believe. The service was about to begin, and she walked down the center aisle, the leather heels of her flats clacking on the stone floor, competing with the pattering of Pater Nosters. After a perfunctory nod towards the altar, she entered a pew north of a claque of anonymous mourners who were fingering the beads of their rosaries. The priest assessed the crowd through the sacristy window as a woman walked into the confessional box, carefully closing the curtain behind her.

Satisfied with the turnout, the priest joined the congregation and was led by his acolyte to the altar. He opened the Biblical text and inserted colored ribbons to mark the passages that were to be read, and then the altar boy handed him a bucket of holy water. The priest retrieved a perforated instrument, the aspergillum, from the water, and spritzed the coffin. A front row parishioner, caught in the crossfire, wiped blessed fluid from his face.

The woman peeled back the curtain of the confessional and looked both ways, checking to see if she had been overheard, and then exited and knelt down in a pew to say her assigned prayers. Nikki remembered her last confession. It was over fifteen years ago, and it occurred after her father showed up at their house, uninvited and drunk, with his new girlfriend. Nikki was in the bathroom, and she heard her mother screaming, begging them to stop. When she came out, he was spinning her mother in her wheelchair while his girlfriend laughed. It was bad enough that he had left her mother after she was diagnosed with multiple sclerosis, but now he had returned just to torment her. Nikki opened the closet door, grabbed one of his old putters, and clunked him on the head. His girlfriend screamed as he fell to his knees, caressing his wound with both palms. They both stumbled out of the house, and she didn't talk to her father again until right before her mother died six years later. It was her last confession, and it was an invalid one because she wasn't sorry for what she had done. Her only regret was that she had used a putter—a pitching wedge would have been more effective.

When she looked up at the altar, the acolyte was taking back the bucket of holy water from the priest, and was handing him the thurible that contained smoking incense which the priest dangled, swinging it like a pendulum. He grasped the midpoint of its suspended chain with his right hand, doubling it over, and swung the censer towards the congregation as it clinked against itself, exhaling puffs of incense through the escape holes. The white smoke dissipated as it wisped towards the vaulted ceiling, and Nikki, encouraged by the fragrance of the incense and the sibilant murmurs of the pious, tried to reconcile Mrs. Lamb's death.

Statistically, she still should be alive. Her breast cancer, a carcinoma-in-situ, had a favorable prognosis, yet she developed metastatic disease, dying only six months after it had been excised. The pundits designated her a statistical aberration, someone who had been victimized by a biologically aggressive tumor. Maybe her surgeon was right when he said that she didn't read the textbook; people don't always respond according to the textbook description. Some patients had outcomes better than predicted and others worse, but there was another factor to consider—the research study. The protocol attached to the front of Mrs. Lamb's chart described a double blind study, evaluating the effect of an experimental drug on cancer patients. The drug was called BrobaGen, and it contained growth hormone, steroids and other substances designed to reverse cachexia—the weight loss associated with cancer—that weakened patients and precluded aggressive therapy. But Nikki was vexed by another possibility: if the drug was able to increase muscle cell growth, then by the same mechanism it could also increase malignant cell growth, which would explain the rapid spread of her cancer.

The priest interjected, "Lord have mercy, Christ have mercy, Lord have mercy."

Nikki echoed, "Lord have mercy." She reminded herself not to jeopardize her career by making premature judgements. Half the patients in the study had received a placebo, and it was not known whether Mrs. Lamb had been given the pharmacologically active drug.

Now was not the time to speculate. She was about to begin a coveted two year rotation in Dr. Stuart Cogswell's lab, the same lab that had sponsored the BrobaGen study. If she had a productive two years, her academic career would be guaranteed, and her dream achieved— an appointment on the oncology staff at Manhattan University Medical Center. If she alienated Cogswell and his team, she would never be able to get a job in cancer surgery, particularly not in New York. Her $200,000 debt accumulated during college and medical school also had to be considered, and she wasn't going to depend on anyone else to resolve her finances.

The priest said, "Now let us give each other the sign of peace."

A woman two pews away made eye contact, and mouthed, "Peace," and Nikki nodded in response, hoping that Mrs. Lamb had finally found peace.

Six professional pallbearers, appropriately dyspeptic, were spurred on by the snap of their leader's hand-held clicker and trudged out of the first pew, lining up on either side of the casket. A second snap of the clicker followed, and they looked to Nikki like actors who had forgotten their lines. The lead pallbearer demonstrated the meaning of the snap by slowly genuflecting, allowing time for the others to catch up. They joined in sequentially, each staying in the kneeling position until all had descended to the same level. They rose as they had knelt, one after the other, and pivoted so that their backs were to the altar and they faced the exit. The congregation watched them wheel the casket towards the exit. When they arrived at the vestibule, they directed the casket down the handicap ramp to the awaiting hearse. After two false starts they managed to coordinate the lifting of the casket and guide it into the back.

Nikki turned and walked back to her apartment. She looked forward to beginning her lab rotation, excused from night call for the next two years, and the opportunity to make a name for herself. Now was the time to concentrate on her own career, and contribute to the treatment of patients with cancer. The BrobaGen study was nearly completed, and she would know soon enough whether her concerns about the drug were justified. But it bothered her that she *was* concerned. After all, Mrs. Lamb was dead, and nothing could bring her back.

Dr. Cogswell's research conference was held on Mondays at 8:00 A.M., and everyone who worked in his lab was expected to attend. Nikki hurried to get some breakfast from the coffee wagon on her corner just two blocks from the hospital.

"Next," the vendor said.

"A glazed doughnut."

He reached towards the pile, and a fly was having its way with the top doughnut. Nikki tapped on the plastic window and pointed. "Not the top one, the second one."

He grabbed the requested doughnut. "You're late today."

"New schedule."

He drew her coffee into a sugared cup, simultaneously pouring the milk, and when the fluid was flush with the brim, snapped on the lid, flicked open a brown paper bag, and screwed the coffee cup inside. A napkin was placed on top of the cover, absorbing the overflow from the perforated lid, rendering it useless for its intended purpose. The doughnut was then placed over the soggy napkin, and he handed her the bag. The napkin pile was purposely placed out of reach of customers to minimize overhead costs, forcing her to make her daily request.

"Another napkin."

He produced the napkin from under the counter, and she put it with her doughnut, rolling the top of her bag closed as she walked to a nearby newsstand. She placed the exact change on the counter, retrieved a *New York Times*—the second from the top—folded it under her arm, and walked to the entranceway of the hospital. A crowd of employees clogged the revolving door, and one by one they were collated onto the other side. A security guard was scrutinizing the I.D. of a staff pediatrician, and Nikki scuttled into a waiting elevator. After repeated stabbings of the seventh floor button, the doors closed, but the elevator didn't move. She pressed the alarm button, but it was mute, and when the doors reopened, she jumped out before she became trapped again. When she arrived in the conference room Dr. Cogswell was showing slides and addressing a group of ten people that included a research nurse, nurse practitioner, two Ph.D's, a drug company representative, one medical student, and a few lab technicians. The room lights were left on to discourage dozing. She took the remaining available seat located near the speaker. When she stooped to avoid the projector's light, three fourths of her head silhouetted onto the screen. Cogswell sighed. His gray-tinged hair, thicker on the sides than the top, framed a face that appeared glazed like her doughnut, as if someone had buffed his shoes, and continued vertically, snapping the cloth against his forehead. Round, tortoise-rim glasses with stems attached at the midpoint gave him an owlish, but trendy appearance. His head, neck and shoulders moved as a petrified unit, burdened by the struggle to unlock the cure for cancer encrypted in the catacombs of his mind. She reached into the bag, grabbed the doughnut, and shoved it in her mouth, freeing her hand to root out the coffee cup. The bag crinkled, causing heads to turn and Dr. Cogswell to blink, forcing her to suspend her search. When he resumed the lecture she removed the cup, placed it on the table, and took a bite out of her doughnut. Cogswell adjusted his bow tie, making sure that each wing was at 180 degrees before addressing the new addition to the team.

"Now that Dr. Moriarty is settled and enjoying her breakfast, maybe she can tell us the translation of the word 'placebo.'"

The definition of a placebo was common knowledge, but Cogswell wanted the exact translation, confident that her education precluded exposure to the classical languages. He raised his head, flaunting his bow tie as if it had been awarded to him for distinguished service to the scientific community.

"It's Latin for 'I shall please.'"

Cogswell looked to her like a schoolyard bully whose victim had unexpectedly fought back, but he recovered quickly.

"That's correct. A 'placebo effect' is a real entity, occurring in up to 60% of patients, and for that reason we need to be rigorously objective in evaluating our study drugs, which is why we only perform double blind studies."

Cogswell acknowledged a raised hand.

"Yes, Dr. Green."

"Question…"

Nikki was befuddled by people who began their question by saying "question"; it seemed redundant.

"…The last patient that died—Lamb, I believe—what was the official cause of death?"

"Pneumonia, with underlying metastatic breast cancer," Cogswell answered.

"I ask the question because I understand she had a positive weight gain with improved immunological parameters suggesting she received BrobaGen. Was there any sign of tumor regression on her chest x-ray or CAT scan?"

"We were encouraged by one of the chest x-rays prior to her death—it appeared there was some clearing of tumor. Isn't that right, Jinny?"

The research nurse responded on cue. "That's correct."

"So the drug was a success, but the patient died," Nikki said.

Dr. Green chuckled while stroking his beard, the only source of hair he had above his neck, and Dr. Cogswell bristled. Nikki realized her mistake, and redirected the conversation.

"Seriously though, I operated on Mrs. Lamb with Dr. McConnachie a year and a half ago for gallstone ileus, and I was surprised to hear that she developed such a rapidly spreading cancer, especially considering her breast biopsy only six months ago showed carcinoma-in-situ."

Cogswell fingered his bowtie. "We were all surprised, my dear, but cancer is a bad disease, often unpredictable."

Nikki hesitated to speak, but she was spurred on by his condescension.

"Any chance the BrobaGen was responsible?"

The medical student nodded in agreement, and the research nurse shifted in her seat, unaccustomed to a resident challenging her boss. Cogswell's response was stalled by a wave of red that seeped from his neck and ascended over his forehead ebbing into his hairline. His complexion returned to its original hue, and by then Nikki knew she had gone too far. The study was nearly completed, and now was not the time to question the malignant potential of BrobaGen.

"Obviously, Dr. Moriarty, that was a concern to all of us. But we failed to see a trend in our preliminary studies. I suspect that either the pathologist made a mistake calling this carcinoma-in-situ, or that the margins of excision were inadequate. I'm going to personally review the histology with Dr. Murphy, our breast expert."

Murphy, a pathologist who had written extensively about breast cancer, had lectured Nikki's class on the subject in medical school. She recalled his published study of breast cancer patients who initially were given good prognoses after removal of their tumor, but inexplicably died of their disease. He discovered that the excised margins of the tumors had been inadequate, and the cancer cells left behind caused premature death.

She regretted that she had spoken—there was nothing to gain by it. It was only her first day, and she was alienating the people she wanted to impress. His explanation was reasonable. And besides, it was possible she didn't even receive the drug. Even if she did, a much larger sampling of patients would have to be studied in order to establish a trend and prove the drug was deleterious, a process that would take years. It was unlike her to voice her opinion without having the facts to support her contention, but Cogswell's hubris annoyed her.

Jinny stood up in support of her boss. "Nikki may not be aware that growth hormone—one of the major components of BrobaGen— is currently being prescribed to reverse the effects of aging, and there haven't been any reports of unexpected tumor growth."

Nikki was familiar with the cadre of physicians who contended that aging was not a natural and inevitable process, but instead a reversible disease. Human growth hormone had become one of the main components of their therapy. She was skeptical of their claims, because the oral form of the drug was ineffective. Their patients were also begun on exercise programs, nutritional supplements, and strict diets. And the resultant muscle gain, fat loss and improved stamina that were attributed to the hormone were actually the result of the lifestyle change. The injectable growth hormone was a different entity. It was effective at increasing muscle mass and decreasing fat, but its influence on tumor growth in humans had not been adequately studied.

"The Medical Examiner signed her death out as pulmonary sepsis secondary to metastatic disease. I see no reason to break the code and disrupt the study. Do you agree, Dr. Moriarty?"

Nikki knew that this was another test question to see if she was a team player—one of Cogswell's toadeaters. Even if Mrs. Lamb had received the drug and not the placebo, it wouldn't prove that BrobaGen had caused her metastases, and stopping the study now would be costly. She had to pick her fights, and this was one she couldn't win. They would know the answer soon enough.

"I agree," she said.

Cogswell's annoyance subsided. He told the group he had submitted an abstract of the first five BrobaGen patients to the International Society of Oncology, and it had been accepted. He also said Biosense, the company that produced the drug, had offered to send the whole team to the upcoming meeting in Hawaii. The announcement was met with applause, and the team turned towards George Lally, the clinical coordinator from Biosense, and thanked him for his company's support. George raised his right hand in a papal gesture of acknowledgement. Dr. Cogswell closed the meeting.

Everyone stood up and filed out of the room, scurrying to have a word with Cogswell as he headed to his office. Cynthia Gornley, the nurse practitioner, inserted a lollipop into her mouth and walked over to Nikki, who was scanning the *New York Times*.

"Nikki," Cynthia said, removing her lollipop from her mouth and gesturing with it to emphasize her words, "what are you trying to do, get fired your first day?"

Nikki looked up at Cynthia's moon face accented with the lollipop stick.

"Just sharing my concerns about BrobaGen," Nikki said.

"Better if you kept those concerns to yourself. Cogswell's got a lot riding on that drug."

"I hear you."

There were two people she needed on her side if she was going to succeed in the lab, and Cynthia was one of them. Cynthia was Cogswell's lieutenant, hired to ride herd over the nursing staff, making sure they pushed the patients through the system in order to shorten hospital stay and maximize reimbursement. They had met last year during her internship when she had rotated on the oncology service. Cynthia had prematurely discharged one of the patients from the ICU, a patient Nikki had insisted needed to remain, and during transport the patient had a cardiac arrest and almost died. Nikki complained that the patient's discharge was dictated by an algorithm rather than by his medical condition, but her complaint was dismissed. Dr. Cogswell had determined the discharge had been justified, and the cardiac arrest had been an unforeseeable complication.

The other key person was Jinny Shay, the research nurse, a fair skinned woman who blushed easily but somehow managed to confine the redness to her neck. Dr. Cogswell was dependent on her to recruit patients for his studies, and to make sure that data was compiled in a timely fashion. All other personnel were expendable, including Nikki.

"Nikki, welcome. Finally we have a resident we like," Jinny said, as she sat down next to her. "So what's the gossip?"

"Gimme a name," Nikki said.

Jinny winked at Cynthia. "How about...Moriarty."

"I don't think we have the time," Cynthia said.

"Very funny. You guys don't have anything on me."

Jinny disagreed. "No? Nikki Moriarty is a dedicated surgical resident, works hard and resents the lowered expectations of her male colleagues. She has proven that women are as committed and as able as men in the program. Currently she is dating an anesthesia resident—not seriously—and has joined Dr. Cogswell's lab for two years to increase her marketability and ultimately secure a position in oncology at the Manhattan University Medical Center."

"Not particularly insightful or revealing," Nikki said, returning to her *New York Times*.

"You want to hear the stuff we made up—it's much better," Cynthia said.

"I'd rather not. By the way, what's with Cogswell's bowtie?"

"What can I say, he's a dork. His wife dresses him funny," Cynthia said, and Jinny high-fived her.

"And what about his new eyeglasses? When I first saw those I almost fell off my chair," Jinny said.

"Every once in a while, someone needs to remind him that he comes from trailer trash," Cynthia said.

"I thought you guys liked him?"

"Who said we didn't like him—he leaves us alone. But he's still a dork," Cynthia said.

Nikki knew why he left them alone—they saved the hospital millions of dollars. The residents no longer decided when the patients were to be discharged from the ICU. Cogswell gave Cynthia the authority because the residents were indifferent to the financial importance of getting the patients through the system, whereas she made it her focus. Nikki acknowledged that putting Cynthia and Jinny in charge was financially beneficial for the hospital, but not always in the patient's best interest. Many of the nurses objected to the policy change.

"How's nursing morale?" Nikki asked.

"We get occasional morale problems, but they're short-lived," Cynthia explained. "I learned something from my mother, who was head of nursing in an Army hospital: 'Commence firing until morale improves.' It works."

"It's not so easy in civilian hospitals. There's a thing called the union," Nikki said.

"True, but we have our ways," Jinny said.

"The bedside nurses don't understand the bottom line," Cynthia said. "Hey, I've been there—I was a bedside nurse, but some of us grow and adapt to the times and others stay stuck. They got to get away from this Florence Nightingale shit. If we didn't make money for the hospital, they wouldn't be able to pay their salaries and the bleeding hearts would be out of a job. They should thank us."

It was obvious to Nikki that last year's complication didn't deter Cynthia from continuing her policy of early discharge, but there was no point in reminding her of her previous mistake.

"Gradually they'll come around. It's get on the bus or get run over by it," Jinny said.

Nurses complained to their supervisors that they were prevented from caring for the patients, that instead they were overwhelmed with paperwork and collecting data for Cogswell's research studies. Their bedside responsibilities and hands-on care were assigned to the Licensed Practical Nurses. The Registered Nurses were told they were valued for their minds, and others could give massages and dole out medication. But it was obvious to Nikki the administration hadn't modified their role out of respect for their intelligence, but rather as a cost saving measure—salaries and benefits for RN's were significantly higher than those for LPN's.

"What's wrong with nurses doing bedside care and being a patient advocate?" Nikki asked.

"It's a waste of talent," Cynthia said. "I want them pushing the patients through the system. Our outcome study showed that since we've been in charge, the patients have had a shorter hospital stay. So you can whine about being a patient advocate, but we're getting the results."

"Yeah, but you have to admit, Cynthia, sometimes you get carried away."

"She's right," Jinny said. "I remember when one of the bedside nurses told you a patient was too sick to be discharged and you told her, 'Dead or alive, I want him out of here.'"

"But don't forget, when she complained to administration, they backed me up," Cynthia said, pointing to herself with her lollipop.

Jinny suddenly became business-like. "Seriously, Nikki, you're coming at a really good time. The studies are rocking and rolling and the lab is well-financed. You'll get a lot done."

"That's why I'm here."

If she had alienated Cogswell during the conference, she knew he would become supportive once she produced abstracts and wrote papers with his name attached. Besides, Jinny and Cynthia were on her side. They would help reverse his opinion. Everybody was going to get along just fine. She could feel it.

When Nikki awakened the following morning she felt refreshed from a second consecutive night of uninterrupted sleep—a perquisite of working in the research laboratory instead of on the surgical service. Her internship had accustomed her to fitful rest, the consequence of nocturnal queries from the staff, and the demands of patient care. Laboratory mice were less needy.

When she arrived in the lobby, she walked out the door and passed a slender figure miscast in camouflage Army fatigues and an Australian outback hat.

"Good morning, Nikki," the soldier said, forcing Nikki to turn around and face him.

"Dr. Cogswell? Is that you?"

He brushed the front of his shirt. "I'm not usually dressed in camouflage."

"You off to a reserve meeting?"

"No, just going hunting."

"It's early for deer season."

"Not deer hunting, something a little more exotic: African Springbok."

"Springbok? Around here?"

"There're a few living on a ranch upstate, an exotic animal ranch.

Here, take a look." He handed her a promotional pamphlet.

The pamphlet was fraught with color photographs of antelope, big horned sheep, Russian boar and American buffalo confined to a 350 acre property enclosed by a chain link fence. The land had previously been used to raise deer until a more profitable business plan emerged: the creation of a club for hunters bored by the lack of challenge posed by domestic animals. Members and their guests were invited to test their skills, the price varying according to their chosen prey. The privilege of killing a Russian boar cost $5000, an African Springbok $10,000, and it included the use of a guide, a four wheel drive vehicle, and delivery of the animal to the taxidermist. Rooms were available for members and their guests for overnight stays, and gourmet meals were provided featuring exotic dishes created from the carcasses of the resident animals. In large letters at the bottom of the last page it proclaimed that leftover meat was donated by The Safari Lodge to area food shelters.

Nikki returned the pamphlet. "I take it this isn't a petting zoo."

"Think of it as a safari without the inconvenience of travel—a wild animal boutique."

"Where'd they get such an eclectic mix of animals?"

"Mostly from zoos. The zoos get replacement animals, and they sell the ones they no longer want. Capitalism at work."

The doorman returned from the curb and walked over to Cogswell. "Doctor, your car's here."

Cogswell inspected the vehicle parked in front of a fire hydrant. It was a black Lincoln Town Car, recently waxed, the windows tinted to assure the privacy of its customers. The company emblem, a blue and white plasticized card, hung from the passenger window identifying it as a member of the Paragon Car Service.

"I'm off, I'll catch you later."

Cogswell followed the doorman to the car, then waited on the curb until the rear passenger door was held open. Through the rearview mirror the driver glimpsed camouflage pants billowing over the top of a leather boot.

"I'm sorry," the driver said, as Cogswell sat down and adjusted his hat that had been clotheslined by the top of the doorway, "I'm here to pick up Dr. Cogswell."

Cogswell glared back into the rearview mirror as if the driver, whom he had never met, should have recognized him. "I am Dr. Cogswell."

Cogswell handed him the pamphlet with the page turned to the directional map. Then he settled back, scanning the headlines of his *Wall Street Journal*. After the car had begun the two and a half hour journey upstate, he glanced at the back of the driver's head and the side of his face. His accent had confused him, but his straight black hair and swarthy skin suggested he was of Indian extraction.

"Where you from?" Cogswell asked, testing his deductive skills.

"Queens."

"I meant originally."

"Guyana."

"You look Indian."

"That's because my grandparents were from India."

Cogswell sat up. "I figured."

"But I'm not Indian."

Cogswell looked skyward, and shook his head. "Genetically, I'm talking—you're genetically Indian."

"May I ask where you're from?"

"America."

"Your ancestors?"

"England."

"So you're English, not American."

"No, I'm American," he answered, the volume of Cogswell's voice trailing to a whisper, "but I guess you could say, genetically, I'm English."

The driver smiled. "My grandparents were transported to Guyana from India by the British. They used my people for slave labor."

The conversation was over. Cogswell did not like his tone—resentful and unappreciative. Without the help of the British, the driver's parents would have died somewhere in the streets of Calcutta, and he would not have had the benefit of a new life in America. It was irritating to him how oppressed people condemned the efforts of the colonialists, even when they benefitted from their presence.

They edged through the rush hour traffic until they entered the FDR drive at 96th Street, where the congestion was confined to southbound cars—suburban emigrants snailing to their jobs. Poor bastards, he thought, Biosense was spending more money on him in one day than most of the commuters would earn in a month. The Springbok alone was $10,000 not including gratuities, and there was also the cost of car service, the taxidermy fee, and lunch—all totaling about $11,000. It was the price Biosense had to pay for the privilege of doing business with the elite of the academic medical community, and Cogswell was a recognized member. Less renowned colleagues had to be contented with a Biosense sponsored golf outing or dinner for two at a local restaurant, a paltry expenditure, but a just one because they were underachievers who had little to offer the company. Stuart knew his value to Biosense—he controlled access to a large cancer population ideal for testing new anti-cancer drugs, and there was nothing unethical about it. Without research there wouldn't be any opportunity for cure, and besides, all participating patients were well aware of the risks.

Cogswell was convinced he was doing God's work and that he did it only to benefit mankind. One could argue, he supposed, that there was some personal gain: his successful experiments advanced his notoriety in academic circles, triggering job offers from competitive medical institutions which forced Manhattan University Medical Center to counter with substantial increases in his salary. And there was also the honoraria—thousands of dollars from Biosense in exchange for each lecture he gave at another institution describing the benefits of one of their drugs. But it was the patients who benefited from his work the most, and that was the way it should be. Make no mistake about it, Biosense could spend all the money they wanted on him, but it wouldn't influence his objectivity, because Stuart Cogswell could not be bought. He did the research, reported the results, and told it like it was. You would never find Stuart Cogswell falsifying data; the results of his experiments spoke for themselves. Even if he chose not to submit his negative outcomes for publication, he reported them immediately to Eric Waddle, M.D., the medical director of Biosense. And anyway, no one published negative results. What was wrong with giving Biosense an opportunity to improve their product without the distraction of a negative press and the burden of a solicitous FDA? Society was the one that benefited from his discretion; he had nothing to gain by it personally. Everything he did was motivated by a hatred for suffering and a desire to find a cure for a dreaded disease.

He closed his eyes and visualized the upcoming hunt, picturing the evasive maneuvers of the Springbok. A television documentary about a herd in South Africa had depicted them as elegant animals possessing a unique skill when threatened—the ability to jump nine feet in the air on four rigid legs. It was called "pronking," and the bouncing herd looked like animated cartoon characters. If he was going to get one, he had to time his shot, anticipate the leap, and shoot above the rising target. The head with its black ringed horns was going to look spectacular in his country house mounted over the stone fireplace.

Two and a half hours after the trip had begun, they arrived at the gate to The Safari Lodge. A uniformed man appeared from a security booth, and after an identification check he opened the gate. The gravel driveway crunched under the tires until they parked behind the lodge. After Cogswell had notified the driver of a three o'clock departure time, he walked to the front of the two story, octagonal building. He studied its stone base and walls of stacked cedar logs that framed floor to ceiling windows. He entered into a large common room featuring a ten foot stone fireplace that cradled a fire redolent of burning apple wood. Oversized leather chairs were occupied by club members, some reading, some discussing firearms, and others looking out the window at the meandering animals. A chandelier of elk horns dropped to the level of the encircling balcony, the second floor location that accommodated overnight guests. A rustic bannister of white cedar, supported by a 'y' pattern of balusters, enclosed the first floor stairwell and balcony. Area rugs from animal hides were scattered over planks of cherry stained hardwood. The heads of horned animals were mounted on the walls with the name of the member hunter and the date of the kill inscribed on a brass plate underneath.

"Right on time, Cogswell."

Cogswell looked up at the stairwell in the direction of the voice, and saw Dr. Waddle staring down at him costumed in an eclectic mix of riding boots, jodhpurs, safari jacket, and Yankee baseball cap. Field glasses suspended from his neck slapped against his paunch as he descended the stairs.

Waddle reached to shake Cogswell's hand. "We've got a perfect day."

"It'll be perfect if I bag that Springbok." They shook hands.

"You're certainly dressed for success, Stuart. We've got four hours to do it; we can't be late for lunch." Waddle released Cogswell's hand.

It was a civilized way to hunt, thought Cogswell: Stalk the animal, make your kill, and relax over a gourmet luncheon while the staff dressed your prey. Their guide sat behind the wheel of an unroofed jeep painted in a camouflage pattern. Two seats in the back faced the rear. Herb was the guide's name, and he gave a perfunctory tip of his cowboy hat to each of his charges. His drooping mustache covered his lips, the weight of the thatch contributing to the burden of conversation.

"Springbok?" he asked, as he handed a rifle to Cogswell.

"That's correct. I don't need one of those, I've got my own," Waddle said, removing a 9 mm semi-automatic, pearl-handled pistol from his holster. He flashed it at Cogswell.

Cogswell reached over and palpated the glistening handle. "Quite a piece."

"I understand the young Dr. Moriarty is quite a piece too."

"She's easy on the eyes," Cogswell admitted.

Waddle stared. "Remember, Stuart, don't shit where you eat."

Cogswell removed his hand from the revolver. "I've learned that lesson long ago."

Waddle climbed into the rear seat of the jeep, and Cogswell followed.

"I've heard some disturbing reports about her," Waddle said, studying Cogswell's reaction.

"Nikki? She's nothing to worry about."

"I don't have to remind you, Stu, BrobaGen is the only breakout drug in our pipeline, and Lally tells me she's asking a lot of questions, questions I thought we put to rest a long time ago."

"Turns out she was the health care proxy for one of the patients in the study, and she thought BrobaGen contributed to her death. I told her she was misinformed."

"What makes you think she believed you?"

"I can tell you she's not going to rock the boat, she's too smart to jeopardize her career."

Herb got into the driver's seat, started the engine, and shifted into the fields. The land was devoid of trees except for an occasional maple, the high grass and shrubs providing the only refuge for the animals. He parked the jeep near a pond in the protective cover of bushes, and directed the hunters to speak low while he climbed a tree stand.

"Gonna see what I can see," he said.

Waddle focused his field glasses and spoke to Cogswell while panning the bank of the pond. "I'm trying to line up five medical centers for the phase three study, the usual suspects, you know—reliable people."

Cogswell had no doubt about who his co-investigators would be. "Reliable" meant investigators whose primary goal was academic recognition through the participation and publication of cutting edge studies. They were comprised of a select group of physicians who welcomed financial support from Biosense, and who possessed an innate optimism about the outcome of the studies before they were begun.

Cogswell nodded and said, "We break the code on the last twenty patients next week, but it's obvious that the fifty percent of patients who gained weight received BrobaGen, not the placebo. When word gets out, you won't have any problem getting other oncologists to study the drug."

"That's what we're waiting for—confirmation." Waddle leaned towards him, peering over his bifocals. "You know how much this study means to Biosense?"

"I understand."

"And Stuart," Waddle said, polishing the pearl handle of his pistol with a paisley handkerchief, "we can't afford to have any surprises."

Cogswell watched him fondle his customized handgun, an act incongruous with Waddle's role as a respected medical academician. He was a man who would still be Dean of the medical school if Biosense had not given him an offer he couldn't refuse.

Herb interrupted. "Get ready."

He backed up, shifted into forward and accelerated across the field towards a distant clump of shrubs. The approaching noise warned the animals of intruders, and they darted from their hiding place, the pack of Russian boar scuttling in all directions. The guide ignored them and drove within sight of a pair of grazing buffalo, continuing onward to four Springbok with arching backs who were about to initiate evasive maneuvers. They sprung away from the charging jeep, but they couldn't outrace it. Herb pulled alongside of the group, signaling Cogswell to shoot. The movement of the jeep prevented him from using the telescopic lens, and he directed the muzzle of the rifle up and down in concert with the pronking animal. He squeezed the trigger, and the wayward bullet missed the Springbok, which responded to the attack by changing direction, separating itself from the others. Herb turned the jeep around.

Waddle shook his head. "They're deceptive bastards."

"I'll get it next time around."

"By the way, I knew her father."

"Whose father?"

"The Moriarty girl. He was a few years ahead of me in the residency program." Waddle adjusted his bifocals with his thumb and forefinger. "He was a deceptive bastard too."

Herb gained ground herding the prey into the open field. Cogswell shot again, skimming its white underbelly. Panicked, it tried to escape the confines of the hunting field, racing towards the border of the property with the jeep in pursuit.

"You got him where we want him," Waddle said.

In desperation, the animal lowered its head and rammed the chain link fence, locking its lyre-shaped horns in the wire mesh. It bucked again and again, attempting to extricate itself, while Cogswell got out of the jeep and aimed. But before he could shoot, all became still. The Springbok slumped against the fence as it breathed its last breath, dead from a broken neck.

Cogswell approached the animal cautiously before reaching down to pat its reddish brown hide, which was separated from the white underbelly by a horizontal band of dark brown fur. He fingered the superficial belly wound, a blood-stained tract that precipitated the suicidal leap.

"Step back," Waddle ordered. He aimed his 9 mm at the head of the dead animal and shot it twice in the neck from two feet away. "Hate to see animals suffer."

When they walked back to the jeep, Herb was pulling the starter handle of a chain saw. It sputtered twice before engaging. Then, with the motor chuffing, he walked to the Springbok and severed its neck.

Blood spurted from the open wound, and the detached torso slumped to the ground. He turned off the chain saw and with gloved hands manipulated the horned head free from the wire mesh. He placed it in a plastic garbage bag.

"For the taxidermist," Herb said, as he swung the trophy head into the back of the Jeep.

"Way to go, Stuart," Waddle said, holding his hand up in a high-five salute, "now we can eat."

After returning to the Lodge, they cleaned up in the men's room before entering the dining area. The waitress led them to a window table.

"Two glasses of champagne in celebration of our Great White Hunter," Waddle said, pointing at Cogswell.

"Congratulations," the waitress said, suppressing a laugh to guarantee her tip. She escaped to the bar to retrieve their order.

"It's not just her looks," Cogswell said, admiring the backside of the departing waitress.

"Please Stuart, not her, I've got to eat here."

"I'm talking about Nikki, not the waitress. She's the top resident in her group, someone to groom for a future position on our staff. The administration's pressuring the department to hire women."

Waddle picked up the newly arrived glass of champagne and clinked Cogswell's glass.

"Cheers," Cogswell said.

"I respect your judgement, but I'm still concerned. We don't want a fifth column in the ranks now that we're on the verge of FDA approval."

"If you're that uncomfortable with her on the team–"

"No, firing her would be worse. All we need now is a disgruntled employee pronking around the hospital, telling people she was fired for criticizing the BrobaGen study. Better to keep her close, just not too close," Waddle said with a wink. "If a problem develops, we'll come up with a solution."

The waitress interrupted to serve the special of the day—Springbok pot pie—and a bottle of Volnay ordered by Dr. Waddle prior to the hunt.

"I haven't told you about our marketing plan. BrobaGen's getting the big push, the largest investment Biosense ever made publicizing a new product," Waddle said, taking out a pen and grabbing a napkin.

He wrote "celebrity sponsor," and explained that the company had hired a well-known individual, a cancer survivor, who was paid to be the BrobaGen spokesperson. Biosense was going to saturate television and radio with soundbites of the celebrity urging the public to ask their physician about BrobaGen.

"What about the FDA? You haven't got approval yet."

"If your results are as good as we think they're going to be, we'll at least get provisional approval—even before the phase three study is done. That's what our FDA insiders tell us. Remember, we're dealing with people who are dying of cancer. We're not asking for approval for some diet drug, we're trying to save lives."

"I hear you."

"This study is going to make you a household name, doctor," Waddle said, raising his glass before he guzzled his wine.

What was the solution that Waddle had in mind if a problem developed with Nikki? Probably money—he would just pay her off to keep quiet. But there was something about him that made Cogswell uncomfortable.

In the car on the way back he kept picturing Waddle standing over the dead Springbok and shooting it in the neck. The man is strange, he thought, always was, but Waddle would never resort to violence. Buy her off, that's it. If she became a problem, he would just buy her off.

It was more than six months since the last time Nikki had met with her assigned mentor. The delay between appointments was not because she was trying to avoid Dr. Luke McConnachie, but rather that he was unavailable. He had been out of work after he had contracted hepatitis from a needle prick that had nearly ended his career. It happened right after his wife had left him.

Nikki entered his office and the secretary was on the phone. She signaled that she needed a moment. Nikki sat down on one of four plastic chairs fused together as a unit, presumably to deter furniture thieves. She pulled out her personal digital assistant to review her operative casebook in which she had documented every operation that she had scrubbed on since the beginning of her internship.

"December 6, 1992- Lamb, Agnes, 54 y.o. white female, History # 48570, small bowel obstruction, gallstone ileus, first ass't-McConnachie, operative surgeon- Moriarty."

It was her first major abdominal operation, and it reminded her of puberty—they were both happy and, at the same time, painful experiences. Happy because she performed the operation, but painful because of the ineptness she displayed in front of the man she wanted to impress.

"I'm sorry, Dr. Moriarty," the secretary said, hanging up the phone, "he had to go to the O.R. for an emergency. Would you like to re-schedule?"

"I thought Dr. Mueller was on today?"

"Apparently he wasn't available."

"That's okay, I'll try and catch him in the O.R."

Nikki was not surprised that Bertrand Mueller had weaseled out of another emergency case—he always tried to dump them on other surgeons because they were associated with increased risks of complication. McConnachie was different. He accepted responsibility and welcomed challenging cases. He wasn't as popular as Mueller, because the residents thought he was too serious. Some groused to Nikki about his penchant for quoting literature and medical history along with his annoying proclivity to spew aphorisms. But they all respected his ability and dedication.

Nikki exited the elevator on the eighth floor, walked to the O.R. locker room, and put on her scrubs. While looking into a mirror, she lowered a scrub cap onto her head, careful not to disrupt her coif, and walked down the hallway towards McConnachie's O.R. suite. She stopped to let a resident wheel a patient off the elevator, the gurney shuddering as it crossed the threshold. The patient grimaced from the pain of peritonitis, exacerbated by the vibrations of the bed.

"Sorry–one more bump," the resident said, before directing the last two wheels off the elevator. The patient braced herself in anticipation.

The wheels quivered. "That should be it."

Nikki thought of Mrs. Lamb, who was also scared and in pain prior to going to the O.R. After she had signed her consent for operation, Mrs. Lamb asked Nikki to be her health care proxy "just in case." She didn't know Nikki, but she trusted her. Besides, there was no one else. If something went wrong, she didn't want to be tethered to life support machinery. Nikki agreed because Mrs. Lamb had reminded her of the helplessness that she felt when her mother was put on life support against her wishes.

Nikki continued down the hallway and passed a circulating nurse huddled over a patient. The nurse held a clipboard while she checked off answers to each question.

"When was the last time you ate?" she asked, as she examined the patient's identification tag on her wrist.

"Yesterday around six o'clock."

"Are those dentures?" she asked, peering into her mouth.

"No, they're mine."

Nikki stopped outside McConnachie's O.R. suite and looked through its windowed door. The anesthesiology resident was sitting on a stool behind the patient's head, filling out a flow sheet and obtaining the relevant insurance information from the chart. When he finished, he loaded several ten-cc syringes with different medications. Then he attached fluorescent colored labels with bold black lettering to facilitate identification. The overhead light was shining directly into the patient's squinting eyes, and after the circulating nurse redirected it towards her feet, the patient mouthed a thank you. The scrub nurse, the only one gowned and gloved, emerged out of the adjacent room in a cloud of steam, carrying her instrument tray that had just been sterilized in the autoclave. She held the tray with toweled hands and placed the instruments on a draped table that was elevated. It required the scrub nurse to use a footstool in order to arrange the instruments. A myriad of clamps, forceps and scissors of various sizes and shapes were sorted, then propped up in orderly rows on their sides. Their handles rested on tightly rolled green towels. McConnachie's preference for suture material was documented on the computer screen. The circulating nurse opened the anticipated packages of silk and chromic catgut sutures, handing them sterilely to the scrub nurse who added them to her armamentarium.

Nikki walked into the inner sanctum of the O.R. and approached the intern.

"Whaddya got?" she asked.

"Acute Abdomen—McConnachie thinks it's perforated diverticulitis. Could be this kid's first colon resection." He raised and lowered his eyebrows like Groucho Marx. "Watch me closely, you may pick up a few technical pearls."

"What size gloves?" the circulating nurse asked the intern, interrupting his self-promotion.

"Seven."

"Go scrub. I'll prep."

Nikki sat on a stool in the corner, electing not to respond to his arrogance. She was a year ahead of him in the program, yet he talked to her like he was her senior—typical male posturing. The anesthesiologist looked up from his charting and leaned over the patient as if he was about to share an intimate revelation.

"Hello dear, I'm Dr. Morris, your anesthesiologist. "

The corner of his eyes wrinkled above his mask, suggesting a smile. His voice slowed into a singsong tone as he began his rote explanation, the one he repeated to all his patients.

"Dear, I'm going to put some EKG leads on your chest so we can monitor your heart. They're going to feel a little cold and sticky, okay?" he asked, placing them on her skin before he had finished the question.

"There we go. Now I'm going to put a blood pressure cuff on your arm, and you'll feel it get tight so don't be surprised, okay?"

After he recorded her blood pressure, he secured a mask over the patient's mouth and nose, adjusting the flow of gases so she was receiving 100% oxygen. He then injected the intravenous with sodium pentathol, and she yawned prior to entering into a deep sleep. An injection of succinyl choline followed, a drug used to relax muscles and facilitate intubation. Her body quivered from the muscle fasciculations precipitated by the drug, and immediately thereafter her muscles became flaccid. She stopped breathing. It was the predictable and desired response. He extended her head and removed the oxygen mask from her mouth. With the thumb and index finger of his right hand, he spread her upper and lower teeth apart and opened her mouth, inserting the laryngoscope with his left hand. He used the blade of the laryngoscope to manipulate her tongue forward and to the side, away from the back of her throat in order to expose the larynx. Two pathways, one on top of the other, were illuminated by the light. The tube had to be guided through the top one, past the vocal cords and into the trachea, assuring that her lungs would receive the requisite oxygen. Nikki watched him insert the tube, then he injected air with a syringe into the balloon port, inflating the balloon at the distal end of the tube. The balloon swelled against the surrounding airway wall, protecting the lungs from any spillage that might occur if the patient vomited. The patient's chest rose and fell in concert with the movement of the bellows of the respirator, suggesting that the tube was in the appropriate place. McConnachie walked into the O.R. as the tube was taped onto the patient's cheeks.

Nikki assessed his hazel eyes, framed by scrub hat and mask, for signs of jaundice. They appeared clear. An ascot of black hair protruded from the V-neck of his shirt, and she admired the way his scrub pants, taut and unwrinkled, cupped his buttocks and separated each cheek into distinct entities.

"We're all set," said the anesthesiologist as he removed the ambu bag and connected the patient to the ventilator.

"I'll go scrub," McConnachie said.

Before he entered the scrub room, Nikki identified herself.

"Dr. McConnachie, it's Nikki, Nikki Moriarty."

"Nikki—I didn't recognize you behind the mask. Sorry I had to cancel our meeting."

"No problem. I've got some time so I came up to watch."

"Great, maybe we can talk after."

He joined the intern at the scrub sink and, after a one-minute wash, opened the door with his back and walked towards the scrub nurse. She handed him a green towel. As he dried his hands the circulating nurse finished her prep, painting the patient's abdomen with an iodine solution beginning at the umbilicus, and continuing circumferentially until the whole abdomen was covered with a glossy brown veneer. The scrub nurse held up his surgical gown with the inside facing McConnachie, and he introduced his left arm in one sleeve and his right into the other. The velcro attachments in the back were fastened by the circulating nurse, as the scrub nurse inverted his glove and directed the opening towards McConnachie. Once he was fully gloved, the circulating nurse detached the cincture from the front of the gown, grabbing it by its paper handle as McConnachie spun so that it encircled him. He then grabbed the string and she removed the paper handle while he tied the string. He framed the painted abdomen with four green towels that were handed to him by the scrub nurse, one by one, while he awaited his assistant for the final draping. The intern entered with his arms raised high in the air, typical of medical students and beginning interns, a maneuver they were taught lessened the likelihood of patient infection. After drying his hands with a sterile towel, he gowned and entered his right hand in the glove, but two of his fingers ended up in the same slot. He attempted to extricate his finger while he placed his left hand in the other glove, but the same thing happened. The scrub nurse recognized his predicament and grabbed the latex digit of the imprisoned fingers, allowing him to pull his fingers back and reinsert them into their appropriate slots. His struggle was going unnoticed until he fumbled his cincture, causing it to cascade out of the sterile field towards the floor.

"Contaminated!" yelled the circulating nurse, exposing another surgical neophyte. "Stand still," she ordered. "I'll pull off your gown and gloves, and then you'll have to scrub again."

The intern, annoyed that the circulating nurse had highlighted his glitch, popped open a sterile alcohol sponge and scrubbed again.

Nikki opened the door to the scrub room and gave him a thumbs-up sign. "Very impressive gowning, I'm recording that as pearl number one." She left before he had a chance to respond.

The folded surgical drape straddled the patient's abdomen, and McConnachie handed the opposite end to the intern after he had been successfully dressed. Together they unraveled the bottom half so it covered the patient's pelvis, legs and feet, and hung like a curtain just above the floor. The top half was directed over her torso, neck and head, and the free end was given to the anesthesiologist, who secured each upper corner of the drape with plastic clips to the I.V. poles on either side of the head of the table. The middle of the drape had a cutout that isolated the painted abdomen, causing it to protrude like a copper cupola. He stood on the patient's left side and sequentially secured the suction tubing and the Bovie cautery to the surgical drape. Nikki anticipated he was about to change sides with the intern, because the surgeon performing the operation was usually positioned on the patient's right side, and interns did not get to do colon operations.

"Have you ever done one of these before?" McConnachie asked.

Nikki remembered her chief resident's admonition to always say "yes" to any attending when asked that question, otherwise she wouldn't be given the opportunity to be the operating surgeon.

"Once," he mumbled.

She knew he was lying, because there was no way he had done a major abdominal operation in his first two months as an intern. It was another example of male posturing. And it was stupid, because he was not going to be able to bluff his way through the operation.

"Okay, give him the knife," McConnachie said to the scrub nurse.

The intern was now the celebrant, not the acolyte, and he was not prepared. The scalpel was handed to him as he stared at the abdomen, searching for topographical landmarks, fingering the surface of the abdomen as if a bell would sound if he touched the correct starting point. McConnachie recognized his apprehension and outlined the incision.

"Start here just above the umbilicus and continue down to the pubic symphysis," he said, pointing to the protuberant tissue just above the vagina.

The intern cut the skin, but failed to incise beyond the epidermis. He tried again, but he lacked conviction.

"Cut, don't scratch. That incision looks like hesitation marks on a wrist after a failed suicide attempt."

The intern laughed nervously, waiting for McConnachie to take over the case, but he didn't. He squeezed the scalpel, and tried again. The tension in his grip was palpable, and McConnachie interceded.

"Wait, let's start from the beginning. You gotta relax; you're squeezing too hard. Hold the scalpel as if it's a bird—you squeeze too hard, you kill it, not hard enough, it flies away."

He had a paternalistic tone that was encouraging, different from his demeanor before the hepatitis. In the past he would have ignored the intern and done the operation himself, but now he was more patient and interested in teaching the craft.

The intern lightened his grip, making a deliberate incision through all layers of the skin as blood oozed over the pouting fat. He curved the incision in a sickle shape around the umbilicus and returned to the midline, continuing down towards the pubic bone.

"That's it, now get the Bovie and go down to the fascia."

The Bovie cautery was handed to the intern. McConnachie compressed the left side of the wound with a cotton pad to slow the bleeding, and the intern similarly compressed his side. With his right hand, the intern deepened the original incision with the cautery, filling the operative field with the acrid smell of burned fat. Smoke trailing the cautery was aspirated with a suction catheter by McConnachie to prevent clouding of the operative field. The coagulated tissue caked onto the cautery tip like remnant of roasted marshmallow on a stick. The scrub nurse scraped it off with a scalpel. A vein spurted blood and McConnachie compressed it with a gauze pad, directing the intern's attention to it.

"Buzz here." He slowly rolled the sponge away from the vessel, revealing the bleeding source.

The spurting vessel hissed in response to the heat of the Bovie tip, followed by a wisp of smoke, and a residue of charcoal-colored coagulum. The bleeding was stanched.

"Let's go through the fascia. Use the knife," McConnachie said.

The intern sharply incised the fascia, a girdle of fibrous tissue that held the organs inside the abdominal cavity, and a thin, diaphanous layer of peritoneum remained—the final barrier to the abdominal cavity.

"Pick up opposite me, and lift up," McConnachie said, using his forceps to pick up the gossamer of peritoneum.

The intern pinched the adjacent tissue and together they elevated it away from the underlying intestines to lessen the risk of injury from the blade. As he nicked the tissue with his knife, an audible puff of air, accompanied by a fecal odor, escaped through the hole, confirming there was a violation of the gastrointestinal tract.

"Smells like a colon injury," McConnachie said.

"Unless Dr. Moriarty farted," the intern said, bobbing from concealed laughter.

"How many of these operations did you say you did?" Nikki asked, silencing the intern who returned his attention to the patient.

The remaining part of the peritoneum was opened, and self-retaining retractors were placed in the wound to widen the exposure by stretching the abdominal incision. The omentum, the apron of fat attached to the transverse colon, was distorted. Instead of draping freely over the intestines, it was pulled to the patient's left side, fused to the hole in the sigmoid colon. McConnachie pinched the inflamed omentum off the colon, exposing the perforation.

"Always amazing how the omentum tries to protect us—the watchdog of the abdomen."

He placed a cotton pad over the hole and lifted the free end of the omentum away from the operative field, placing it onto the chest wall. Nikki stood on a stepstool and looked over the intern's shoulder at the loops of small intestine, a slithering nest of albino eels.

"What do you want to do now?" McConnachie asked, pushing him to make a decision.

"Sigmoid resection?"

"Okay, let's do it."

According to the textbook, removal of the perforated segment of colon was recommended, but it was obvious the intern didn't know how. He had read the steps of the operation in the surgical atlas, and watched others resect the colon, but leading the way was different. It was similar to looking at a map the night before a car trip, confident of the directions until you're on the road, unsure which turn to take. McConnachie recognized his paralysis and interceded.

"Let's identify the ureter so we don't injure it."

He showed him how to expose the left ureter, a worm-like tube connecting kidney to bladder for the purposes of transporting urine.

"That's the ureter?" the intern asked.

"Watch," McConnachie said. He compressed the muscular wall of the putative duct with his forceps, and observed it squirm in response. "See that? That's how you know it's the ureter."

He traced its course over the pelvic brim, separating it from the environs of the inflamed colon. Nikki remembered that injury to the ureter was one of the major complications that occurred with sigmoid resection, particularly when the operative field was obscured by inflammation. McConnachie mobilized the sigmoid colon by cutting away its peritoneal attachments with a Metzenbaum scissors, while maintaining tension on the colon, pulling it towards the right side. She watched, relieved he was taking charge, and the intern appeared relieved also. Approximately one and a half feet of colon needed to be removed, and after placing a pair of bowel clamps at the proximal margin and a similar pair at the distal margin, he outlined the V-shaped piece of attached mesentery, the membranous tissue that contained the blood vessels, lymphatics, and nerves which fed the bowel, and which would also have to be removed. He scored the mesentery with his scalpel, and then poked a hole with a clamp into the incised mesentery, avoiding injury to the blood vessels that supplied the segment of colon to be resected. Another hole was created an inch from the first, and he enveloped the tissue between the holes with his opened clamp.

"Clamp opposite me," he said to his assistant.

The intern was handed a clamp by the scrub nurse and he placed it as directed, through the same holes adjacent to McConnachie's, and clamped it closed.

"Okay, cut between the clamps."

The tissue was cut, and the clamp that contained the severed blood vessels feeding the colon was then encircled with a silk suture. McConnachie tied the suture and directed the knot underneath the tip of the clamp as his assistant elevated the tip so that McConnachie could ascertain that his tie was secured completely around the clamped tissue.

"Okay, off," McConnachie said.

The intern released the clamp as the knot was snugged around the tissue, then he cut the redundant strands of silk just above the knot.

"Nothing like the excrement of a worm," McConnachie said.

"Excuse me?"

"Silk—it's excreted by worms. It handles better than any of the synthetic sutures."

After the remaining mesentery and its vessels were tied, the colon was severed between the bowel clamps and the diseased segment with its attached piece of mesentery was removed.

"Now what do you want to do?"

"A sigmoid colostomy?" the intern asked.

"That's the correct answer when you take your boards, but I think we can do this patient a favor and safely avoid a colostomy."

Nikki knew that joining the two cut ends of colon together in a field where there was fecal spillage and inflammation increased the risk of leakage from the suture line—a life threatening complication. Colostomy was the recommended procedure for patients with perforated diverticulitis, because in the hands of the average surgeon it was the safest option. She wondered if McConnachie was more interested in the technical challenge and proving the surgical poobahs wrong than in the patient's well-being. But if she was the patient, she wouldn't want a colostomy either. The omentum had plugged the hole, minimizing fecal spillage, and the cut ends of the bowel appeared healthy. It was probably safe to do an anastomosis. But if it leaked there would be no defense for not following the standard of care.

McConnachie performed the two-layer anastomosis, allowing the intern to place some of the sutures, and once the two ends of the colon were joined together, gas and colonic contents were milked through the colon as they studied their suture line for any sign of leakage. Confident in the integrity of the anastomosis, they returned the abdominal organs to their normal positions, then they irrigated and suctioned the abdominal cavity with several liters of warmed saline solution to dilute any bacterial contamination before they sutured the fascia back together.

"There's a thirty percent chance of a wound infection, so watch for it, and don't hesitate to open the wound if it occurs," McConnachie warned, as he held the skin edges together with forceps, and the intern stapled them together.

When they arrived in the recovery room, the pungent odor of Drakkar Noir cologne signaled that Dr. Bertrand Mueller was nearby. Nikki sat down at a desk awaiting McConnachie's arrival, and Mueller emerged from the coffee room, his scent intensifying with each approaching step. The residents postulated that his liberal use of cologne was an attempt to distract staff members from his incompetence, a hypothesis that Nikki thought had merit. He spoke with McConnachie while Nikki studied the intricacies of Mueller's combover, baffled by how a remnant of hair could paste itself across his entire scalp. It looked like it was held in place at gunpoint.

He thanked McConnachie for covering for him, complaining about all the administrative duties that separated him from the joy of operating. After McConnachie apprised him of the operative findings, Mueller expressed admiration for his courage to proceed with an anastomosis instead of relegating the patient to a colostomy. As soon as McConnachie left the recovery room, he pulled the intern aside and whispered his concerns.

"I don't know why he did that. It's exactly what you're not supposed to do. It's not safe. He put this lady's life at risk. It's not your fault—you're just an intern, but you need to be aware for your own good that he did the wrong operation. I wish I could've done it myself, and you would've learned the right way to do it. Just watch her closely."

He walked away, shaking his head, and then frisked his scalp to determine if his head movements had disrupted his coif.

The textbook was clear about the operation of choice in such a situation, and Nikki knew that Mueller was right—a colostomy should have been done. She suspected he was on his way to alert colleagues in the Department of Surgery that McConnachie had performed an anastomosis in the presence of fecal spillage, priming them for the expectant leak.

"Great case," Nikki said to McConnachie.

"I think we'll get a good result. You want to meet in my office in around fifteen minutes?"

Nikki agreed and went to the locker room to change. He was a good looking man, pleasant, and an exceptional surgeon. So why did his wife leave him? She didn't know the answer, but people are different behind closed doors. Everyone respected her father too, and look what a bastard he turned out to be.

She entered the stairwell, descended to the seventh floor, and walked into McConnachie's office.

His secretary greeted her. "Hi, Dr. Moriarty. I'll check and see if he's ready for you."

As she opened the door, Nikki could see him sitting upright at his desk with his eyes closed.

"He'll only be a few minutes," the secretary said.

"Those catnaps really help."

"He wasn't sleeping, he was meditating."

"Meditating? Like with a mantra?"

"I guess—he does it twice a day."

Nikki couldn't visualize McConnachie as the type who would sit in the lotus position and open his mind to flowing thoughts. Before he became sick he would have scoffed at the idea, but disease can do strange things to a person's mind. If he had said no to Mueller when he asked him to cover that patient with a gun shot wound to the abdomen, he never would have gotten sick in the first place. But, Nikki reasoned, if he had refused, he wouldn't be McConnachie.

"You can go in now." The secretary replaced the intercom phone on its cradle.

Nikki scanned him for signs of chronic disease, but there were none. "You look fully recovered."

"I feel good. Everyone should have six months off—it helps put things in perspective."

"Your secretary said you were meditating," she said.

"My internist recommended it. I find it helpful."

"I tried it a couple times in college, but I just ended up making mental lists of things I needed to do."

"It takes practice like anything else."

Nikki shifted in her seat, concerned he had lost his ambition and was wasting his time on New Age remedies instead of concentrating on his career.

"How does it help?"

"It helps you look at life objectively, see why things happened the way they did."

"Disease happens, you can't control it."

"To some extent you can. I've come to believe you create your own reality."

"What about a baby with cancer? The baby didn't create that reality."

"I don't have an answer for fetal and newborn disease except the ones that result from the choices made by mothers while pregnant. With me I know I wasn't cautious, maybe even reckless. Never wore a double layer of gloves even though we all know the trauma population are frequent carriers of AIDS and hepatitis. And reaching blindly for a needle tip was suicidal."

"But you saved a patient's life."

"If I waited, put pressure on the bleeding site, and sucked out the blood so that I could visualize the field and see the needle tip, I wouldn't have gotten stuck and still saved his life."

"You're not suggesting that you wanted to get hepatitis or AIDS, and that you purposely imbedded your finger into the needle?"

"Not consciously, but perhaps unconsciously."

He was obsessing about his disease, and his self-criticism bordered on the absurd. She attributed it to his prolonged absence from work combined with the loss of his wife, someone who helped him put things in perspective.

"But why would you unconsciously stick yourself?"

"That's what I spent six months trying to answer. In a way it was a gift, because I started to focus on what's really important."

"A gift? I don't think I would've handled things as well."

"I didn't handle it well at first. I went through the Kubler-Ross stages of dying—you know, 'why me,' and finally 'acceptance.' You have to deal with the cards you're dealt. It's a waste of energy to try and change things that can't be changed."

"I agree with that, but I still have trouble with the idea that you were somehow responsible."

"That's why meditation helps. It helps you to awaken the mind, free it from any preconceived notions so that you can recognize the truth. Ever read Emerson?"

"Not really. I know he was a transcendentalist like Thoreau, but that's about it."

"Right. He said 'We bring back from the Indies what we take to the Indies.' We see what we want to see rather than what is really there. I'm sure you noticed it in the lab. Some researchers conclude what a study is going to show before they begin, and when they review the results, they look for confirmation of their biased beliefs rather than looking objectively at the outcome. Often we don't like to face facts."

She enjoyed talking with McConnachie, but a relationship with him would never work. He was a surgeon, self-absorbed like herself, and emotionally unavailable. Besides, she knew he would never violate his responsibility as mentor by hitting on her because he was too uptight. But it was all for the better, because if she got involved with him she would never be able to focus on her career—he required too much nurturing. Fred was less interesting to talk with, but he fulfilled her sexual needs without compromising her independence.

Nikki got back to business. "Not to change the subject, but do you remember Mrs. Lamb? We operated on her for a gallstone ileus."

"I remember."

"She died recently of metastatic breast cancer."

"That was quick. She didn't have evidence of breast cancer when we operated on her—unless we missed something."

"I was afraid of that too, but I reviewed her chart. She never had a palpable breast mass; it was picked up six months ago on routine mammogram, and excised. Turned out to be a carcinoma-in-situ."

"Carcinoma-in-situ? She should've been cured with the local excision. How did it spread so quickly?"

"I don't know. But I must say I'm concerned about the study she entered after she developed cancer. Before I started in the lab, Cogswell was testing a new drug from the Biosense company—BrobaGen—

that's supposed to stop the cachexia associated with cancer patients. But it doesn't only stop patients from wasting away, it actually increases their muscle mass, and improves their immunological response."

"That would be great, if it works."

"Problem is, if she got the drug, and I don't know if she did, it may have increased the growth of the tumor as well. It contains growth hormone, growth hormone releasing factor, insulin-like growth factor, steroids, and I'm not sure what else."

"Makes sense. Growth hormone could theoretically increase the doubling times of tumor cells. But I guess they would've seen a trend of unexplained tumor growth with other patients in the study."

"So far they claim there's no trend, and that Mrs. Lamb is just an aberration—a statistical outlier. They're reluctant to interrupt the study, not only because of the expense, but the FDA and the Health Department would get involved."

"Maybe they should."

"But when I brought up the possibility that the drug spread cancer, it was dismissed. I guess it's like what you said about Emerson—they may not want to see the truth."

"So what are you going to do?"

"I raised the possibility and it was rejected. So there's not much more I can do. Besides, Cogswell could be right—there's always the chance that she's one of those patients with a biologically aggressive tumor, and there's a fifty-fifty chance she didn't even get the drug."

"I see."

In the past, Nikki could always read McConnachie, but now she didn't know if his "I see" meant that he agreed with her assessment, or if it was code for "bullshit." She felt a need to defend her wait-and-see approach.

"Cogswell is going to review the original biopsy slides with a breast pathologist, and see if the tumor was more advanced than the original reading or inadequately excised. The study is almost over anyway, so the code will be broken soon."

"Let me know if there's anything I can do," McConnachie said, before changing the subject. "By the way, I reviewed all your evaluations from the senior residents and the attending staff over the last six months. They're superlative."

"That's good to hear."

"Have you run into any problems?"

"Not really—nothing I can't handle."

"You should come up to the country before the fall is over, and bring your boyfriend. It's Fred, isn't it, the anesthesia resident?"

"Yep, it's still Fred."

"Leaves are starting to change color, and the two of you could get out of the city. If you'd like, why don't you guys come Sunday for dinner."

"Now that I have more time, that'd be fun," she said, wondering who else would be there. If he's already got a girlfriend, then they were probably getting it on while he was still married. Maybe that's why his wife left him.

"I've got to make rounds in a few minutes. If I can be of any help with that other problem, let me know."

Nikki got up and walked to the door, realizing that the rumors about a mental breakdown were just hospital gossip instigated by envious colleagues and staff. His personal introspection was an uncommon surgical trait, and one that she initially found unsettling. But what appeared to be a weakness she now saw as a strength. Regular meditation or reflection was something she might benefit from also. Nikki reached out her hand.

"It's great having you back. It's great for the program."

McConnachie shook her hand and smiled.

He was different than before—serene and more peaceful. She headed back to the laboratory, gratified she had not dumped him as her mentor, not only because it would have been disloyal, but because he was one of the few attendings in the program she still admired.

A flyer advertised free pizza in the conference room, and when Nikki entered she overheard George Lally promoting one of Biosense's overpriced antibiotics to a chief resident. The resident glommed a second slice while George tried to capture his attention.

"Could you use tickets for the Mets?"

He nodded both in agreement to George's offer, and as a means to separate himself from a tenacious strand of mozzarella cheese that tethered his mouth to the pizza. After the head maneuvers subsided, George continued his pitch.

"How about two tickets for Saturday?"

"Fantastic."

"It should be a great game—they're playing the Braves."

"Baseball? I thought you asked if I could use tickets for the Met—the Metropolitan Opera. I don't have any interest in baseball."

"I don't know what's wrong with me, I knew that. Let me make a call and get back to you."

"I'll give you my cell, you can call me direct," the chief resident said, pulling out a pen and his prescription pad.

The thought of opera tickets compelled him to acknowledge George's drug promotion, and he asked if it had been approved for use by the hospital's formulary committee. George assured him that approval was imminent, now that Dr. Brunner, an avid Mets fan, had become the committee chairman.

With his fixed smile and helmet of hair, George looked like a politician campaigning in front of a subway station, trying to engage the eyes of indifferent commuters. He panned the room for other targets. Nikki felt him looking at her as she poured a cup of coffee.

"Dr. Moriarty? I'm George Lally, the clinical liaison for Biosense. Looking forward to working with you, heard a lot of good things." He offered to get her a slice of pizza.

What a bullshit artist, Nikki thought, while fingering her abdominal collop, a barely noticeable roll of fat that fluctuated in concert with her lapses of dietary discretion.

"I'll have one with spinach."

George placed a slice on a paper plate and handed it to her.

"Spinach—so you're into health food," he said and smiled.

"I tolerate health food as long as it's on a carrier of pizza—with the exception of lima beans."

"You don't like lima beans?"

"No, they taste like velvet buttons."

She took a bite, pursing her lips as she pulled the slice away from her mouth. George glanced at her hair, sensibly styled in a tightly coiffured roll, and ogled her athletic figure. He looked through his briefcase for a suitable potlatch that he could offer her, but his supplies were depleted.

"Could you use a penlight?"

"Not really, I'll just end up cannibalizing it for the batteries. I use them for my beeper."

"Great idea—instead of penlights, give out batteries to the residents stamped with the Biosense logo. Less wasteful. I'll run that by marketing."

The gift-giving to physicians by pharmaceutical representatives was a practice that Nikki had witnessed since the beginning of her internship. Competing companies manufactured equivalent drugs, and pharmaceutical representatives used whatever means necessary to promote their product. Interns and junior residents were lobbied with token gifts commensurate with the minimal influence that they possessed, but as they progressed through the program, they were wooed with expensive dinners and free tickets to a variety of cultural and sporting events. The drug companies attributed the outlay to the cost of doing business, and attendings who supported the product line were rewarded with free trips to medical meetings. The academic elite were the most heavily recruited group, particularly those in charge of disease-specific patient populations—physicians like Dr. Cogswell. He provided the producers of anticancer drugs with a human testing field, and in exchange for access to patients, Biosense financed his entire lab, a multimillion dollar investment.

She took another bite of pizza while George watched her chew. It was obvious he was attracted to her, but the interest wasn't mutual.

George assumed a somber expression. "It was unfortunate that Mrs. Lamb passed away. I know you were close to her."

"It wasn't unfortunate at all," Nikki corrected. "She had extensive disease, and significant pain—it was merciful that she died."

George, impressed with her imperturbability, decided to suspend the niceties and cut to the chase.

"You were concerned her cancer spread so quickly."

"I raised the question."

"Our staff shared your concerns about BrobaGen's potential to spread indolent tumors, but we're all encouraged by the outcome of the pilot study."

"Hopefully, the numbers will hold up."

George smiled and then excused himself, explaining that he was about to speak to the staff about the economics of producing drugs like BrobaGen, and he hoped to talk with her again after the lecture. Nikki considered leaving the room, but she wanted another slice of pizza. The audience, comprised of residents, nursing staff, and members of the research team, hunkered down with their food, bracing for a lecture they felt obligated to attend in exchange for the free lunch. Cynthia arrived as the lecture began, sat down next to Nikki, and offered her a lollipop. Nikki flashed her slice of pizza. She placed the lollipop back in her pocket.

"Does anyone know the cost of producing a drug like BrobaGen? I'm talking from the very beginning—the synthesis of the drug up until it's placed on the drugstore shelf?"

"Question," someone said, with a raised hand.

George identified the source. It was the bald man with the beard.

"Yes, Dr. Green?"

"Including the cost of promotion?"

"Yes."

"Two hundred million."

"Too low. It takes twelve to fifteen years at a cost of 750 million dollars."

The cost of doing business included a twenty-billion-dollar yearly investment for research, and the frustration of knowing that only five out of the 10,000 compounds synthesized by their company ever get to the point of testing on patients. Nikki was skeptical of his numbers, and she suspected that the cost estimates were padded by Biosense to gain support for their drug prices. George explained that it took ten years from the time BrobaGen was synthesized until it was tested on human volunteers in the phase one study. After it was proven to be well tolerated in humans, the phase two study was begun to determine if patients with weight loss from cancer benefited from the drug. The three year study by Dr. Cogswell was almost completed, and he was optimistic about the results. He thanked the research team for their hard work, and he was hopeful that Biosense would obtain preliminary approval from the FDA before the phase three trial was completed. Nikki knew the phase three trial would involve several institutions evaluating the drug simultaneously, and it would be another few years before they could collate the results and seek FDA approval—assuming that the drug maintained its efficacy. It was in Biosense's best interest to get approval as soon as possible.

"Question," Dr. Green said again.

"Yes, Dr. Green."

"So you're saying that if for some reason the study was stopped— a detrimental effect on patients an obvious example—then the company would be out 500 million bucks."

"Something like that. But even though the loss would be exorbitant, if we truly believed a drug was detrimental, then we would withdraw it at whatever stage of development. Litigation is very expensive these days, and lawyers would like nothing better than for us to release a drug that they could prove shortened someone's life."

Cynthia whispered to Nikki, "I've got to get out of here. I'm going to relieve one of the nurses for lunch so she can come in here and suffer instead of me."

"I'm following you."

They both got up, walked out and headed towards the nurse's station. Cynthia continued into a patient's room to free a nurse for lunch, while Nikki began looking through a patient's chart. The oncology beds were full as usual with patients referred from the tristate area. It was the busiest cancer service in the country, with a patient population essential for testing drugs. Physicians who referred their patients to the oncology service at the Manhattan University Medical Center knew if a breakthrough in the treatment of cancer was to occur, it was going to happen there. Cogswell and Biosense had a symbiotic relationship—he had the patients, and they had the drugs. He needed the experimental drugs to attract the patient referrals, and they needed the patients to prove efficacy and obtain FDA approval. It was a win-win situation. His steadfast loyalty to Biosense was rewarded with the company's support, both technical and financial, enabling him to complete cutting edge studies. He was on the forefront of cancer care, a member of the academic elite. It was an enviable relationship that he had established, and one that Nikki someday hoped to arrange for herself.

The floor clerk called to her. "Dr. Moriarty, Cynthia needs you in room twenty-one right away, it's Mr. Washington."

Nikki put down the chart and scurried towards the room, wondering who Mr. Washington was and why Cynthia was calling her instead of the resident assigned to the floor. When she walked in, Cynthia was standing near the head of the patient, calmly placing an ambu bag over the patient's nose and mouth. The overhead monitor beeped a pulse rate of forty-four, and the patient appeared unconscious and not breathing.

"Cynthia, what's going on?"

"I think I've got things under control. He just started to struggle and his pulse dropped, but he should respond to this."

She proceeded to bag the patient with 100% oxygen, while Nikki turned to the nurse standing in the doorway.

"Get the arrest cart in here. We need an amp of atropine stat."

His chest expanded with each compresson of the ambu bag, and Nikki knew he was being adequately ventilated. She watched the monitor to see if his heart rate increased in response to the oxygen while silently reviewing the most likely suspects that could cause such a sudden change in the patient's condition. If his lung collapsed—a pneumothorax—it could inhibit his oxygenation and decrease his heart rate. She would have to insert a chest tube to evacuate the air around the lung that prevented it from fully expanding. She grabbed a stethoscope that was hanging from an I.V. pole and listened to the right side of his chest. Definite breath sounds. She then listened to the left side, and there were also breath sounds, which made the diagnosis of pneumothorax unlikely. She considered other possibilities such as the aspiration of stomach contents, pulmonary embolus, a mucus plug, but before she committed herself, the patient's heart rate increased in response to the improved oxygenation. He began to initiate his own breath. The nurse outside the room rifled the drawers of the arrest cart, pulling out an ampule of atropine, but it was no longer needed.

"Hold everything," Nikki said, "it looks like he's responding."

The patient awakened, confused but breathing comfortably, and Cynthia removed the ambu bag and placed an oxygen mask over the patient's mouth and nose.

"I'll set the oxygen at one hundred percent for now, and we can lower it if he remains stable," Cynthia said.

Cogswell entered the room, fortified by the knowledge that things were under control.

"Cynthia, what's going on?" he asked.

She reassured Mr. Washington before walking out of the room to respond.

"Unclear. I was covering for Carmen, who was at lunch, and Mr. Washington had a dying spell. Fortunately, Nikki was on the floor, and thanks to her we were able to get him back."

"Nikki, what do you think happened?"

"Most likely a mucus plug. We need to get a chest x-ray and EKG to sort things out."

"Good job, Cynthia, but where were the residents? Nikki's supposed to be in the lab, not taking care of patients."

"They're in the conference room with George Lally. I would've called them, but Nikki was nearby, and I knew she could handle it."

Cogswell nodded and walked off the floor, impressed with Nikki's ability. It was important to keep the mortality rate low in order to continue to attract patients, and he was pleased that disaster had been averted. Cynthia always seemed to be there to address life threatening problems on the unit, and he was fortunate to have her on the team.

Carmen Gonzalez, Mr. Washington's nurse, returned from lunch and was surprised to see the arrest cart outside her patient's room.

"What's going on?"

"Your patient wasn't getting the respiratory therapy he needed," Cynthia said. "He plugged. I keep telling you guys to work with these patients, make sure they're using the incentive spirometer, deep breathing, and getting chest p.t. Luckily, Nikki was on the floor, and turned things around."

"He was breathing fine before I went to lunch, and his chest x-ray was clear this morning. He didn't have any secretions. I don't understand how this could've been a plug."

"Carmen, I don't want to argue with you, but we were here. Let's get another chest x-ray and we'll talk about it later," Cynthia ordered, and then walked back to the nurse's station.

Mr. Washington was responsive, but groggy, as if he was suddenly awakened out of a deep sleep. Carmen examined him in front of Nikki, and he appeared oriented to his surroundings, unaware of the recent events. He couldn't recall any chest pain or difficulty breathing, just a sudden weakness and inability to keep his eyes open. His brisk deterioration and quick recovery were hard to understand, and she looked at Nikki for insight, but she was equally confused.

"I guess it was a mucus plug," Nikki said. Carmen shook her head and returned to her patient.

Nikki had witnessed patients suddenly deteriorate from the consequences of a mucus plug, but they were patients who were producing large amounts of mucus, and who hadn't been adequately suctioned. It was also strange how Cynthia gave her the credit for Washington's recovery. It wasn't deserved, and she wondered what motivated her to do it. She walked over to the nurse's station and sat down beside her.

"Cynthia, you handled that well."

"No big deal."

"Thanks for the compliment in front of Cogswell. It wasn't deserved."

"All minorities have to stick together, women included. I can imagine what it must be like to be a female resident in the department of surgery—always suspect, never getting the credit you deserve."

"It hasn't been that bad, but I know what you're talking about. If I'm not on the floor they assume I'm shopping at Bloomingdales."

"And worse. We hear it all the time from the residents who rotate through here. You know what they say: 'Surgery isn't a specialty for women, they lower the standards. Other specialties are more their type, more feminine.'"

"I ignore that crap. Some of the boys do a lot of talking, but ultimately it comes down to patient care and your ability in the O.R., and I don't have any problem being compared to anyone in the program, male or female."

"I know you can hold your own, but it doesn't hurt for us women to support each other. It balances out the old boy's club that runs the department of surgery. By the way, a few of us are getting together after work to celebrate the full moon, we do it every month. It'd be great if you could stop by. You know where we are, the staff building, apartment 6N."

"Let me check and see what's going on. I'll try and stop by."

George Lally came out of the conference room and smiled at Nikki. He told her he'd heard about Mr. Washington, and that they were lucky to have her on the team.

"After you get settled, I'd like to show you our headquarters in New Jersey so you can see the complete operation. I think you'll find it fascinating."

"Some day, after I get settled."

He wanted to continue to talk, but she was preoccupied with the circumstances of Washington's arrest. And she needed a sugar boost. She walked to the basement and entered the alcove that housed the vending machines. Sample choices were visible through the plastic window, and as she debated her selection, she decided it must have been a mucus plug. Cynthia had suctioned him prior to assisting his ventilation and probably dislodged the mucous obstruction of his airway. He responded so quickly that she was hardpressed to come up with a better explanation. Cynthia's quick and confident response under pressure was impressive, and she realized how valuable it was to have a nurse practitioner on the floor who was capable of dealing with emergencies. Perhaps it would be a good idea to stop by her apartment after work, bond with some of the people she was going to be working with for the next two years.

She inserted three quarters into the coin slot and pushed the button under the chocolate almond Hershey bar. As she bent down to pick up her cache, she heard a familiar voice.

"You know they've done carbon-14 labeling on the candy in that machine."

"I like my candy aged." She turned and smiled at Fred.

He was wearing green scrubs underneath his lab coat, and instead of a "no pain" button on his lapel that was de rigueur amongst anesthesiologists, he had one that said "pleasure." Nikki had suggested he lose the button—it was unprofessional—but Fred thought that "pleasure" was more proactive and more encouraging to patients.

"O.R. quiet today?" she asked.

"Not overwhelming. And you?"

"Still getting oriented. I'll tell you about it tonight, you going to be around?"

"About eight."

"I'll come by a little later. I'm going to bond with some of the staff."

"Sounds good. Walk with me to the Trauma ICU, I've got to pre-op a patient."

They entered and found McConnachie finishing his teaching rounds. Nikki sat at the nurse's station within earshot while Fred evaluated his patient.

McConnachie spoke to the team of residents. "Have we seen all the new admissions?"

"We missed one, bed five, but he's really a Neuro patient," the chief resident said, leading McConnachie and the other residents to the bedside to prove his point.

The patient, an African-American, was intubated. Cotton pads covered his eyes, secured with paper tape. A plastic tube, approximately the circumference of a pencil, protruded from his right nostril, and was connected to a suction apparatus that intermittently removed yellowish green stomach secretions, routing the fluid into a plastic cannister to prevent inadvertent overflow into his lungs. He was dependent on a respirator that was attached to a thumb-sized tube protruding from his remaining nostril. His chest expanded rhythmically, every four seconds, with the bellows of the respirator. A penile catheter captured the urine from his bladder and directed it into a collecting bag attached to the bedrail. The amount of urine was recorded hourly by the nurse, and documented on a flow sheet so the team could determine if he was receiving an adequate amount of intravenous fluid. His skull was wrapped circumferentially with a roll of cotton gauze, his extremities were flaccid and motionless, and the heels of his feet hung over the end of the bed.

"This is a sixteen-year-old black male, six foot ten inches tall, admitted last night after he shot himself in the head. He was intubated and resuscitated in the E.R., and remained stable; however, he had a Glasgow Coma Scale of three with extensive intracerebral damage. He hasn't shown any signs of responding since admission."

"Sixteen years of age?" McConnachie asked. He shook his head and walked over to the bedside.

"That's what we're told. Neurology is supposedly on the way to determine if he meets brain death criteria. It looks like that'll be a no-brainer—so to speak."

McConnachie ignored his last comment, but a few of the other residents smirked and shuffled their feet.

"He's a big kid," McConnachie observed. "A basketball player."

McConnachie removed the cotton gauze covering his eyes and raised the right eyelid with his left thumb. He leaned over the patient, shining a penlight directly into his eye. The patient's pupil did not react to the light.

"His pupils are fixed and dilated."

He then placed a pen over the the nailbed of the patient's middle finger, compressing it forcibly, looking for a withdrawal reflex, but there was no reaction. He continued his exam, like an interrogator of a recalcitrant prisoner of war, trying to elicit information. With the middle knuckle of his right hand he identified the patient's sternum and rubbed it forcibly back and forth, but the patient made no attempt to recoil. Finally, McConnachie detached the respirator tubing from the endotracheal tube and held his hand over the aperture to feel for any movement of air. But after a full minute it was clear the patient was unable to initiate any respiratory effort.

"We need to have neurology do a formal apnea test and confirm that he's brain dead. How's the family holding up?"

"There's no family, but he has a legal guardian who's in the waiting room."

"Did you discuss the prognosis with him?"

"We were waiting for neurology."

"It's best not to keep him hanging, we should let him know that things look grim. Why don't you introduce me and we can bring him up to date."

McConnachie was one of the few attendings on the Trauma service who was willing to discuss bad news with the families instead of relegating the responsibility to the housestaff. A medical student went to get the guardian from the waiting room, and the resident summarized the history he had gleaned. He told McConnachie that the boy's guardian was also his high school basketball coach, and that the kid didn't have any prior history of depression. He was described as a popular athlete, highly recruited by several major universities to play basketball. McConnachie did not understand why someone with so much going for him would want to kill himself.

"Dr. McConnachie, this is Mr. Crowe, the boy's legal guardian."

"Actually, he's my adopted son," Mr. Crowe corrected.

"I'm sorry, Jinny told me—"

"No problem, I was his guardian, but a few weeks ago got the papers. Adopted both him and his brother," Mr. Crowe said to the resident.

A white coach adopting two black brothers—he had to be an exceptional person. Nikki decided she was not altruistic enough to adopt a child, much less one of another race.

"Mr. Crowe," McConnachie said, "we wanted to bring you up to date."

"Call me Coach."

"I know you're aware of the seriousness of this injury. We were hopeful there would be some sign of brain recovery but, unfortunately, that hasn't happened. We're waiting for confirmation from the neurologist, but it appears your son has suffered irreversible brain damage. Things don't look good."

"That's what I expected. I appreciate you being upfront with me, Doc. He was a great kid, a superb athlete, and every college coach in the country was licking his chops trying to recruit him. And I don't mind telling you that several college athletic directors wanted me as their coach—a sort of package deal."

"Did he appear depressed?"

"Occasionally he would get a little blue, but everyone gets a little blue, nothing out of the ordinary."

"We'll continue to monitor him closely. The neurologist will also evaluate him. But it's my impression he's not going to recover, and I want to prepare you for that."

"I understand."

McConnachie took a deeper breath than usual. "When brain injury is irreversible, there really is no point in keeping someone artificially alive."

"You don't have to convince me, I agree."

"If he meets the criteria for brain death, he could potentially help several people through organ donation."

"I understand where you're coming from, but he's suffered enough—no organ donation. I just went through this with my wife three years ago. She died of cancer right here, in this hospital. Nothing worked, not research drugs, not vitamins, nothing."

"I respect your feelings, but as far as the autopsy, that's up to the Medical Examiner. They have the right to perform a post mortem exam on anyone who suffers a traumatic or suspicious death."

"Whatever they have to do, Doc. You don't understand what a shock this is, it doesn't make sense. I just completed editing a video of his basketball highlights as a kind of promotional package for interested college coaches. You see him play and you're blown away, the kid was that good."

When Nikki heard him say that his wife was in a cancer research study, she wondered if she had been one of Cogswell's patients. The hospital computers were interconnected so that the clinical course of study patients could be upgraded by team members anywhere within the hospital network. Nikki rotated the monitor at the nurse's station towards her and booted up. She entered the password limited to active members of the research team, clicked onto patient profiles, and scrolled down until she highlighted the coach's last name. According to the information that had been entered, his wife had been diagnosed with breast cancer, and also had a documented 20%

loss in body weight which qualified her for the BrobaGen phase two study. She died of pneumonia the following year, but her weight loss was reversed with the study drug. It was unclear in the computer as to how extensive her disease was prior to receiving the drug, but her profile was similar to that of Mrs. Lamb. She watched McConnachie return to the patient's bedside with his entourage and finish his assessment.

"His unusual size could be the result of a pituitary tumor, a craniopharyngioma."

"We have the official reading of the CAT scan, and no brain tumor was identified, just extensive intracerebral damage," the resident said, ruling out McConnachie's diagnosis.

"Just for the hell of it, send off a growth hormone level anyway. I'd be curious to see if it was elevated."

"I don't know if the HMO will pay for it with a negative CAT scan. And it's not a routine test. Besides, how's it going to change the outcome?"

McConnachie was miffed by the resident's concern about saving money for the HMO rather than finding out if the patient had an unusual hormonal abnormality. A lot had changed in the six months he'd been away from the bedside, but he reacted calmly.

"It probably is a waste of money. And you're right, it won't change the outcome. But I'm curious about the answer. If you contact the research department, one of the techs will run it for us. They're doing work with growth hormone."

Jinny, the research nurse, entered the ICU as the coach was leaving, and they exchanged a prolonged hug that appeared to be more intimate than professional. They looked and held each other as if the boy's death was a shared loss, and in a way it was. Nikki calculated that Jinny had known the family since she had entered the wife in the study three years ago, and she witnessed his wife's death and now his son's. She was a constant during the most tragic period of the coach's life, and it was understandable that they clung to each other in search of consolation. Jinny walked out with the boy's father and a few minutes later returned alone. She sat down next to Nikki.

"Sad case. He loses his wife and now his adopted son. I guess you know the family?" Nikki asked.

"Very well. I entered his wife in the BrobaGen study."

"Raising an adopted kid by himself, he must be a good man."

"Two kids."

"That's right, I forgot about his brother. Another basketball star?"

"No, he doesn't even play, too short. He's only five foot ten." Jinny grabbed her laptop and stood up. "I hear we may see you tonight."

"I'm going to try and stop by."

"You should. I think you'll find it interesting."

As Jinny left the ICU, Nikki walked over to Fred, who was writing in a patient's chart.

"Finished?"

"Yup. How about we get some lunch and go back to my place. We can discuss my research proposal," Fred said, pointing to his "pleasure" button.

"Fred, you'll never have a research project approved in this hospital. In fact, you're lucky if you don't get arrested by the religious police for moral depravity."

"What's wrong with studying the pleasure response and how to enhance it? All anyone in this department is interested in is pain. It must be their puritan heritage."

He pronounced "pleasure" more like "play-sure," slowly and with reverence, as if he was unwilling to leave the word and go to the next.

"Let's get out of here, and go do a 'pleasure' pilot study," he suggested.

Nikki smiled. "Only in the interest of science."

Nikki entered the lobby of Cynthia's apartment building at 5:30 p.m., walked past a doorman who ignored her, and took the elevator to the sixth floor. After ringing the buzzer outside apartment 6N she waited for a response. There was none. She turned the door knob, which was unlocked, and entered the vestibule. Guided by the drone of chanting, she continued into the living room, which was illuminated by an assortment of candles of various sizes and shapes. A group of women, mostly hospital employees, were seated cross-legged in the middle of the room with their eyes closed, uttering unintelligible ditties. It was reminiscent of a séance she had attended in college, her first and her last, and she decided to leave while everyone was preoccupied. But before she could turn around, the chanting ended and Cynthia saw Nikki in the doorway.

"Our guest has arrived. Everybody, I want to introduce the goddess, Nikki."

The introduction was followed by a medley of responses from the assembly that included, "Welcome," "We love you," "Thanks for coming," and "Join us." The "goddess" reference was strange, but Nikki dismissed it as a dig at surgeons who were frequently caricatured as minor deities. She felt as if she had entered a women's A.A.

meeting, the members awaiting her lurid account of a life dominated by the demon alcohol. The circle enlarged and Cynthia directed Nikki to sit down next to her.

"We welcome Nikki to the Lunar Club. Feel the power."

The group responded enthusiastically to Cynthia's exhortation, repeating together, "Feel the power."

"What power are we supposed to be feeling?" Nikki asked.

"The power of female unity, the power to challenge the oppression of the male medical establishment," Cynthia said.

The group nodded in agreement, like cult followers who had sacrificed their individuality for the common cause. Members in the circle spoke of their shared experiences of discrimination by both male physicians and hospital administrators. A woman identified as Gabrielle reminded everyone that not long ago a nurse was expected to stand up when a physician walked into the room, but nurses today had learned to assert themselves. Caregivers were no longer dependent on an M.D. to make all the treatment decisions.

They looked at Nikki, waiting for her to reinforce their collective experience of persecution. Sexism certainly existed in surgery like everywhere else, but Nikki never felt oppressed. She agreed that health care had improved with a more balanced approach to the patient by a team of providers rather than exclusive reliance upon the physician.

Cynthia spread her arms. "We have ventured beyond the boundaries imposed by the fathers of medicine, and it has been this support group and others like it that have given us the strength to overcome our fears." The other members nodded.

It was clear to Nikki that this get-together was more than an informal gathering of friends. They categorized the Lunar Club as a "female empowerment group," abbreviated FEG, and members were considered of equal importance, eliminating any hierarchical authority. All FEGs were not the same, each focusing on different priorities. In this group the emphasis was on health care and the need for change in the health care delivery system.

"We don't receive a proportionate amount of societal recognition for the amount of work we do, and we definitely aren't adequately compensated," Cynthia said, as the others in the congregation nodded. "We're not saying that physicians like yourself shouldn't earn a good living, we're just saying that we should too."

Jinny added, "Everyone contributes to the care of the patient, both doctors and nurses, but it's a male-controlled industry, and men are more concerned with competition than with helping the patient. They are obsessed with who gets the credit."

They had a point. Within the affiliated institutions of MUMC, Nikki was aware of many talented scientists, each trying to find a cure for cancer, but refusing to share critical information. It was more important for them to secure patent rights in case they hit upon a commercial product rather than working together. If no one cared about individual glory or monetary gain, cures would be available for diseases currently thought incurable.

Patient care had improved with the advent of a more active nursing role, but Nikki was uncomfortable with Cynthia's belittlement of her colleagues. The more she talked, the more it became clear that she had disdain for all physicians, both male and female. It was as if women physicians were sleeping with the enemy, conspiring to maintain the status quo. Cynthia's solution was to usurp physician authority, replacing it with a gynecocracy led by nurse practitioners.

A goblet of wine traversed the circle of participants, each person taking a sip before passing it on in a clockwise direction, and then Cynthia ended the formal monthly meeting by kissing Jinny on her cheek, who in turn kissed the next person until the kiss had completed the circle.

"Before we break, we would like to remind our guest that there remains prejudice against women, especially female activists united in principle. We know that Nikki would have the discretion not to reveal to anyone the members of the Lunar Club."

"I understand and respect your concerns."

They got up from the floor, and Cynthia approached Nikki with a glass of wine which she accepted and sipped, silently identifying it as a Puligny Montrachet. It was one of her favorite white wines, but too costly to enjoy on a regular basis. They had good taste, but it was not enough to convert Nikki to their cause. Cynthia encouraged her to consider joining their community, and explained that the time commitment to participate was minimal. Meetings only occurred once a month during the full moon.

"The ebb and flow of the tides at full moon are symbolic of the menstrual flow of women," explained Cynthia. "All our members are so in tune, we share the same cycle."

"How convenient, you can borrow each other's tampons." Nikki waited for a laugh or at least a smile, but Cynthia and the members remained nonplussed at her attempts at humor. Their solemnity, a hallmark of fanatics consumed by a cause, disturbed her.

"We don't belittle men, but we certainly don't put them on a pedestal. The history of medicine is rife with stories of the 'great men,' and surgery in particular doesn't honor women."

"Things have improved," Nikki said quietly. "There're more women in surgery than ever before, and one day we'll get the credit we're due. But you're right, it's subtle. There's still prejudice."

"You guys are disparaged for taking the time to have babies, and robbing 'dedicated' men from positions in surgical training programs," Cynthia said.

"Women in the past often put down the scalpel once they got married and had a family, but that doesn't happen much anymore."

"But you're not respected like the men."

"Some women in the program complain that when they call the attendings about a patient who needs to go to the O.R., the attending asks for another resident's opinion—a male resident's."

"The only women who are accepted by their surgical mentors are those who subjugate their femininity and adopt a male attitude towards life and their profession. I think that's a mistake and a big loss for society," Cynthia said.

Nikki partially agreed. The role models were predominantly men, and it was hard to break the cycle of dependence. The process began during her orientation: surgical interns were isolated from their social network of friends and family by the demands of the job, stripped of their individual personality, and replaced with the personality of those they were dependent upon for their professional advancement. It was a variant of the Stockholm syndrome in which hostages, threatened by their aggressors, identify with those in control, adopting their likes and dislikes. Women who encroach on the male dominion morph into a replica of them. The best example, Nikki thought, was Karen Ball, the most popular woman in the surgical program. She always tried to outmale the males, bragging to the staff about her sexual conquests, and challenging her male counterparts to drinking contests at liver rounds. When one of them didn't keep up, she called him a "wimp", and then taunted him with her favorite surgical aphorism: "Can't drink, can't fuck, can't operate."

"It's important that competent physicians like yourself achieve positions previously reserved for men—particularly in surgery." Cynthia went on. "Women strong enough to value their intuitive female talents and break the tribal mold."

"I haven't found that intuition is a desirable trait in the training program."

"And you won't, not until there're more women in positions of power who support each other."

Nikki saw a lot was happening. Cynthia was annointing her as the poster girl for "women in surgery," because she was the most knowledgeable and technically proficient resident in her group. And she wasn't planning on going into breast surgery or plastics like all the other women in the program. They wanted her to become the apotheosis of surgery, flaunting her female qualities. But it was a role she had neither the time nor the desire to pursue. All her effort was focused on becoming the best at what she did, and taking on the surgical establishment was something she wanted to avoid. Securing a position on staff at the Manhattan University Medical Center would be the most effective way to act as a role model for women, but—and it was a big but—that would only happen with the help of Cynthia and Jinny. She had to have a productive research experience, and win over the confidence and support of Dr. Cogswell.

Cynthia said, "Eventually, Cogswell will realize your power. He's learned not to fight us if he wants a productive team. Individually, we're weak, but united we're a force."

"I appreciate how he depends on all of you," Nikki said, careful not to alienate anyone.

"I have a feeling you're not interested in joining the Lunar Club at this time, and that's fine, but we also hope you'll respect our views."

"I support people's right to speak their minds, it's just that I can't commit to any group right now, but maybe that'll change."

"Whatever you decide, we'll be there for you." Cynthia handed Nikki a gift-wrapped box and instructed her to open it.

Nikki unwrapped the box and removed its contents—a pendant of a moon and a star with "Lunar Club" inscribed on the back, and also two green candles. As she tried to look grateful, Jinny explained the significance.

"We burn green candles because they represent money. Material wealth unites us, and by burning the green candles, it's our hope that you'll share in our material success. Wear the pendant in good health."

"From your mouth to the goddess's ears," Nikki said and smiled.

"Open the envelope," Cynthia said.

Nikki opened the manila envelope, and inside was a document which she read out loud as the group looked on. It was a stock certificate naming her the owner of 200 shares of the Biosense company.

"We're not pushing you to join us, so don't take this the wrong way," Cynthia said.

"You've got to be kidding. This is worth a lot of money."

"Soon it'll be worth a lot more."

They had bought the shares in Nikki's name, gathering the requisite personal information from a copy of her CV. She felt uncomfortable accepting the gift, especially after she had told them she wasn't going to change her mind about joining the club. But they didn't care. Cynthia explained they had formed an investment group and pooled their resources, acquiring Biosense when it was ten, and now it was twenty-one. Sharing profits was one of the tenets of the Lunar Club, because doing good deeds for people creates good Karma—something they all could benefit from in the future.

"I'm overwhelmed. I need to go home and take this all in."

"Remember, it's just between us." Cynthia kissed her on the cheek, and other members followed and did likewise.

After a flurry of good-byes, Nikki left the apartment and waited for the elevator thinking about the gift, unclear of its significance. She was happy they liked and supported her, but she was concerned that ownership of the shares could be perceived as a conflict of interest. The research lab tested and evaluated Biosense products, and if she was a shareholder, she could lose her objectivity. It was a difficult decision.

Fred's apartment door key was the last key on her chain, and when she entered, he was sitting on the couch, dozing in front of the television.

"Fred, wake up."

He moved slowly, opening his eyes and rubbing them with the back of his hand.

She shook his shoulder. "What are you doing sleeping at this hour? I hope you weren't self-medicating."

"Give me a break, I was on last night, remember? What time is it anyway?"

"Eight-thirty."

"How was the bonding?"

"Pretty intense. They're a tight group; they even menstruate together."

"That means they get PMS together—I'd stay away from them."

She showed him the candles and explained their significance, which he dismissed as candlemaker's propaganda. Before revealing the stock certificates, she swore him to secrecy.

"Who'm I gonna tell?"

She handed him the manila envelope. He pulled out the Biosense stock certificates listed in her name.

"Whoa. They gave you this?"

"Whaddya think?"

"I think they're serious lesbians who want you badly."

"Do you have to see everything in terms of sex? You can't make an assessment without consulting that homunculus between your legs?"

"Then explain to me why co-workers would give a new member of the team a gift worth thousands of dollars."

"I admit it's strange, and I'm also concerned about owning stock in a company that I'm going to be doing research with. It's probably best I return them."

"What for? If they want to give you the shares, why fight it? Go with the flow. You can own shares in a company you're doing research with, you just have to reveal it if you present a paper, and I got news for you, most people don't."

"If we have positive results with a Biosense product, and I reveal that I'm a shareholder, people are going to doubt our findings."

"Maybe at first. But if the results are reproducible then the doubts will disappear. If you believed in a drug and had the foresight to anticipate it would be successful, then you'd be stupid not to own stock in the company. Believe me, there're plenty of well known academicians in medicine who made a lot of money from their association with drug companies. Shit, I could use four grand."

"I'm not so sure the shares are going to go up. The pilot study had positive results, but that may change after they analyze the results of the twenty patients, and particularly if the multi-centered study doesn't go well."

"If Cogswell is about to report positive findings, then I'd hold onto them until after they peak. You can always dump them later."

"Sounds easy."

"It is. Why don't you introduce me to your new friends and see if I'm their type?"

"I don't think you are."

"Then I was right—they are lesbians."

"Whatever," she said, straddling Fred's lap and silencing him with a kiss.

Fred was right. The stock price would increase if the results of the BrobaGen study were positive, and that outcome would be known soon. If she held the shares until the stock went up, she could sell them for a profit, and return the original investment to the Lunar Club. The monthly loan payments for college and medical school were burdensome, and the profit from her transaction would alleviate her credit card debt. No one would get hurt, and there would no longer be any perceived interference with her objectivity. It was common for investigators to make money off the pharmaceutical companies sponsoring their research. This wouldn't be the first time. But Nikki decided against it. She was not going to be beholden to Cynthia, the Lunar Club or Biosense. The shares were going back in the mail tomorrow with her regrets.

She pulled the bowstring of Fred's scrub pants and reached inside, liberating his penis. He responded reliably, with the emotion of a battery-powered dildo, and as they made sex, she looked over his head thinking about McConnachie.

Dr. McConnachie was correct——the kid's growth hormone levels came back off the wall. The result was consistent with a growth hormone producing tumor, most likely a pituitary adenoma, which must have been missed on the CAT scan. The medical examiner elected to proceed with the autopsy, citing the need to confirm the putative cause of death. Nikki had never attended a post mortem examination before, and she decided to take advantage of the opportunity and satisfy her curiosity about the source of the boy's excessive growth hormone production. If the CAT scan was correct and there wasn't any tumor, then the kid must have had access to a drug that mimicked the effects of a growth hormone producing tumor—a drug like BrobaGen.

Nikki left the hospital and joined the line in front of a hot dog stand. Frankfurters were ideal for ambulatory eating, and she needed something in her stomach before she went to the Medical Examiner's office.

She waited for the overweight dietician in front of her to collect her order, and then Nikki spoke to the vendor. "One with mustard."

Nikki admired his work ethic—forking tubed offal relentlessly into an awaiting bun six days a week, and never abandoning his stand.

She marvelled at the abyss of his bladder that provided him with the ability to hold his urine all day. Some colleagues had postulated that he didn't have to urinate because he had kidney failure and received dialysis after work, but Nikki had her own theory, which was rendered concrete as she watched him fill her order. Warm water from the vat that contained the cooked hot dogs splashed onto his wrist, which was followed by a frisson of relief on his face that lasted thirty seconds. He diverted attention from his physiological need by the desultory prodding and poking at his franks. After he had finished relieving himself, he speared a hot dog, directed it into a bun, painted it with mustard, and reached for a bag. Nikki hesitated to take it, because he hadn't washed his hands, but then she realized that there was no need.

She took the hot dog out of the bag and walked away, concluding there were two possibilities: he either wore an incontinence pad or a catheter. An incontinence pad was unlikely because the winter chill would make it particularly uncomfortable, the cold urine chafing at his skin and distracting him from his work. A condom catheter was a more plausible explanation, probably procured from one of the urology residents who frequented his stand. The condom was attached to a catheter that drained into a bag secured to his thigh, allowing him to urinate freely. At the end of the day, he simply removed the bag and emptied it. Nikki continued down York Avenue, satisfied with her solution of one of the many urban conundrums that had perplexed her.

The buildings along the way were functional but without charm until she got to Sutton Place, where an enclave of town houses and corner apartment buildings provided visual relief. At 53rd street, Sutton Place ended and she continued her trek along First Avenue. When she arrived at the door of the M.E. office, she went inside and interrupted a receptionist who was reading a tabloid.

"I'm Dr. Moriarty, I called about the post on Angus Crowe."

"Must be an interesting case. Another doctor's waiting for the same one, should start in about ten minutes."

"Who's the other doctor?"

"A Doctor McConnachie?"

Nikki wasn't surprised that McConnachie had come to the post mortem, because he made a habit of going to the autopsies of every patient who died while on the trauma service.

"He's upstairs in the museum. You can go there if you want while you're waiting for the case to start."

"Thanks."

The museum was comprised of a macabre collection of organs obtained from patients who had suffered unusual deaths. She recognized McConnachie on the other side of the fluid-filled encasement.

"Dr. McConnachie."

He looked up from a penetrating wound to a heart, immortalized in a vat of formalin.

"Nikki, what are you doing here?"

"I was curious about that kid who shot himself in the head. I was in the ICU when you were making rounds."

"Is this your first time here?"

"First time here, and first post anywhere."

"It's a worthwhile experience. Kind of crude compared to the O.R."

They walked by the plexiglas encasements that housed the suspended organs, and Nikki was doubtful there was any educational value in the display. Pathologists like to collect anything unusual, the more bizarre the better. She remembered a pathology professor in medical school who had a prurient interest in rectal foreign bodies. Any time a surgeon removed a foreign body from the rectum of a patient, he classified it, labeled it and displayed it on a shelf in his office. They ranged from tubers, the most common food group, to tapers of various sizes and shapes. His most prized artifact was a statue of the Virgin Mary which he labeled, "The Immaculate Insertion."

They sauntered past the display cases and descended to the autopsy room located in the sub-basement. The lower half of the stairwell wall was adorned with peeling paint of institutional gray that blended seamlessly onto the stairs. The color contrasted with a faded yellow on the top half of the wall that butted up against a white ceiling.

"I'll meet you in the autopsy room. There's an entrance through your locker room," McConnachie said.

The female locker room had a table with boxes of protective paraphernalia, and she picked out a one-size-fits-all paper jumpsuit. After climbing into it, she identified a zipper at the crotch. She coaxed it to the top and slipped on two nylon shoe protectors over her loafers. The shower cap, the only available head cover, was lowered over her hair so as not to disrupt her coif, and she molded the metal support on her face mask over her byzantine nose before securing the ties. She reflexively looked for a mirror, but fortunately none was available. Then she grabbed two rubber gloves pouting from a cardboard box before walking through the door labeled "To Autopsy Room." Elastic bands cinched her paper suit to her ankles and wrists. The remaining material ballooned and chafed between her thighs, whooshing with each step.

The diener, the medical examiner's assistant, was wheeling a new arrival towards the wall of refrigerated drawers, a giant file cabinet for cadavers. After he had identified a vacant slot, he opened its door and withdrew a steel slab on wheels. The hands of the deceased were tied at the wrist with gauze to prevent the arms from catching in doorways during transport. An identification card with its attached string encircled his large toe. It was always tied around the large toe, and Nikki surmised that the natural gap between the large toe and second toe made it the easiest digital target for the orderly to lasso. After he had maneuvered the stretcher parallel to the drawer and cranked it slightly higher, he lifted the feet off the stretcher and transferred them onto the end of the refrigerated drawer. He then went to the far side of the drawer and reached over to the deceased's right arm and jerked him from the stretcher. His head whiplashed and clunked onto the metal table, causing Nikki to shudder.

The diener, realizing he had an audience, leaned over the patient and barked into his ear, "Take two aspirin and call me in the morning."

"Get some new material," Nikki said.

She continued her journey to the final door that separated her from the abattoir. Before entering, she looked around as if expecting to see a three headed dog guarding the entrance. When she opened the door her nostrils flared, jolted by the reek of feces mixed with formalin. After stifling a retch, her brow furrowed, and her breathing was redirected exclusively through her mouth, her mask pulsating with each exaggerated exchange. She panned the room and observed eight tables, four of which had bodies on them in various stages of the examination process. She spotted two blimp-like figures standing at the other end of the room, tentatively identifying them as

McConnachie and the medical examiner. Then she walked in their direction, stopping to witness the work in progress. Each metal examination table had perforations punched throughout its surface that allowed the patient's fluids and uncollected offal to flow into a sloped basin supplied with a continuous irrigation system that directed the waste into a drain. Suddenly her hot dog repeated, and she gagged silently as she thought of its components. She walked past the remains of an unrecognizable body that was later identified as a young white female who had died of an overdose of heroin. The organs of her chest and abdominal cavity had all been removed, and her remaining torso looked like the shell of a crab on a beach after it had been picked clean by sea gulls. A physician's assistant replaced the sampled organs into the body cavity. He approximated the edges of the chest wall with a hand-held needle that was curved, and had a long piece of attached twine. He began at the corner of the chest wound, placing the needle tip through the cut edge of skin and fat and proceeded to the other side, then continued downward using a baseball stitch, inverting the skin edge of the abdominal wall, unconcerned about the cosmetic outcome of a wound that would never be seen.

McConnachie saw Nikki approach. "Sid, this is Dr. Moriarty, one of our surgical residents."

Sid Sorel, the medical examiner, stirred the dottle of his pipe with a paperclip as he nodded in her direction, unaffected by the odor of putrefaction.

"We don't see too many residents down here," he said, "and except for you, Mack, not too many attendings either. Why all the interest in a teenage suicide?"

"He had elevated growth hormone levels consistent with a pituitary adenoma, but no tumor on CAT scan. We're trying to figure out the source for the abnormal levels," McConnachie said.

The other thing that bothered McConnachie was the suicide itself. He told Dr. Sorel that the boy was a sixteen-year-old high school basketball star, heavily recruited by college coaches, and who had everything to live for. It didn't make sense that he committed suicide. Dr. Sorel listened while he looked at the boy's mottled skin and his half-opened mouth.

The boy's head was cradled on a convex wooden block, and his eyes stared blankly in whatever direction his head was turned. The medical examiner looked closely at the entrance wound to the scalp, stepped back from the dissecting table, and sucked on his pipe. He spoke through the smoke. "Ever hear of Richard Corey?"

"The poem, I hear you. Things can look great on the outside, but you never know what's going on in people's heads," McConnachie said.

Dr. Sorel nodded, and began his dictation.

"Angus Crowe is a well-built, sixteen-year-old black male, who measures eighty-two inches tall and weighs 100 kilograms."

He walked over to the right side of the table and turned the boy's head with a gloved hand, and shaved a patch of hair surrounding the head wound.

"An entrance wound is noted over the right tempero-parietal region accompanied by the presence of powder burns consistent with a close range gunshot wound. No exit wound is noted."

The pathologist wore loose fitting gloves, thick like those used for household cleaning, and with a large bladed scalpel he made a crude Y-shaped incision beginning from one armpit and extending to the other. He then continued it vertically from the midpoint of the chest incision all the way down to the pubic bone. It was a bloodless field except for the ooze of dusky fluid.

"We use the Rokitansky method—remove all the organs en bloc like a cluster of grapes, and then we examine them individually."

The skin and fat overlying the chest were pulled towards the head as he cut their attachments to the chest wall. A handheld electric saw was applied to the rib cage, buzzing through fingers of bone on either side of the sternum, and continuing vertically to divide the clavicles. The freed up segment of bone was then removed, exposing a still life of his pericardium, heart, pleura and lungs.

"I wish I could work through an incision like that, it would make our job a lot easier," Nikki said.

"As long as you don't have to close it," McConnachie said.

"You may get a few patient complaints about the scar," the medical examiner added, looking at the exposed entrails like a diviner about to make his prediction. "As you can see, the organs don't appear particularly enlarged, but we'll weigh them."

The diener worked simultaneously to expose the brain. His incision arched from just above the top of the right ear to just above the top of the left ear. The skin and its thick covering of hair was elevated from the skull with a flat bladed instrument, a periosteal elevator, and pulled down over his face to the bridge of his nose. The posterior flap was similarly pulled down to the vortex, his skull propped up on the wooden block like a boiled egg in its shell waiting to be cracked.

The medical examiner cut the spleen from its attachments deliberately and without concern for injury, and walked over to a ceiling scale and dropped it into the basin.

"It's two hundred and eighty grams." He looked at Nikki as if he was a butcher waiting to see if she wanted more or less, or would take it as is.

"I don't know the normal weight of organs," she said.

"It's within normal range for his size. Patients with giantism, particularly acromegaly, have disproportionately enlarged organs, but I don't see that here."

Their discussion was interrupted by the whirring of the electric saw as the diener applied it to the skull. The blade skated over bone, its scream ranging from a lifting soprano to a crescendo whine, grating as it encountered the resistance of the cortex. The noise subsided as it broke through the inner cortex and entered the space between skull and brain. When he had completely encircled the skull, he removed the top segment of bone and placed the bony skullcap on the table, exposing its protected contents. The bruised and bloodied brain was manipulated from its boney mausoleum, sloshing like a boot in mud, and once he had severed it from the spinal cord, it was placed on the dissecting table. The fingerlings of tissue quivered like an aspic mold, its presentation undermined by the damage from the missile that had traversed it. A deformed bullet was identified by the diener, retrieved, and clinked into a glass jar.

"Hey chief, we got another death from lead poisoning," he said, looking at Nikki.

His macabre humor drew uncomfortable laughter from most visitors, but Dr. Sorel was unamused, like a waiter at a comedy club. The M.E. picked up the glass jar containing the bullet and held it up to the light, studying its configuration before making his assessment.

"A dum-dum bullet."

"What's a dum-dum bullet?" Nikki asked, unsure if she was about to be the victim of an inside joke.

"I don't know where the name came from. Mack, you're the ballistics expert."

"That's the name of a town near Calcutta, India where it was first manufactured."

McConnachie picked up the bullet and pointed out to Nikki that it was a non-jacketed, hollow point bullet which expanded on impact, causing more tissue damage than the copper-jacketed bullets which tended to go right through the victim.

"It wasn't a cry for help, he really wanted to get the job done," Dr. Sorel said. "Calvin, let's look at the sella turcica and see if there's a pituitary tumor. That's what everyone's interested in."

The diener dissected the pituitary gland free from its surrounding bone and handed it to his boss.

Dr. Sorel made a cut through it. "The gland is normal in appearance. I don't see a tumor. It looks like the CAT scan was right. Any drug history?"

"Just vitamins, according to his father," McConnachie said.

"He must've taken growth hormone. The parents are the last to know," Dr. Sorel said, as if he was talking from experience.

The heart was normal size, but Dr. Sorel explained that if he had lived longer, the continued exposure to growth hormone would have caused it to enlarge, often a fatal complication.

"Giantism occurs before puberty from overproduction of growth hormone, and if it persists and becomes chronic, acromegaly results—enlargement of the hands, feet, face and organs. Many of those people die in their forties from cardiac arrhythmias."

He made serial slices through the right lung with a long knife, scraping the cut surface with the blade, looking for evidence of disease.

"His lungs appear grossly normal. No pneumonia. I don't see any evidence of chronic disease. No tumor in the pancreas or other abdominal organs. We'll take sections of all the organs, of course, but I don't think we're going to find much."

The diener replaced the ransacked organs into the body cavity and began closure of the skin.

"So for now, Sid, the only findings are a self-inflicted gun shot wound to the right temple with extensive intracerebral damage,"

McConnachie said.

"That's correct, but I'd change the wording to 'a close range gunshot wound, presumably self-inflicted.' We need to wait for the ballistics results and the rest of the police investigation before it can be assumed to be self-inflicted."

"Sid, thanks for your time."

"Dr. Sorel, thank you," Nikki echoed.

"My pleasure. I'll send you both a copy of the official report once it's completed."

They walked towards the locker room. Nikki was relieved to get away from the odor of decomposition. McConnachie took off his gloves, mask and cap, placed them in a garbage can lined with a red plastic bag, and climbed out of his jumpsuit looking like a member of the pitstop crew at the Indy 500. Nikki removed her cap, massaged her hair, and placed the protective clothing into the receptacle before they both walked out the exit to the stairwell.

"Why don't we get a cup of coffee," McConnachie said.

"Coffee, I might be able to handle," Nikki said, placing her hand over her abdomen.

"The autopsy room takes a little getting used to," McConnachie said.

"The smell—I don't see how pathologists tolerate it. Even his pipe didn't help. I need fresh air."

They walked into a Greek coffee shop, sat in a booth, and ordered two coffees.

"Only one explanation for his increased growth hormone levels—the kid had to have been self-medicating with growth hormone. It's readily available on the street," McConnachie said.

Nikki nodded. It was common practice for young athletes to take drugs to increase their size and strength, but not their height. Studies had shown the injection of growth hormone to be effective in increasing height only in children who were growth hormone deficient—pituitary dwarfs. Increased muscle mass and fat loss had been demonstrated, but the data suggesting growth hormone could increase height in normal sized individuals was contradictory. Most likely he was genetically predetermined to be tall, and the increased levels were just a red herring, a serendipitous finding that didn't have any substantive effect on his ultimate size. If his parents were tall, he may have been within his projected growth rate. Growth hormone alone couldn't have been responsible.

"But even if he took the injectable form, kids of normal stature only grow one or two inches," Nikki said.

"I agree, unless there's something else out on the street, another drug that we don't know about."

That was the other possibility that concerned Nikki—another drug not previously available that was more effective than growth hormone alone, a drug such as BrobaGen. It had never been studied in patients of his age group, and Nikki knew he had access to the drug from his mother, who had been in the BrobaGen study. When he observed how she had responded to the injections with increased weight gain and muscle tone, he may have decided to try it himself.

"Maybe the coach has some information from the orphanage about the size of the kid's parents. If they were tall, then it would put an end to our speculation," Nikki said. She thought about the corollary of her statement—what if his parents were below average in size? Then there would have to be a pharmacological explanation for his unusual size, and growth hormone alone wouldn't do it. It would mean that BrobaGen was most likely the causative agent.

Indolent tumors in the younger age group were relatively rare. Therefore, the risk of spreading cancer would be less than in the older population. Every athlete and every wannabe athlete would be taking it as a performance-enhancing drug, and it would open up a whole new market. The shares of Biosense would take off. Maybe she should've listened to Fred and held onto the stock a little bit longer. No use thinking about it; they were somewhere in the mail system on the way to Cynthia.

McConnachie said, "If his parents were tall, it would mean he took growth hormone causing his increased blood levels, but it probably didn't have anything to do with his size."

Nikki agreed, and decided it was premature to share her speculation about BrobaGen until after Cogswell broke the study code. It wouldn't be known until after he tabulated the results as to whether BrobaGen increased weight and size in humans. And for now it made more sense to try and find out about the size of his parents.

"There must've been signs of depression that were missed," McConnachie said, looking at her over his coffee cup, "perhaps caused by the drugs. We just need to let the coach know, because other members of the team could be taking drugs, particularly his brother."

Psychotic episodes could result from steroids, Nikki knew. It happened to a patient she had helped take care of last year, and it was not unreasonable to think the drugs Angus had taken had precipitated his suicide.

"I'll talk with the social worker and arrange a meeting with his father. I know you're busy, just getting back and everything. I'll go over the post findings with him."

"Thanks. Call me if I can be of any help."

They finished their coffee, satisfied with the agreed-upon plan. He had resumed his mentor role of advising Nikki, remaining aloof, their interaction confined to medical topics. He did invite her to his country house for dinner, but he invited Fred also, something he would not do if he had a personal interest in her. But, Nikki thought, it was better that way.

McConnachie went to a dental appointment, and Nikki returned to the hospital ruminating over the autopsy findings. If Angus had taken BrobaGen, it had to have been prior to puberty, approximately three years ago, when his epiphyseal plates were still open. Once they're closed, the bone can no longer lengthen in response to the drug and cause a growth spurt. Someone must've injected him with his mother's BrobaGen years ago, or had at least shown him how to do it. Jinny was the most likely candidate since she was the one injecting his mother at the time. But it was all conjecture. If she made accusations without proof, she would incur the wrath of both the Biosense executives and Cogswell—a career ending move. Before making unsubstantiated allegations, she needed more data, and for now it was best simply to inform the coach about the post, and just do her job.

When Nikki arrived at the hospital, she walked into the nurses' lounge and poured herself a cup of coffee. An audience of one, an ICU nurse, tried to ignore Jinny's rant while Nikki sat down out of view of the speaker and sipped her coffee. Jinny whined that Cogswell took credit for her work, enjoying an international reputation because of her efforts.

"He's treated at the cancer meetings like he's the Second Coming, but what they don't know is he didn't have anything to do with the study," Jinny said.

Her last comment aroused her listener, Carmen Gonzalez, one of the better nurses on the team, who had been subjected to Jinny's self-promotion on more than one occasion.

"He could replace you with another research nurse and not miss a beat," Carmen said.

"No one can recruit patients like me, and he knows it."

"That's because you tell them what they want to hear."

"The risks are spelled out on the consent form. We're not running a remedial reading program. No one forces them to sign up."

Carmen was right: Jinny skated over the consent form with patients, minimized the risks, and signed up patients for studies at a rate uncommon for most research facilities. It was a major reason why Biosense was so supportive of Dr. Cogswell's lab.

"I got to tell you, there's something wrong with paying research nurses for every patient they enter," Carmen said.

"Who told you they pay?"

"Gimme a break, that's why you're always hustling patients."

Jinny didn't deny it. Nikki knew that drug companies paid capitation fees to ensure that their studies were given priority, prodding the researchers to approach all available patients. It was similar to the gift-giving by the drug representatives, or the payment of honoraria to physicians—monetary inducements to ensure loyalty and prevent distraction. It was an accepted cost of doing business, but Nikki was aware of the inherent danger: the payments influenced the recipients, consciously or subconsciously, causing them to overlook factors that would eliminate patients from a particular study—patients like Mrs. Lamb. Her hospital chart contained a nurse's note documenting that Mrs. Lamb's ten pound weight loss resulted from a diet confined to tea and soup because of loss of appetite from depression, and not as a result of the catabolic effects of cancer. She wasn't a candidate for the study, but Jinny ignored the recorded history and wrote her own version.

"One of these days it's going to backfire. A patient or their family is going to realize they weren't fully informed, and your ass is grass," Carmen said.

"It's all spelled out for them in writing."

Technically she was covered. Cogswell was the senior investigator and it was his responsibility to oversee the research team, making sure all the protocols were followed and the patients were properly screened. If an unqualified patient had been entered into a study by a research nurse, he should have caught it and prevented it, not only to protect the patient, but also to justify the results of the experiment. Data collected from a patient population that did not meet criteria for admission into the study would be misleading and the conclusions unreliable.

"We have to be able to defend what we do, and not just hide behind a consent form or blame the M.D.," Carmen said.

"It's the other way around—physicians blame the nurses. You don't understand, I was married to one and I know how they think."

Jinny viewed herself as the critical catalyst to the research project, but underappreciated and underpaid. Her enmity towards her husband had spilled over into the workplace, explaining her resentment of physicians, and Cogswell in particular. Nikki was appalled at her duplicity.

Jinny continued, "If I had M.D. after my name, believe me I'd be treated differently."

"Why don't you go to medical school then?" Jinny responded to Carmen with a deprecating wave of her hand before getting up to leave.

On the way out, she saw Nikki sitting in the corner.

"Nikki, whassup?"

"I went to the post on the coach's son," Nikki said.

"I thought they refused," Jinny said with practiced indifference.

"They did, but every traumatic death is automatically an M.E. case."

"That's something I never understood—an obvious suicide and they still do a post."

Nikki informed her of the absence of a brain tumor. Without a pulmonary adenoma to explain his elevated growth hormone levels, McConnachie and she had concluded that the kid was taking growth hormone on his own. Jinny readily agreed, citing the rampant use of street drugs by that age group, particularly performance-enhancing drugs.

"If he was injecting growth hormone or whatever, his brother or a friend, someone would've known about it," Nikki said, as she watched Jinny for any sign of complicity, but she remained unruffled.

If Jinny had injected him with the BrobaGen, she had no intention of disclosing it.

She disavowed any knowledge of his biological parents, and claimed that the brothers were in foster care prior to their adoption by the coach. Nikki explained that she was concerned about both his brother and his friends, who may have been exposed to the same street drugs, drugs which could have precipitated his suicide. It was important to apprise the coach of the need to make the others aware. Jinny agreed, and promised to discuss the problem with the coach when she saw him.

A few minutes after Jinny had left, Carmen returned. She poured herself a cup of coffee, added a splash of two percent reduced fat milk, and sprinkled granulated chemicals from a paper packet into the solution. The color of the mixture was too light, and she added more coffee. Satisfied, she gulped a sample and sat next to Nikki.

"Have you got a minute?" Carmen asked.

"Sure, go ahead."

"I've got to get something off my chest, and I feel I can trust you."

Nikki became uncomfortable that an acquaintance had chosen her as confidante, but she agreed not to repeat what she was about to tell her. She braced herself for her disclosure.

"That respiratory arrest the other day—Mr. Washington—I've tried to put it together and there isn't any good explanation."

"A mucus plug," Nikki said, relieved that the nurse's angst was related to a patient care issue rather than a personal matter.

Carmen remained unconvinced about the diagnosis, but Nikki attributed her misgivings to self-defense. Cynthia had reprimanded her for not providing the patient with adequate chest physical therapy, and Carmen was denying responsibility for the complication. She tried to remove blame from Carmen by saying that they would never know the cause for certain, and that there were other possibilities such as a cardiac arrythmia. Carmen produced the rhythm strip that was recorded at the time of his arrest, and the only abnormality was the bradycardia—the slowing of his heart from the decrease in oxygen.

"I guess that's another reason why mucus plug is the most likely diagnosis," Nikki said, while Carmen shook her head.

Carmen pointed out that the patient didn't have any reason to have a plug. He had been steadily improving, and just before his arrest he was sitting in a chair, waiting to be discharged from the ICU to the floor. His chest x-ray that day had been clear, and he had just completed deep breathing exercises with an incentive spirometer before she went to lunch. Nikki conceded the precipitating event for Mr. Washington's arrest remained obscure; it was a medical conundrum they were never going to solve.

"Whatever the cause, the important thing is he survived," Nikki said, and she started to walk out.

"It isn't the first time something like this has happened," Carmen said to the back of Nikki's head, causing her to stop and turn.

"What are you trying to tell me?"

"Over the past three months, two other respiratory arrests were presented at Nursing Q.A., and both involved Cynthia."

"And the cause for those arrests?"

"Same thing, a plug. But Cynthia leads the discussion of the patient complications, and no one questions her."

"There's really no other explanation."

"Just one," Carmen said.

Nikki found herself sitting down, suddenly tense. Carmen described what happened after she returned from lunch. She saw the rhythm strip in the waste paper basket, and she bent over to pick it up. When she stood up she brushed against the sharps container on the wall, and something rattled inside. She didn't think anything of it except she remembered that just before she went to lunch, housekeeping had placed a new container on the wall and removed the old one. It should have been empty, but after hearing something inside, she turned it upside down and retrieved a used ampule which she handed to Nikki.

Nikki read the label. "Fentanyl."

"You know we only give Fentanyl to patients who are in severe pain, and it wasn't even ordered for Mr. Washington."

"Someone probably used it on another patient and dumped it into his sharps container."

"Nobody carries needles or ampules with them from one room to another, they're all paranoid about AIDS, and what happened to Dr. McConnachie and everything."

"Maybe it was already inside the container when housekeeping put it in the room."

"The container was new, and I saw the housekeeper remove the seal before placing it on the wall. Believe me, I wanted to think there was another explanation, but nothing else makes sense."

Nikki liked Carmen and trusted her. But she knew she had issues with Cynthia, and perhaps her emotions were interfering with her objectivity. She tried to dismiss the suggestion that Mr. Washington had been injected with Fentanyl, causing his respiratory arrest, but she struggled to find a more plausible explanation. The first thing to do was to check the medication chart and see if another patient had received the drug. They walked over to where the narcotic records were kept and confirmed that another patient, Mrs. Cummings, had received Fentanyl. Carmen checked the narcotic sign out sheet. Cynthia had been the one who had picked up the Fentanyl.

"Maybe she gave it to Mrs. Cummings and neglected to discard it until right after she relieved you for lunch," Nikki said.

"Unfortunately, Mrs. Cummings is still on a ventilator, so she can't verify that Cynthia had injected medication into her I.V."

"You're thinking she signed out the medication for Mrs. Cummings, but gave it to Washington instead?"

"Exactly."

"The Fentanyl would explain Mr. Washington's sudden deterioration, and his quick recovery, but why would she do it?"

"The only thing I can think of is she was trying to make herself look like a hero, you know—Cynthia saved another patient."

The administration was willing to pay top salaries to key personnel, and they had identified Cynthia as one of those people, someone adept in crises. A retrospective review of the outcome of patients who had suffered cardiac arrest during their hospital stay showed that patients resuscitated by Cynthia had done significantly better than those resuscitated by the resident staff. And Cynthia wasn't shy about bringing the results to the attention of her superiors. If Carmen was right about the contrived patient arrests, it would explain Cynthia's unparalleled success at resuscitation. But the evidence was circumstantial, and, undoubtedly, Cynthia had documented on Mrs. Cummings' flow sheet that she had given her the Fentanyl. There was no basis on which to dispute her claim. The administration was behind her, and as long as the paper work was in order, nothing else mattered.

"By any chance did you send off a sample of Washington's urine to see if he had Fentanyl on board?"

"Yesterday. We should have it back in a couple of days."

Nikki advised Carmen that she and her colleagues should refuse Cynthia's offers to cover for them for now. The results of the urine sample would determine their next move.

"I feel better I shared this with you. There aren't too many people around here I trust," Carmen said, and she left the lounge to return to the bedside.

Nikki was upset by Carmen's hypothesis, because it made sense and explained why Cynthia had been so calm when Washington had arrested. It was a controlled arrest, and she knew exactly when she had to intercede. She ventilated him with one hundred percent oxygen to correct the bradycardia, knowing that the half life of Fentanyl was short, and that he would start breathing on his own within minutes. It was a practiced routine, but dangerous. It was just a matter of time before someone didn't respond as planned, and died as a result of her self-promotion.

If Nikki was going to accuse Cynthia of having injected a patient with a drug that caused a respiratory arrest, she had to be able to prove it. The urine sample was essential because if it came back positive, it would prove he had received the drug. The Department of Health would have to be notified, and the administration would not appreciate the bad publicity. If she didn't want to jeopardize her career, she had to proceed cautiously. It was best not to share what Carmen had told her with anyone at this point until there was more data, not even with McConnachie. Everyone would know soon enough.

On her way out of the hospital, Cynthia frisked her left hip, retrieved her two-way, and messaged Jinny to meet her right away at
D.O.A., a nearby hangout. She crossed York Avenue, walked half way
up the block towards First, and entered the bar. The lunchtime crowd
had dwindled, and she proceeded to the back, settling in a booth
isolated from the few remaining customers. A bartender, supporting
the medical theme of the establishment, wore a green scrub suit,
accented with a stethescope around his neck. The shelf on the wall
behind him displayed replicas of the liter bags of saline solution found
in hospitals and used for intravenous therapy. But instead of saline,
these were filled with scotch, bourbon, gin or vodka. The waitress,
outfitted in an abbreviated nurse's uniform that included an anach-
ronistic white hat, handed Cynthia a menu entitled "CPR."

Cynthia handed it back before speaking. "I'm waiting for someone, but I know what we're gonna have."

"Fire away."

"We'll have 'Last Rites' for two."

"My favorite," the waitress said, raising her eyebrows, and smiling before leaving.

Cynthia scooted off the banquette and walked towards the bathroom past a display of medical artifacts that included a human skeleton propped up on a corner barstool, its skull crowned with a Tam o'Shanter. A sculpture comprised of fused surgical clamps was spotlighted in a corner alcove, and a pair of cardioversion paddles was mounted on the bathroom door. She opened the door, locked it behind her, adjusted the water temperature, and began scrubbing her hands. God knows what hospital bacteria had taken refuge in the crevices of her skin, she thought, while washing her hands for the third time. A ladybug escaping the cool fall weather landed on the mirror, and Cynthia counted nine spots on its orange colored back. They were pretty insects, and beneficial to the environment. Her stepmother claimed they protected her homegrown tomatoes from juice sucking aphids, but who knows if it was true. If she had been allowed in the garden during her annual July visit, Cynthia thought, maybe she would have seen for herself.

After drying her hands, she picked up the insect between her thumb and index finger and pinched it. It emitted an odor to ward off predators, but it was too subtle for her to smell. She squeezed harder, coaxing it to increase its secretions, but Cynthia was unable to appreciate the deterrent. The ladybug extended its wings from its tail, poised for flight, and Cynthia reached into her pocket, retrieving a surgical clamp. With the jaws of the metal teeth, she grasped the wings and avulsed them. Now that it was fully aroused, she smelled again, but still nothing. The experiment was over, and she concluded that only insects could appreciate the pungent discharge.

Without wings, it lay in the sink, dependent on the mercy of others. Cynthia compressed it with her thumb against the resistance of the the plaster basin and splashed water on it, watching as the remains swirled down the drain. She washed her hands three more times.

When she returned to her seat, she opened the manila envelope. It contained the Biosense shares returned to her by Nikki along with a letter of explanation. It didn't make sense. How could she worry about a conflict of interest as a Biosense shareholder when she wasn't even involved in the BrobaGen study? Besides, by all reports, she was in debt. And people in debt don't return shares worth $4000.

Jinny arrived and slid into the booth opposite Cynthia. "Whassup?"

Before Cynthia could answer, the waitress returned with a wide-mouthed glass bottle filled with a combination of vodka, Southern Comfort and a splash of cassis responsible for the reddish hue. She inserted a rubber stopper with a plastic tube connected to its metal spout, and turned the bottle upside down. A wire handle at the bottle's base was hooked onto a wall peg, and the fluid filled the tubing, which bifurcated into two distinct teats, each with its own stopcock. She placed an ice-filled glass in front of each customer.

"Enjoy," the waitress said, before retreating into the kitchen.

"We're starting early today," Jinny said, as they each picked up their respective tubes.

"For good reason. We've got problems."

A red flush appeared on Jinny's neck. "What kind of problems?"

"The worst kind—financial," Cynthia said. They each raised the tubes and released the stopcocks, squirting approximately 100 cc's into their respective glasses.

"Problem with the stock portfolio?"

"No," Cynthia said, waving the manila envelope. "Nikki returned her shares."

"That just means more money for us," Jinny said, her red chevron fading.

"If she was stupid I wouldn't be worried. But something about her gives me bad vibes."

"You gotta remember, she needs us more than we need her."

Jinny still didn't understand the potential problem that Nikki posed, but it wasn't surprising. Jinny was well-intentioned but not street smart, a consequence of her Connecticut upbringing.

"I've been going over in my head things she said, trying to find some clue about what she's up to," Cynthia said.

"Maybe nothing."

"I don't buy that. She says she returned the shares because of a conflict of interest, but there wasn't any."

"You know how much she wants an appointment on staff when she finishes her training. She's paranoid about being labeled a mercenary."

"I agree, but I still think there's something else going on."

They both took another sip of their drinks while Cynthia reviewed Nikki's character profile, which was inconsistent with her current behavior. Their research revealed two things about Nikki: fierce ambition and heavy debt. She couldn't afford to alienate people who could help her career, and she also couldn't afford to return the money. Her unpredictable behavior did not bode well.

"Now that you mention it, she's been asking a lot of questions lately," Jinny said, staring down at the table.

"What kind of questions?"

"You know, stuff about the kid. Who are his biological parents, how tall are they?"

Cynthia slapped the top of the table with the palm of her hand, startling Jinny. "Dammit Jinny, when the fuck were you planning on telling me this stuff?"

"Whaddya want me to do, page you every time she says hello?" Jinny's neck became fully flushed. "It's no big deal, I handled it."

Cynthia controlled her anger. Yelling would only cause Jinny to edit her responses and prevent her from disclosing other information. "Sorry, I didn't mean to lose it."

Jinny nodded, and Cynthia resumed her questioning. "Can you think of anything else she said?"

"She mentioned that the post on the kid didn't show any brain tumor."

"She went to the post?"

"That's what she said."

"Strange, I mean it wasn't as if the kid was her patient or anything."

"She's curious, that's all. Wanted to confirm that it was suicide, not murder."

What an idiot. How did she ever tolerate working with such stupid people? It wasn't that Cynthia didn't trust Jinny, she certainly was loyal to the cause, but there was something missing—she lacked intuitive skills. Medical curiosity about whether the kid's death was a suicide or a murder did not explain Nikki's presence at the autopsy. More likely it was because she suspected the kid was on BrobaGen, and she went to confirm her suspicion.

"No question she's curious, but curious about what?" Cynthia asked, gently trying to awaken Jinny to the obvious.

"I don't know, but McConnachie was there too. Maybe she's boinking him."

"That loser? First his wife leaves him, and then he pricks himself with an infected needle. Who'd want a piece of that?"

"I got news for you, a lot of people. Come on, admit it, he's a piece of ass, and it doesn't hurt that he makes the big bucks."

"Don't tell me you're going after him, not after what you've been through," Cynthia said, knowing how to push Jinny's buttons.

"I told you I don't do doctors anymore, too self-absorbed. But if I did–"

"What about that anesthesiologist that she was getting it on with?"

"You mean Fred? I hear he's hung like a donkey."

"Yeah, Fred. What happened to him?"

"They're still together, but that doesn't mean she isn't sampling McConnachie."

Cynthia took another drink. She didn't like what she was hearing about Nikki's interaction with McConnachie. He was a bad influence, a real pain in the ass, and was probably the reason why Nikki had returned her shares. She remembered the do-gooder had petitioned the administration to bar pharmaceutical representatives from the hospital, because he didn't think it was appropriate they gave gifts to the residents as a stimulus to prescribe their products. He overlooked the fact that the administration also benefited from ties with the drug companies. They turned down his request.

The waitress walked over. "Guys, I can see your vital signs are improving. Can I get you anything else?"

"Not now, thanks," Cynthia said, watching the waitress walk away. "They need to come up with some new lines, besides 'your vital signs are improving.' They say that shit every time you have one of their fucked-up drinks."

Jinny nodded while she swallowed another squirt. "It does get tiresome."

"So what's their explanation for the kid's increased growth hormone levels?" Cynthia asked.

"He had to be taking it. What else are they going to say?"

"Did she mention anything about BrobaGen?"

"No, just growth hormone. Cynthia, don't you think you're making more out of this than there is?"

Cynthia shrugged her shoulders. "Maybe."

She didn't want to disagree with Jinny and put her on the defensive again. It was important to gather the facts and base a course of action on as much information as possible. Cynthia got up from the booth and walked over to the waitress and asked her for some peanuts or potato chips. A wicker basket labeled "hyperalimentation" was produced, and it contained Pepperidge Farm Gold Fish. She grabbed a handful, tossed them into her mouth, and placed the basket on the table in front of Jinny.

"When Nikki asked you about the kid's parents, what'd you say?"

"What could I say? I never met them. That reminds me, she wanted to talk to the coach and tell him that the kid was taking growth hormone."

"We're fucked if she talked to him. That hayseed probably told her Angus was on BrobaGen, and he got it from you."

"Take it easy, I took care of it. I told her that I would talk to the coach myself."

"Good, but make sure you warn him that she may still try and contact him. Let him know she could jeopardize his coaching opportunities."

"I know how to handle the coach."

"Did you mention Angus's brother?"

"All I said was he had a brother. I didn't mention that he was a twin."

"Smart." Cynthia gulped her drink. "And tell the coach if he shoots his mouth off about the twins, he's gotta know he not only screws us, he screws himself. If there's an investigation, he can kiss off any college jobs."

Jinny nodded. Cynthia knew that the coach would sell his first born to advance his career. The only reason he adopted the two black kids was because he thought they were going to help his all-white basketball team. If it wasn't for BrobaGen, his team would still be in last place.

Cynthia filled her glass again from the I.V. bottle and walked over to the juke box. She scanned the selection and inserted a quarter, which clinked its way down the coin slot, and she punched "It Wasn't Me" by Shaggy.

Jinny still didn't get it. She was too complacent about Nikki, and unappreciative of the damage she could do.

McConnachie, damn him. She never liked that prick with his holier-than-thou attitude, and if he was so great, why did his wife leave him? He had a bad influence on Nikki, and if they kept snooping around, eventually they would put it all together. If they discovered that the kid was on BrobaGen, an investigation would follow, and Jinny would fold under the scrutiny. She would disclose the twin experiment, and bring everyone down with her. Nikki had to be stopped now, before it was too late.

Cynthia returned to the booth, smiling at Jinny as she sat down. "I didn't mean to overreact before."

"Hey, no big deal," Jinny said. She began to sing the words to the song, the alcohol eliminating her inhibitions. She laughed when Shaggy sang that his girl friend walked in on him while he was banging the next door neighbor on the bathroom floor, and even though he was caught in the act he still protested "It wasn't me."

"There's a lesson to be learned with that song," Jinny said. "No matter what happens, you got to deny it. Just like Clinton, and just like Shaggy."

"If you lie enough, people start to believe you," Cynthia said, staring at Jinny's lips, two thin red lines that gave her an angry appearance.

"Whaddya thinking?" Jinny asked.

"Just trying to figure out the best way to handle things. Can you remember anything else?"

"I told you everything. I was in the coffee room, I talked to Carmen and then Nikki."

"Carmen?"

"Carmen Gonzalez."

"Was she talking with Nikki too?"

"I guess, after I left. Why?"

Cynthia leaned in. "That bitch tried to send a drug screen off on Washington after he arrested."

"And?"

"She was trying to prove that someone overdosed him with Fentanyl, namely me. Can you believe that shit?"

"You know Carmen, she's in denial. She can't admit that his arrest was her fault. She's lucky you were there."

"Tell me about it. I canceled the test, but I gotta tell ya, just the idea of it pissed me off. I thought about suing her ass."

"You shouldn't have canceled it. When it came back negative, it would've proved what an asshole she is."

"I guess you're right," Cynthia said, satisfied that Jinny never suspected Washington's arrest was contrived. It was important for her to have the respect of her peers; it facilitated the accomplishment of her goals. "When's the next time you gonna meet with the coach?"

"I'll call him Monday."

"Just make sure he doesn't talk with Nikki."

"I know, I know," Jinny said, with her eyes closed. "What about George Lally, should we let him know Nikki may be a problem?"

"No, I don't want the Biosense people spooked. If they think there's going to be a problem, they may postpone the promotion of BrobaGen. We need to let the stock bounce, and then get out. Let them think everything's cool."

"I hear you."

"Don't forget, it's not just our money. The Lunar Club has over a million bucks invested, and half of it is on margin. If Biosense goes south, the sisters lose a fortune."

Carmen had probably shared her hypothesis about Washington's arrest with Nikki, Cynthia thought, and now Nikki and Carmen would be watching her. But so what, let them watch and let them talk all they want, they don't have any proof that she gave Fentanyl to Washington. Cynthia would just have to be careful around them. It was important to be aware of your enemies.

"We should let Cogswell know she's not working out," Jinny said.

"Not yet. It'd be better if she left on her own."

"No way. She's not the type to quit."

"She might be if she felt threatened. And I'm not talking about career threats."

"Whaddya gonna do, beat the shit out of her?" Jinny asked, shaking her head before draining the remains of the bottle.

Maybe I will, Cynthia thought, and maybe I'll beat the shit out of you sitting there with that fucking lime-colored Polo shirt and khaki skirt.

"I thought we'd start off with a few anonymous phone calls."

"She'll recognize your voice."

"Not with a voice scrambler. She'll probably suspect it's some goon hired by Biosense to protect their investment."

"I wouldn't be surprised if Biosense did do something about her."

"Obviously. You're talking a potential windfall for the company of billions of dollars if BrobaGen hits. They're not going let some resident screw things up. That's why we need to do something before it gets out of hand."

"What if she goes to the cops?"

"As the song says, 'It wasn't me, it wasn't me,'" Cynthia said. "Anyway, I'm not doing anything yet, but we have to have a contingency plan in place."

"How far are we going to go with this, I mean if she doesn't back off?" Jinny asked.

Cynthia stared at Jinny's chicken shit face, focusing on her bridgeless nose. It was freckled, like the back of the ladybug.

"One step at a time," Cynthia said.

"It's too bad she had to get so uppity. She had everything to gain by just being cooperative."

"It all started with that Mrs. Lamb. She had some sort of weird attachment to her. Hey, Nikki, she's dead. Get over it."

The waitress placed the bill, enclosed in a leather folder, on the table.

"We don't accept any third party insurance, just Master Card, Visa, American Express or cash. And make sure that both of you return for your follow-up appointments," the waitress said, and smiled before returning to the bar.

Cynthia placed enough cash inside the folder to cover the check and a twenty-five percent tip. The medical theme was not the waitress's fault, she was just doing her job. Cynthia liked it when people did what they were paid to do.

The daylight startled them when they opened the door, their pupils constricting as they walked down the block singing, "It wasn't me, it wasn't me."

Biosense Pharmaceuticals was located in Northern New Jersey amongst the world's leading drug companies, a consequence of available farmland, proximity to New York and favorable tax breaks. The aroma of recently cut grass suffused the gated campus. The grounds were landscaped with spirea, barberry and juniper bushes with a backdrop of ornamental trees. Nikki climbed the marble stairs to the columned entrance of the four-story building and entered the lobby.

A security guard sitting at a desk greeted her. He requested two pieces of identification, one with a picture, as he reviewed the computerized list of expected visitors. After he had cross-referenced her name, he reached for a camera and took her picture. He then produced a handheld metal detector and combed her perimeter before approving her admission. The polaroid was attached to her temporary I.D. card, and both were inserted into a plastic holder suspended on a metal chain. Nikki bowed as he draped the chain over her head and instructed her to wait while he called her escort. Before he had finished dialing, George Lally appeared. George welcomed Nikki and walked with her out of the lobby and down a hallway.

"I hope you didn't mind the security check," George said.

"The strip search was a little much."

"Strip search?"

"Just kidding."

George laughed, but confided that it wouldn't have been the first time it had happened. An unauthorized visitor had tried to get by security last year, but she was stopped and the police were called. She was armed with pepper spray, and after they had completed a strip search they discovered she was wired with a tape recorder and a hidden camera. She was a member of PETA—People for the Ethical Treatment of Animals—and she had planned to document animal abuse, spray the lab personnel and free the animals. It would have been years of research down the drain. The security precautions had intensified since that episode. Tours of the facility were strictly limited.

They walked through two more automated security checks, the doors opening in response to radio waves emitted from his badge. They entered a large warehouse-like room that was subdivided by a labyrinth of counters creating individual work areas for over thirty scientists, and they climbed a flight of stairs to a catwalk that encircled the work area below. A few of the investigators talked in groups, while others worked independently. Nikki learned that the researchers were all promising scientists who were paid three times the salary earned by colleagues in academic institutions, and they were also privileged to work under the auspices of two Nobel Laureates. Drugs that they synthesized, and that became commercially successful, increased the value of their shares in the company. And that's why the employees were so enthused about their newest product—BrobaGen.

They walked down the stairs and passed through two doors before arriving at the "small animal research facility."

George paused before opening the door. "Labs that experiment on mice usually aren't bothered by anyone."

"Sounds like the animal rightists are discriminatory."

"They are. If you do research on cats, dogs or primates, forget about it."

It was ironic, but Nikki concluded it was easier to get approval to do studies on humans. You give a patient a consent form and they either sign it or don't sign it. But once they agree, the investigator is covered. Lower forms of life had defenders, but people were on their own. If there was a PETH—People for the Ethical Treatment of Humans—then maybe Mrs. Lamb would still be alive.

A familiar looking woman in a white labcoat approached them. George introduced her to Nikki. Her name was Gabrielle, and she was a post-doc who had agreed to continue the tour while George attended a pre-scheduled meeting.

"I leave you in good hands," George said before he left.

"Welcome, we meet again," Gabrielle said, shaking Nikki's hand.

"I'm sorry, but where do I know you from?"

"Cynthia's apartment. You were at our last Lunar Club meeting."

"Right, the Lunar Club."

Gabrielle told her that as an inducement to join their club, she was going to take her on the private tour. They entered an elevator, exited onto an unmarked floor, and confronted an armed security guard who sat at a desk in front of a locked door. He recognized Gabrielle. She explained that she was taking Nikki on the V.I.P. tour. He checked Nikki's I.D. before he allowed them to pass through the doorway, which opened into a plexiglas-enclosed primate lab. It housed a variety of monkeys including macaques, orangutans, and chimpanzees. Gabrielle apologized for all the security precautions, but explained that visitors were not allowed in the primate lab, and that her friend, the security guard, had done her a favor.

Two chimpanzees were separated from each other in adjacent cages, but they looked completely different. One was robust and healthy, while the other appeared listless and wasted as if it were dying. Gabrielle told her they were siblings, and both had been exposed to Simian Immunodeficiency Virus—the monkey version of the AIDS virus.

"The CD4 cells in the one dying were normal three weeks ago, and now they're down to fifty."

Nikki didn't understand why the CD4 cells, the cells that held the virus in check, were so low only six weeks after exposure, a process that usually took many years. The normal count in humans was around 1000, and once it dropped to less than 200, opportunistic infection occurred, causing the patient's death.

Gabrielle observed Nikki's perplexed expression. "If you're wondering why the CD4 cells dropped so fast, it's because the researcher spiked the virus."

"What about the one that looks healthy?"

"They both inhaled the virus, but the one that's dying was exposed to the souped-up virus."

"I thought HIV couldn't be transmitted as an aerosol?"

"That was true up till now. We altered it so it can permeate the nasal mucosa."

Researchers had further modified the virus, enabling it to replicate at such a rapid rate that the host's immunological defense mechanisms were overwhelmed within six weeks, a process that in the past took ten years. Nikki was shocked that a leading pharmaceutical company was trying to accelerate the growth of a killer virus rather than trying to eliminate it.

"Why would anyone spend time trying to develop a better way to spread HIV?"

"Part of a Defense Department contract."

"What's the plan for its use?"

"That's up to them. We don't get involved in the politics. We get paid to do the science, and we leave the moral wrangling and the ethical debates to others."

It was the next generation of biological warfare—a supercharged AIDS virus that could be placed in biological warheads and fired from scud missiles into civilian populations. Whoever inhaled the virus would be unaware that they had acquired it, and they would spread it unwittingly to family and friends, attributing their symptoms to the flu.

"What if a terrorist gets hold of a cannister?"

"Scary, but that's why I figure it's better in the hands of the United States than some third world country."

An odorless, colorless spray that could be released by terrorists in the subway and inhaled by unaware commuters. It would spread exponentially, and by the time people sought treatment it would be too late for protease inhibitors to be effective.

"The substance added to the virus, it wouldn't be BrobaGen, would it?"

"Can't say, it's under military contract."

It had to be BrobaGen. The drug caused the virus to replicate faster, and by the same mechanism increased the doubling times of malignant cells. Its ability to disseminate HIV eclipsed BrobaGen's anabolic effect on muscle metabolism, resulting in weight loss and opportunistic infection. The chimpanzee experiment also demonstrated that BrobaGen could be delivered as an aerosol instead of an injection, which would increase its popularity. Teenagers, hoping to improve their athletic performance, would demand it.

"We better get going. I could catch hell if they find out I took you into a restricted area."

They walked past the security guard, who told Gabrielle she didn't have to bother signing out, and they returned to their starting point where George was waiting.

"Enjoy the tour?"

"Gabrielle was very informative."

"Good. I want to show you our marketing department, a combination of Hollywood and Madison Avenue all rolled into one."

Nikki said good-bye to Gabrielle and walked with George to the elevator, which they took to the third floor. A series of passageways led to a double door with an unlit, neon "On the Air" sign. When they entered, there was a revolving stage that was divided into three different sets. The first one recreated a hospital room with all the appropriate monitoring equipment. The second one portrayed a physician's consultation room with an imposing mahogany desk and a backdrop of bookcases filled with leatherbound books. And the third scene featured a podium with the words "University Hospital" inscribed in large lettering along with twenty chairs filled with white-coated, lifelike mannequins.

"This is where we shoot our video news releases."

Nikki had seen their products advertised many times on the evening news: an actor posing as a patient in the ICU bed while a simulated physician touts the breakthrough drug. In the next sequence, the doctor is in the consultation room, discussing with the fully recovered patient how fortunate he was to have received the drug. The major scientific breakthrough is then summarized in the final scene by the research physician standing at the podium, while a voice-over urges the audience to request the drug from their doctor.

George told her their videos were directed by a former network news editor, someone who spoke the television language and knew exactly what the television producers were looking for. All the promotions were carefully scripted so they didn't look like blatant advertisements, and could be inserted into the nightly news without the need for editing. The segments were done so well that the television directors took credit for the story, electing not to identify that the material was supplied by Biosense, a trend the drug company encouraged.

Nikki saw a familiar-looking actor talking to the set director, and George explained his presence.

"We have a stable of celebrities we choose from, matching their personality with the specific drug. They become our spokespeople."

It made sense: prospective patients, influenced by their admiration of the celebrity, ask their doctor about the drug. If there's no contraindication, the physician prescribes it to keep them happy.

Nikki disliked the strong-arm tactics. "Doctors should advise their patients about medication, not the other way around."

"This program has effectively changed that interaction."

"Any physician resentment?'

"Minimal. In the real world, if a patient asks you for a drug that's not contraindicated, and you don't give it to them, they get upset."

It was self-preservation, and Nikki knew that patients received physician evaluation forms from their HMO. If they submitted enough negative evaluations, a doctor could be discontinued as a provider and lose a significant percentage of her clientele. The drug companies appealed directly to patients with "Ask your Doctor" ads, and the physician was compelled to prescribe the drug to avoid alienating her patients.

Nikki had to admit it was a well-thought-out strategy. It began with synthesis of the compound, and ended with the promotion of the drug to the public. In between, the company cultivates relationships with investigators like Cogswell at leading medical centers to evaluate their product with the caveat that the company has the right to review the researcher's results prior to publication. If an investigator's conclusion is negative, the company sponsoring the study pressures the individual not to submit the results to a medical journal. Those who don't comply lose their financial support. When a positive result is produced, the marketing department takes over and launches a two-pronged attack: It targets physicians, convincing them that the company's new product is superior to their competitors'; and also the public, saturating them with advertisements directing them to ask their physician for the drug.

"Sounds like you got things covered at both ends—patients and physicians."

"We try. Speaking of covering both ends, did I ever tell you about Dudley?"

George proceeded to describe the legend of Dudley, their drug "advance man of the year." Biosense had targeted an influential gastroenterologist with one of the busiest practices in New York. He refused to allow any drug representatives into his office, and his secretary was under strict orders to keep them out. None of the usual maneuvers to lower physician resistance worked. He rejected offers of tickets to Broadway shows, free dinners at four-star restaurants, and paid trips to medical meetings. Dudley called his personal physician and had his secretary schedule an appointment for him with the gastroenterologist for a colonoscopy without sedation. While undergoing the procedure he pitched the drug, and the physician had no choice but to listen until he completed the exam. After it was over, he still refused to prescribe it.

"The gastroenterologist was right—there're better drugs—but that effort earned our man a well-deserved promotion," George said.

Nikki was still preoccupied with the Biosense facility and its promotional juggernaut, rather than listening to tales of Dudley. BrobaGen couldn't fail with this kind of promotion. Every cancer victim's family would be demanding the drug from their oncologist, at least until there was clear cut evidence that it was deleterious. With FDA approval, Biosense will turn their focus onto teenagers. The market for a performance-enhancing drug was limitless, and it would be years before a pattern of harmful side effects could be proven.

They walked by a warren of offices used by the graphic designers and passed a soundproof room where the voice-overs were recorded, stopping at the office of a PhD and his secretarial staff. He was a former employee of the FDA, an expert in statistics who had been a critical decision maker in determining whether a drug received FDA approval. Now he was a highly paid employee of Biosense, and his friendship with his former colleagues helped achieve favorable reviews for Biosense products.

George told Nikki that approval times for experimental drugs had decreased, ever since the pharmaceutical companies agreed to donate millions of dollars to subsidize the FDA so they could hire additional personnel. A protease inhibitor that had decreased mortality from AIDS had been approved by the FDA within seventy-two days. In the past the same process would've taken years, and recently there had been record approval times for some cancer drugs.

"Expediting the review process is essential because once we get the blessing of the FDA, we can go directly to the public."

The final stop on the tour was a large room with several compartmentalized spaces, each containing desks with computers and ergonomic chairs.

"We use this room to fill prescriptions over the internet."

"How do you do that without getting a history and examining the patient?"

"Easy. We have a combination of nurse practitioners and physician assistants under the auspices of an M.D. who interview the patients over the internet. They review their history and current medications, and if there aren't any contraindications, they give them the prescription."

With all the paraprofessionals hired to perform the screening, Nikki estimated, the physician is able to prescribe over 200 prescriptions per hour, receiving a fee for every prescription she authorizes.

"When we get FDA approval for BrobaGen, we're going to triple our staffing in anticipation of the demand," he said. "Aren't you happy to be part of this team?"

"Can't you tell?"

It was a well-oiled machine geared to saturating the market with their drugs. They had big plans for BrobaGen, even though there wasn't any statistically significant data that proved BrobaGen was responsible for the patients' weight gain. If Cogswell didn't prove an advantage for BrobaGen over the placebo in the phase two patients, it would be the end of the drug, especially if other investigators questioned its effect on the doubling times of cancer cells. Its role would be restricted to use as a biological weapon. On the other hand, if Cogswell's phase two study shows that it increases muscle mass and doesn't spread cancer, then Biosense would shift to a broader market—aspiring athletes. With the imprimatur of the FDA, physicians will be at liberty to prescribe it at their discretion.

"You haven't met Dr. Waddle, have you?" George asked.

"Who's Dr. Waddle?"

"He's our Medical Director, brilliant guy, president of all the biggest academic organizations, including the American Oncological Organization. A former Dean at an Ivy League medical school, and he knows everyone in academia. Good friends with Dr. Cogswell."

"Is he involved in the research?"

"Indirectly. He establishes relationships with the academic institutions, negotiates contracts for clinical studies, and makes sure that the studies get done."

"What if one of the centers has a bad outcome? What happens to their contract?"

"We haven't had that problem yet, so I don't know. Dr. Waddle chooses reliable people to participate, people that he has relationships with, and who have a pretty good idea what they're going to find even before the study begins." George gave Nikki a wink and a nod. "Can I take you to lunch?"

"Thanks, but I've got to get back to the hospital."

"Duty calls. We'll do it another time."

"Another time."

She thanked him for the tour and walked out to the parking lot. Their operation was impressive, but she reminded herself not to be taken in. It was important to remain objective about the results of any patient studies she participated in, and not let her interpretation of the data be influenced by her relationship with Biosense or any other drug company.

Before leaving the parking lot she took out her cell phone and called her answering machine for messages. There was only one, and it was delivered by an unidentifiable voice, robotic sounding and gender neutral. The message was, "Leave while you can." Nikki repeated it to herself, perplexed by the warning. Leave what, leave where? It didn't make sense. It had to be a wrong number. At least she hoped it was.

Nikki glanced at the directions to McConnachie's house and confirmed the exit before continuing onto the Taconic Parkway. She had spent four years of college in Poughkeepsie, and she retained fond memories of the Hudson River Valley. Every summer she returned to attend a festival and sail with classmates under a quilt of hot air balloons. It was her annual respite from urban blight.

The parkway was narrow but untrafficked, and the turns were lined by trees including maple, oak, and linden, their leaves offering an early orange, red, and yellow. Roadkill distracted her. Crows pecked away, survivors that fed on the misfortune of others.

She couldn't believe Mr. Washington's urine sample had been discarded. How did Cynthia find out a sample had even been taken? She must have seen it sitting at the nurses' station before it was picked up for delivery to the lab. The clerk said Cynthia was livid, screaming that whoever requested such a test was irresponsible since Fentanyl had never been ordered for Mr. Washington.

You have to pick your fights, and there was no way to win this one. It would only ensure her own failure. She had worked too hard to throw everything away and sacrifice her career. Shut up for now.

Go with the flow.

She got off the parkway and continued northeast towards Amenia. The roadside alternated with horse paddocks and farmland, reminiscent of the mid-west, and she watched a colt frolic across a fenced-in meadow. Galloway cows munched on hay. A field of stubble recalled the corn harvest.

McConnachie's property was identifiable, as she had been warned, by a barn-red mailbox. She turned onto his driveway, a road lined with a wall of rhododendron bushes that had long since bloomed, and she came upon a yellow colonial with black-shuttered windows. After she parked the car she walked to the front of the house. A handwritten note addressed to Nikki and Fred was posted on the door. It directed them to follow the path into the woods. It was signed "Luke."

She walked down the hill behind the house and headed toward a footbridge that forded a creek. In the middle of the bridge she paused and studied the gurgling whitecaps created by jutting rocks. The rocks had been abraded smooth by the current. On the other side of the water a Virginia creeper spiraled up a dead elm. The pathway, blanketed with dried leaves, crepitated under foot.

A rustling startled her, but it was just a squirrel. She was about to return to the house when she spotted McConnachie. He was perched on a rustic chair cobbled out of cedar, looking out at a savannah of wetland.

"Mack," she called.

He stirred from his meditation. "Hey, you made it. Where's Fred?"

"Couldn't come, had to take call."

"Too bad."

"Not really, we find separation mutually beneficial." McConnachie grinned, and Nikki sat down next to him. "And where's your significant other?"

"I'm not seeing anyone right now."

The question rattled around again. What had provoked McConnachie's wife to leave him? Probably something banal like a sexual dalliance with a hospital employee. He had plenty of opportunities. But Nikki decided now was not the time.

"You've got a beautiful place."

"It's funny, I never came here before I got sick."

"So there were some positive aspects about getting hepatitis."

"I guess there were. I learned from it."

"The only lesson I learned was to avoid taking care of trauma patients."

McConnachie smiled and pointed over Nikki's shoulder at a doe and her fawn walking through the wetland. Every few yards they would stop, motionless, with their ears erect and their nostrils flaring, sniffing the air. The doe's hide had camouflaged itself, preparing for a leafless winter. The fawn's spots had begun to fade. Twigs cracked beneath Nikki's shifting feet and the deer pounced away, their white tails upright. She watched them disappear into the high grass.

"Graceful. I don't think I could ever kill one." She turned to McConnachie. "You don't hunt, do you?"

"No, but I enjoy tracking them, taking pictures."

Someday she would have the time to hang out in the woods and gaze at animals meandering in their natural habitat.

"How do you track animals anyway?"

"You follow their prints and look for scat."

"Scat? As in Satchmo and Ella Fitzgerald," she said, smiling.

"Different kind of scat—the animal's stool."

He pointed to a pile of congealed pellets nearby. "Those are fresh deer droppings, shiny and slightly moist."

"Gastroenterologists would be good trackers. They're all closet coprophiliacs."

"Coprophiliacs?"

"You know, shit lovers."

McConnachie laughed. "They probably would be good. Those deer tracks over there are also a giveaway," he said, pointing to two crescent-shaped impressions in the dirt separated by a ridge, formed by cloven hooves.

He walked over to a maple sapling and signaled Nikki to join him. The bark had been scraped away as if it had been sandpapered, leaving a smooth, denuded surface.

"Another sign of deer. That's from a buck."

"His horns?"

"Just before they rut, they rub the tree with their forehead and antlers. It leaves a hormone that warns other bucks that the females in the area are already spoken for."

"I wish that was all we had to do to protect our turf. Leave your scent, and other oncologists would stay away from your patient population."

"Protection of turf is more subtle with physicians."

"Rumors and gossip rather than confrontation." Nikki hesitated to share the hospital rumors about McConnachie's sudden departure, but decided it was better he knew. "Like when you left, the reasons ranged from liver failure secondary to hepatitis up to and including a nervous breakdown because of marital problems. I'm not telling you that to upset you, but I think it's important. Set the record straight."

McConnachie, familiar with hospital palaver, was unaffected by Nikki's disclosure.

"There was a time when I'd be interested in responding to rumors, but there's a Buddhist saying: 'See it to be a lie, and you have already dealt it a mortal blow.'"

More of his Zen. It was an interesting philosophy, she thought, but it was ineffective in dealing with the competition of professional life in New York. He needed to be proactive or his enemies would swallow him up.

"But rumors can do a lot of damage, even to the point of affecting your practice," Nikki said.

"You can't spend your time worrying about rumors, lies and what other people think. You become paralyzed."

He just didn't get it. His reputation had been trashed, and he was being grandiose, taking the moral high road, a strategy that would just play into the hands of his enemies.

"I still think reputation means a lot for a surgeon. You've worked too hard to ignore the consequences."

"We worry about our reputation and what people think instead of just living our lives. It reminds me of a parable by a Zen master..."

Again with the Zen. His newfound passivity was inconsistent with the surgical personality. If someone attacked Nikki, she attacked back harder, or else she wouldn't have gotten as far as she had. Zen Buddhism may be effective on the grounds of a monastery isolated from the real world, but it doesn't work on the grounds of the Manhattan University Medical Center. McConnachie had been spending too much time in the woods; he needed to regain his fighting edge.

"Zen master, Hakuin," McConnachie continued, "was respected in his community and recognized as someone who lived a pure life until the daughter of a neighbor became pregnant and identified him as the father."

"It's always the ones that act so pure."

"The parents were outraged and accosted him."

"Obviously he denied it; it was before DNA analysis—no proof."

"He didn't deny it or admit to it."

"That means he did it."

"All he said to the parents was, 'Is that so?'"

"He's lucky her father didn't kill him."

"When the baby was born, the parents brought the baby to him and told him that the child was his responsibility, and he had to raise him."

"What about the mother?"

"She was very young and went on with her life, and didn't have any contact with them. His reputation was ruined, but it didn't matter to him. He raised the baby to the best of his ability and continued to live his life one day at a time."

"If he wasn't responsible, he would've denied he's the father and refused to raise the baby."

"A year later the girl confessed the real father was someone else. The parents were distraught that they had accused Hakuin, and asked for his forgiveness."

"I hope he told them to get lost."

"Instead of being angry, all he said was, 'Is that so?'"

"Didn't they have lawyers in those days? I would have hit that family with a libel suit, the likes of which they'd never seen before."

"He knew he hadn't done anything wrong, and that was all that mattered to him. Life's short, and he wasn't going to waste his time trying to convince others that he wasn't responsible for the child."

"With that attitude, there'd be a lot of lawyers out of a job. What happened to the baby?"

"He gave it back to the family, and went back to his life."

"You have to admire someone like that, but there's no way he would survive in the real world, at least not in New York. You haven't become a Buddhist, have you?"

"No, but I think you can learn something from every religious tradition or philosophy of life."

"I agree. God has to be more broadminded than to confine herself to one religion over another."

"I had an opportunity while I was on leave to read about Zen, and Transcendentalism, along with my long forgotten Catholic teachings."

"Why not combine all three, Transcendentalism, Zen Buddhism and Catholicism? You could call it TransZenCatholicism."

"Something to consider. Seriously, I know it's impractical to try and adopt a purely Buddhist view, and still live and work in New York. But the teachings can be very helpful."

"Like what?"

"Mindfulness, for example. Focusing your mind on whatever is before you. Living in the moment."

"Surgeons do that every day in the O.R."

"Right, but sometimes we get distracted and don't do the operation that's best for a particular patient."

"What do you mean?"

"For example, I've done operations because they fit the standard of care and, therefore, are beyond criticism, ignoring perhaps a better approach."

"But if everyone did what they thought was right, there'd be chaos."

"I don't mean that you act on a whim, or that you ignore the collective experience of the surgical profession before making a decision. You have to be knowledgeable of all the recommended treatments. But keep an open mind, and think of the patient. Don't tailor the patient to the operation, tailor the operation to the patient."

"Once you find that something works, you tend to stick to it."

"That's fine, but what worked on one patient may not necessarily be the best approach for another patient."

"You mean like the operation I watched you do last week."

"Exactly. It wasn't the standard of care at that time, but I was confident we could accomplish it safely and the patient would benefit."

"I guess if you wanted to avoid criticism, you would have given her a colostomy."

"We become fixed in our ways, closed to new ideas. André Gide said, 'Believe those who are seeking the truth, doubt those who find it.'"

There was merit in what he said, Nikki thought, and his quotations and aphorisms were entertaining. But his philosophy was not realistic. If that patient had a major complication, he would've been sued, and there would have been no defense. His choice of operation was a deviation from the standard of care, and it didn't matter how well-intentioned it was.

A groundhog ascended from his burrow, raised himself on his haunches, and stretched his neck as if he was trying to see over a wall. He held a medley of vegetation in his paws, which he munched nervously as he listened for interlopers. Uncertain of his safety, he waddled to his nearby plunge hole and dove into the earth.

McConnachie got up from his chair and walked with Nikki towards the house. She had viewed him as the embodiment of the dedicated surgeon—able, affable, and available—but now disease had turned him into a wimp.

When they arrived at the house, McConnachie stopped at a planter made out of a wine cask and broke off twigs of rosemary and thyme. He placed them on a counter by the sink in preparation for cooking.

"Need any help?" Nikki asked.

"Why don't you cut the garlic in half, and I'll get the chicken ready."

"I think I can handle that, but I have to warn you that I haven't cooked dinner since I began my internship. I'm the only one in New York that has a sign on my door requesting Chinese menus."

"I remember those days. Residents eat out of necessity, not out of enjoyment."

"I like to eat, I should learn to be a better cook."

"If you can operate, you can cook. There are a lot of similarities between great chefs and surgeons."

"Both are on their feet for long periods."

"You definitely need stamina. And both have to tolerate long training programs."

He compared the recipe to the steps of an operation, and in both cases it was essential to have a full understanding of each before beginning. Unfamiliarity with the procedure or working out of sequence could have fatal results for both the patient and the soufflé.

McConnachie felt the garlic bulbs, assessing their firmness, and then smelled their cut surface. "Good chefs and good surgeons use all their senses."

"One major difference," Nikki corrected, "surgeons aren't dependent on taste."

"Thankfully, it's one sense that has a limited role in surgery."

McConnachie trussed the chicken with a large needle loaded with a piece of twine. He pierced the flesh of the leg and continued through the carcass and out the other leg. Then he made a u-turn and directed the needle through the wing, carcass, and out the other wing, so that he held both ends of the string on the same side of the chicken. He tied the two ends with a surgical knot and the chicken became taut, braced for the oven.

"What is this dish called, 'Chicken in Bondage'?"

"That would catch the eye of restaurant critics."

"Seriously, why do you tie it up?"

"It just keeps the chicken legs and the wings from flopping around when you turn it, and it allows the chicken to cook evenly."

A dollop of butter mixed with sea salt was then placed on its breast, which he massaged into the skin, and continued rubbing onto the legs and both wings. A second helping of the concoction was inserted inside the carcass. He smeared the salted butter onto the inner surface, over the ribs and spine, as he stared at the ceiling. He looked to Nikki like he was performing an internal exam, except that he didn't warn the chicken it was going to be "a little uncomfortable."

"Is that one of those hormone treated chickens?"

"Organic, no antibiotics, no drugs."

Nikki thought about Mrs. Lamb's death. Also organic. "I never used to care about organic, free range, whatever. But then you read about five-and six-year olds developing breasts and menstruating because they ate estrogen-injected chickens."

"That worries me too. The chickens are bred to have large breasts, and they are so top heavy they can't even mount each other to reproduce."

"I've always made it a policy: Don't eat any animal that can't screw."

"The Department of Agriculture should adopt that as their slogan."

"I'm not kidding, next thing you know they'll be injecting chickens with BrobaGen."

"I believe it."

McConnachie grated freshly ground pepper over the bird and placed it on its side in the broiling pan surrounded by four halves of garlic. Two stalks of rosemary and thyme, retrieved from his herbal pot, were added before inserting the pan into a preheated oven set at 425 degrees.

"You have to season the chicken with sea salt and freshly ground pepper both before you put it in the oven, and after you take it out. No dried herbs, only fresh. Just like in surgery, details count."

"You know, thinking about that kid who shot himself, I'm convinced he was taking BrobaGen."

"Why do you say that?"

"When you were making rounds, I overheard the coach say that his wife had cancer of the breast and had been a research patient. I looked up the BrobaGen patients. Turns out she was one of the first to be entered into the study."

"You think he took his mother's BrobaGen?"

"After seeing her increased muscle mass, I think he decided to try it himself."

McConnachie lifted the chicken and placed it breast side up in the broiling pan. "BrobaGen would explain his elevated growth hormone levels, but it's hard to imagine that a thirteen-year-old kid would inject himself with an unknown drug."

"Maybe he didn't inject himself. You know Jinny, the research nurse?" McConnachie nodded. "Jinny was treating his mother. She could've given it to him."

McConnachie was confused. "Why would she risk her license by giving an experimental drug to a minor? Especially since growth hormone has only been marginally effective in average-sized kids."

Nikki leaned over the table. "But BrobaGen isn't just growth hormone. It has huge doses of growth hormone releasing factor, Insulin-like growth factor, steroids, DHEA and who knows what else. The combination of substances makes it more effective than growth hormone alone."

"There could be a synergistic effect. But his growth spurt could also have been genetically predetermined and have nothing to do with the drug."

"And that won't be easy to prove since both he and his brother are orphans." Nikki picked up a piece of rosemary and sniffed it. "Smells like mentholated pine."

"It adds to the flavor of the chicken."

"Who taught you to cook?"

"My father."

"Your father was a chef?"

"A firefighter, but he cooked for his firehouse all the time. He was lieutenant in an engine company in Brooklyn, and they took their food seriously. Sharing a good meal strengthened the bond between them."

"You never know when it's going to be their last one," Nikki said.

"True." McConnachie looked down at the floor.

"I take it he's no longer alive."

"No, he died when I was fourteen—a building collapse," he said, walking over to the bookshelf and picking up a framed newspaper account of the tragedy. She read it to herself while he opened the oven to baste the chicken.

"'Forty-two-year-old Fire Lieutenant Jimmy McConnachie, responding to a woman's plea to save her baby, ran back into her burning house in the Brownsville section of Brooklyn and suffered life-threatening burns along with internal injuries. Battalion Chief Marty McGlaughlin had just ordered everyone out of the building because of uncontrolled fire on the top floor, when the hero firefighter ignored the command and returned in a desperate attempt to find the baby. His search was prolonged by heavy smoke, and tragically ended when the top floor he was standing on gave out, and he crashed along with it through each succeeding floor, mangled and trapped in the burning basement.'"

Nikki looked up at McConnachie. "I can't imagine falling into a fire. What makes them go into those burning buildings anyway? I mean I can see hosing the building down with water, and extending ladders on the outside to help people escape, but that's it."

"They're trained to perform a search when they think someone's trapped inside."

She shifted in her seat and continued reading. "'Members of Rescue 2, led by firefighter Lee Balzano, responded to McConnachie's Mayday call and extricated him from the superheated rubble. He was rushed to the New York Firefighter's Burn Center and remains in critical condition.'

"Thank God they got him out."

"Not before he suffered a sixty-five percent burn and multiple fractures."

It suddenly made sense to Nikki why McConnachie was so interested in Trauma. "How long did he live?"

"Forty days. He would've made it but he had a bad inhalation injury—that's what killed him."

"Amazing he hung on that long. The baby died?"

"I guess you didn't read the last paragraph."

Nikki returned to the clipping. "'The baby was presumed dead, and once the fire was controlled, a final search for the body was begun. It ended when the woman screamed, "My baby is alive, my baby is alive," and she ran over and picked up her dazed but viable, calico cat.'"

"The woman's baby was a cat?"

"A cat."

McConnachie said his mother made him promise after he burned his legs that he would give up on being a firefighter, and so he went to medical school and became a trauma surgeon—medicine's version of firefighting.

"Thank God for your mother," Nikki said.

"That was a hard decision. I loved hanging around the firehouse with my dad. Going to probie school was a natural for me. I still have friends who are firefighters. They're a good group." He paused to collect his thoughts. "Your father, he's a physician, right?"

"Some call him a physician, I call him an asshole."

McConnachie remained silent, and she felt obligated to explain her unresolved anger towards her father. She told him her father was a well-respected psychiatrist who advised couples about relationships, but he himself was incompetent as a parent and husband. He had abandoned the family when she was twelve, and upgraded to a nurse who was twenty years younger than him right after her mother's health began deteriorating from multiple sclerosis. Her mother lived for another five years, but died the summer before she entered college. During her decline, Nikki had the opportunity to listen to her mother's fears and concerns, and resolve issues between them. This allowed her mother to accept her fate peacefully. At her mother's request, they composed a living will which emphasized that under no circumstances was she to be put on life support, and Nikki promised she would make sure she was kept comfortable. When her mother slipped into unconsciousness portending an imminent death, Nikki called her father's office out of obligation. She got his tape, and left a message that if he wanted to pay his last respects, now was the time. Within thirty minutes a team of paramedics appeared at the door and began resuscitating her mother. Nikki told them to stop, but they would not listen because her father, Dr. Moriarty, wanted everything done. She tried to pull them away, but they pushed her to the side and threatened to have her arrested. When she arrived at the hospital's ICU, her mother had morphed into a helpless cyborg, unresponsive and intubated, lullabied by the trill of the monitors. Her father insisted that the living will was invalid, because he was the next of kin and responsible for her care. He stood by the bedside holding her mother's limp hand, like a caring husband devastated by his partner's impending departure. Her father refused to allow the physicians to curtail treatment, and the nurses admired his compassion, unaware that his ex-wife's wishes had been ignored. His colleagues filed by and patted him on the back, admiring his steadfast devotion as he stood by the bedside every day from two to two fifteen. Her death was prolonged an additional three weeks, and Nikki was distraught that she had called her father, because by doing so she had betrayed her mother's last wishes. He didn't care whether his wife lived or died, he only cared about his image.

McConnachie shook his head. "I'm sorry you had to go through that."

"The next time he called me was after I graduated from medical school. I didn't talk to him then, and I have no desire to talk to him now."

"I understand."

"I wish I did."

She didn't understand her father's paroxysms of parental concern, when most of the time he acted as if she didn't exist. He would introduce her to colleagues at national meetings like a carnival barker announcing an unusual phenomenon, and when the meeting ended she was returned to her handler as he resumed saving the world. His family was a career enhancer, testimony to the outside world that he was a caring person. But it wasn't a true family, it was just two people on retainer, she and her mother, available on command.

"Unfortunately, people often marry out of societal expectation rather than love," McConnachie said.

"It would've been better if they hadn't married at all. Did I ever tell you my idea to solve the problem of emotionally absentee fathers?"

"Castration?"

"That's one option, but I had something less radical in mind: Moriarty's Time Share Families. It's a business that would obviate the need for workaholics to procreate and thereby spare children emotional turmoil."

"Sounds interesting. How does it work?"

"Simple. My concept is based on the one popularized by owners of vacation condos, but instead of living space the participant is provided with a family. The first phase of the business plan targets surgeons right before major meetings. For a reasonable price, they're supplied with a presentable spouse during the designated week of their annual meeting along with two well-behaved children, one of each sex, trained to make appropriate conversation with his colleagues, and attest to his parenting skills. When the meeting ends, the leased family is deposited at the airport along with the rented car, and the surgeon returns to his work unfettered by the banal responsibilities of family life. The same family is available to him/her the following year, and all participants are able to trade weeks with other members if mutually agreed upon. If the member chooses a different time period the following year, availability of the original family will not be guaranteed."

McConnachie laughed. "I like it, you'd be sold out your first year."

"Definitely."

"Anyway, you said you wanted to learn to cook, so why don't you come over here."

Nikki watched him remove the partially cooked chicken from the oven and baste it. He explained it was important to cook it twenty minutes on each side, and twenty minutes with the breast up. Turning the chicken ensured it cooked evenly and was less likely to dry out.

He opened the oven, filling the room with a warm fragrance. Each halved garlic was tanned on its exposed surface, and the taut skin of the bird glistened a golden brown. He removed the pan to the top of the stove, accompanied by a crescendo of crackling fat.

"How can you tell if it's done?"

"By looking at it, but that comes with practice. Generally, I cook a four pound chicken about an hour and fifteen minutes. You can also stab the leg with a fork and when you see clear fluid come out it means it's done, but I haven't found that to be a reliable technique."

He elevated the tail of the chicken by placing an overturned plate under the pan, and then covered the chicken with aluminum foil.

"I'm sure there's a reason why you're doing that."

"I'm letting the juices flow into the breast before carving. It keeps the meat moist. Meanwhile I'll show you how to do the potatoes."

He rinsed several small, red potatoes in cold water to get rid of some of the starch, and after drying them in a towel, he cut them into quarters. A tablespoon of congealed fat was then scooped into a hot pan, and it liquified, covering the cooking surface.

"Whatever you just put into that pan can't be approved by the American Heart Association."

"You're right, it's duck fat. Every good restaurant's secret. They use it when they sautée potatoes. It gives them a much richer taste."

He placed the potatoes into the hot fat and allowed them to brown on each side. A minced garlic clove was added during the final minute of cooking, and the pan was removed from the stove.

"That's it."

McConnachie dismembered the chicken, placing a limb and a slice of its breast on each plate along with a portion of potatoes. A bottle of red wine was uncorked, and the food was brought to the table. After they were seated, McConnachie picked up the bottle and hovered over Nikki.

"Wine?"

"Absolutely."

"It's a Brunello. A patient gave me a couple of bottles not too long ago."

It was a simple dish, but it had exceptional taste, the crisp skin contrasting with the moist meat and the crunchy potatoes speckled with garlic. The wine complemented the meal, and the conversation slowed as they ate and drank. It was a welcome change from her usual diet of handheld foods, and the roast chicken was as good as the one she had had at David's in Paris. They discussed French and Italian cooking, their appreciation of food, and the improved dining experiences that had evolved in recent years throughout the United States. McConnachie attributed the change to the professional training offered at schools such as the Culinary Institute of America, and the demands of heightened palates exposed to European travel. The combination had resulted in a marked improvement in the quality of American life.

When she reached for her wine glass, it had been refilled.

"I may be out of line, but I don't understand why your wife left you. You're too good a cook."

"She did like my cooking, but there were bigger issues."

"I'm sorry, it's none of my business."

"No, it's okay. I feel comfortable talking to you about it," he said, shifting in his seat.

"A surgeon's life, it's a strain on any relationship," she said, offering a generic opening.

"That's true, she needed a lot of nurturing, and I wasn't available."

"Didn't you realize what she was like before you got married?"

"Sort of, but I guess I deceived myself."

"Did she give you an ultimatum?"

"I've never told anyone this, but–"

"Another man."

"I decided to surprise her and come home for lunch. When I got there, I found her in bed with another woman."

Nikki reached over and squeezed McConnachie's hand. "I'm sorry."

"I should've seen it coming—not the lesbian part—that I never expected."

"Maybe it was a one-shot deal. There were women like that in college—LUGs—lesbians until graduation."

"We weren't sleeping together, and she was spending a lot of time up here writing while I worked in the city."

"What did she say when you walked in on her?"

"They both acted like they hadn't done anything wrong."

"Any chance for reconciliation?"

"She claimed I never gave her the attention and nurturing she deserved and needed. I guess it didn't matter to her whether she got it from a man or a woman."

"Sounds like she has some serious issues."

"I guess we both do."

"But she knew the demands of your practice."

"She did and she didn't. It's different when you're dating, the lifestyle's better tolerated."

"I guess."

"It was weird. The woman's face was familiar. Turned out she was a staff gynecologist."

"Unbelievable."

"The more we drifted apart, the more time I spent at the hospital. And when I wasn't at the hospital I was writing papers."

"It's hard to find a balance in medicine."

"I should've concentrated on my family and on my patients, rather than publishing, trying to make a name for myself."

"Academic institutions want their name out there."

"I know, the institution comes first."

Nikki wanted to hold him and place his head on her breast, but instead she stood up and kissed him on the cheek. He tightened his lips, and she returned to her seat. She didn't think he could handle anything more.

When she finished her wine, McConnachie got up to clear the table, refusing Nikki's offer to help, rinsing the dishes before he placed them into the dishwasher. When he returned, he said, "I still don't understand why anyone would risk doing a study that wasn't sanctioned by the I.R.B."

Nikki, nurtured by the meal and perhaps the wine, had an urge to share her theory—thoughts she had planned to keep to herself. She explained that cachectic cancer patients were a narrow target audience, especially compared to healthy teenagers. Biosense was looking for a new market. Cogswell's study, if positive, could result in provisional FDA approval of BrobaGen, and then it could be prescribed at the discretion of physicians. It was the old "bait and switch"—get approval for one indication and prescribe it for another. Aspiring athletes would be petitioning their physicians for the drug.

"What about its effect on tumor growth?"

"That hasn't been proven yet, and it'll take several years before any trend can be established."

She reminded him that kids didn't think about risks, especially if the product is something that can make them more attractive or better athletes. They smoke cigarettes, abuse alcohol, take drugs—including steroids—even though the consequences are well known. They don't care about the potential risks of a drug that can make them bigger, especially if it is conveniently packaged as an aerosol.

"What do you want to do about it?"

The old McConnachie wouldn't ask what to do, Nikki thought, he would be knocking at Cogswell's office door demanding an explanation.

"Tomorrow morning I'm meeting with the coach in the social worker's office. I plan to tell him about the autopsy findings and discuss the kid's growth hormone problem. See if he has anything to say."

"If your theory is correct, it could get ugly," McConnachie said.

"It gets worse. Last week Cynthia and her friends welcomed me to the team, and gave me 200 shares of Biosense."

"The shares are in your name?"

Nikki nodded. McConnachie slid back in his chair and took a deep breath.

Nikki said, "It's not an issue. I gave them back."

"I think that was smart."

"I know, but it's going to be painful to watch the stock go up," she said, thinking about her college and medical school debt.

"There'll be other investment opportunities."

Maybe she had said too much, but he had that effect on her—a desire to share her thoughts. At least she hadn't repeated what Carmen Gonzalez told her. If he heard about that, he would expect her to report the incident to the State Health Department. And since there was no proof, an investigation would only end up alienating Cogswell and his staff. It was good she had left some things unsaid.

They finished their coffee, and she faced him, thanking him for the meal.

"I'm glad you were able to come," McConnachie said, looking towards her feet.

Nikki wanted to throw her arms around him, but she held back, afraid it would make him uncomfortable. Instead she stood on her toes and kissed him on his lips, careful not to linger.

"I'd like to do this again sometime," Nikki said.

"I'm sorry if I've been a little distant, but I guess I'm still going through a transition–"

"Don't apologize, you need more time. I understand."

They walked to her car. She started the motor, waved good-bye, and exited the driveway. It was unfair, she thought; he was too good to have a wife treat him like that. His marital problems affected his concentration, and probably resulted in his injury from an infected needle.

Nikki liked him, she liked him a lot, but caring for someone was not what she planned for herself at this point in her life. She had a career to think about. But being with him was different than being with others; she wanted to spend more time with him. And Nikki wasn't sure if that was good.

Joy, the social worker, had an office located adjacent to the ICU, and it was where she met with the patients' families and discussed the discharge plans. Her duties included procuring clothes for the hospitalized homeless, arranging for their shelter upon discharge, and instructing patients without insurance how to obtain Medicaid coverage to cover the costs of their care. Nikki arrived for the scheduled meeting with the Crowe family. She saw a boy sitting outside the office with his head bowed, elbows on knees, and hands clasped as if he was in the midst of silent prayer. When he looked up, his face had an uncanny resemblance to Angus's.

"I'm Dr. Moriarty. I work with Dr. McConnachie, one of the physicians who took care of your brother."

He nodded, then looked away.

"I'm sorry there wasn't more that could've been done. How you holding up?"

"Okay, I guess," he said, sitting up straight in the chair, and exercising his neck by twisting it.

"I know it must to be unbearable to lose a brother. Depression is a terrible disease."

The brother furrowed his brow. "Depression? He wasn't depressed, college coaches were fighting over him."

"So what happened?"

"Voices. He started hearing voices. I told the coach, he didn't believe me at first."

"What kind of voices?"

"Telling him he was evil, and had to be punished."

"What did your father think?"

"He told him he was just feeling stress from all the coaches calling him. He said after the season he wanted him to see a shrink."

"But he never got to the psychiatrist."

He shook his head. "Shot himself right before the last game."

The coach, consumed by his basketball schedule and the possibility of a better job, had been negligent. He had ignored a psychiatric emergency—an acutely psychotic boy with auditory hallucinations. Proper medication and psychotherapeutic support would have prevented his suicide, but there was no reason to burden his brother with her thoughts.

"You play ball too?"

"Not basketball, too short," he said, sitting up in the chair.

"Maybe you'll shoot up like your brother did."

"Don't think so, that happened to him three years ago. The only scholarship I've a shot at is an academic one."

"Nothing wrong with that."

"Girls like jocks."

"That'll change. How old are you?"

"Sixteen."

Nikki gave him a double take. "Sixteen? You're the same age as your brother?"

"Most twins are the same age."

"I'm sorry, I didn't know you were twins." "Sometimes I wonder myself."

The disparity in their sizes was misleading, but Nikki had to admit that his face was an exact replica of his brother's.

"How did he get so much bigger than you?"

He shook his head and looked at the floor. "I wish I knew. I ate what he ate and more. We did the same exercises, but he got tall and I didn't."

Nikki hesitated to ask her next question, but it was important.

"Did he take any drugs?"

"You mean like steroids? No way. He hated drugs. Never drank or smoked either. Only drug was our vitamin medicine."

"What kind of vitamin medicine?"

"I don't know, you inhale it. Coach called it our 'supervitamin.' My brother's was a brown bottle and mine was white, so we didn't get them mixed up."

It all made sense. They had unknowingly participated in the ideal controlled study—an experiment on identical twins. They had the same DNA, the same home environment, yet one grows a foot taller than the other. His brother's color-coded inhaler contained BrobaGen, and the other one was the placebo. There was no longer a need to find out about the size of the biological parents; the disparity in the size was drug-induced.

The office door opened and Joy walked out, said "hello" to Nikki, then spoke to the boy.

"I'm sorry, I have to leave, there's a problem with one of the families on the floor. All your brother's clothes and personal belongings should be in this black bag." He nodded and Joy turned to Nikki. "Feel free to use the office when his father arrives. I'll join you later if I can."

"Take your time, Joy. We'll be fine."

"One more thing before I forget. Jinny wants Mr. Crowe to give her a call, says it's important, so in case I miss him..."

"I'll give him the message," Nikki said.

The brother reached inside the bag, sorting its contents. There was a pair of sneakers, sweatpants, and a sweatshirt stiff with frozen rivulets of dried blood. After emptying the bag, he continued to look through the clothes.

"Are you missing something?"

"The inhaler. Coach said to make sure it's there."

It was strange that the family wanted to keep his blood-soaked clothes and his used inhaler. Out of the corner of her eye, she observed the coach walking down the hallway on his toes, like a puma ready to pounce. His hair was crewcut short, and he had a jutting chin, daring someone to punch him in the face. He had the demeanor of a drill sergeant, someone who sees the world as either black or white, his way or the highway.

While nodding acknowledgement to Nikki, he placed his hand on his son's shoulder.

"Did you get everything?"

"Everything but the inhaler."

"Look again. I want to keep everything as a remembrance."

"Mr. Crowe, I'm Dr. Moriarty. Joy had contacted you on my behalf so we could discuss the autopsy findings of your son."

"Glad to meet you, Doc. Call me Coach," he said, shaking her hand until she started to speak.

"If you're ready, we can sit down in the office?"

"I'm as ready as a dairy cow at eleven o'clock in the morning that ain't been milked," he said, palming his chest with both hands. "Son, why don't you wait here and we'll be right out."

Nikki walked into the office and the coach followed. She closed the door and he walked behind the desk, leaving the windsor chair for her.

"I'm sorry, did I take your chair?" he said after sitting down, and making no attempt to get up.

"Not a problem."

"Being the coach, I guess I'm used to sitting behind the desk—you know, when I advise the boys."

"I understand," Nikki said, while collecting her thoughts. "We were concerned that Angus had hyperpituitarism."

"Hyperwhat?"

"I'm sorry. He had elevated levels of growth hormone in his blood. When that occurs in kids before puberty, they can grow over seven feet tall. If there is prolonged production of excessive growth hormone, they're not only exceptionally tall, but their hands, feet and jaw become disproportionately enlarged."

"Like that wrestler, André the Giant."

"Yes, he had the same disease."

"A couple people in the NBA too, making millions. I don't think they'd call it a disease."

"It's a disease because it causes premature death as a result of abnormalities of the heart. That's why André the Giant died in his forties."

"If you're going to die early, it's not so bad if you at least got to be an NBA star. Those guys have the life." He clasped both hands behind his head and leaned back in the chair.

It was obvious to Nikki that he didn't get it. Big was beautiful, and nothing else mattered. If he had the opportunity to obtain a drug that would increase the size of his athletes, he would give it to all his players.

"The most common cause for the increased production of growth hormone is a tumor at the base of the brain, but Angus didn't have one."

"So you're saying he was making a lot of that growth hormone stuff, but there was no tumor to explain it."

"Correct. Which means he had to be taking a drug, either growth hormone or another drug that would elevate his growth hormone production."

"Makes sense." The coach looked at his watch.

"Our concern is that the side effects of these drugs over time are not well-defined, and if your son had access, other kids did too."

"I hope so."

"You hope so?"

He held up his hands. "Don't get me wrong, Doc; I don't push drugs, not the ones that make you high anyway. But if there's a drug that can make you bigger and stronger, I'm all for it."

"Even though you don't know what the side effects are?"

"Listen," he said, sitting up in his chair, "we know what the side effects of cigarettes are, and we stand by and watch millions of kids smoke."

"I agree, cigarettes should be illegal."

"But a drug that can improve athletic performance, that's a positive. I guess I feel like Abe Lincoln—give a case of it to all my generals," he said, and repositioned his feet onto the wastepaper basket.

"Were you aware that he was taking drugs?"

"Only the 'supervitamin.'"

"The same drug that your wife received?"

"The same drug that my wife received, or didn't receive. I guess they'll break the code soon, and then we'll know, but I'm sure she got the real thing."

"Why do you think so?"

"Because before she got the injections, she looked like one of those models that starve themselves. You know..." he said, sucking in his cheeks to replicate the gaunt face of starvation.

"You mean an anorexic."

"Right. But after the injections she gained weight and started to get some muscle back. I told Jinny I had players who could benefit from something like that."

"The players were injected?"

"No, my guys are scared of needles, and it wasn't available except for cancer patients. We were lucky. Jinny's people came up with a nasal spray."

"Did she tell you what was in it?"

"The same thing my wife got, the special vitamin."

Either Jinny lied to him about BrobaGen, or he was in denial. Nikki figured it was a combination of both.

"How many players tried it?"

"He was the only one so far. First they needed to see if it worked, and I'm proud of that boy, he proved it did."

"You told both sons that they were getting the same drug?"

"That way they didn't know who got the drug, and who got the placebo. I think they called it a blinded study."

"Did he sign a consent?"

He shook his head. "My wife did, but Jinny didn't think that another one was necessary for Angus."

Of course she didn't. The last thing she wanted was a paper trail that would prove she was conducting unauthorized studies.

"How often did they use it?"

"Every six hours."

"And it worked?"

He looked at her wide-eyed. "Did you see his brother? They were the same size up until they were twelve. I was only sorry I couldn't give it to both of them."

"That way you would've had an even better team. Those college coaching jobs are pretty lucrative these days."

He took his feet off the wastepaper basket and sat up in the chair. "Let's get one thing straight, Doc. I care about my players. And for many of them, basketball is their only ticket out of the ghetto. Whatever it takes to help them succeed, I'll do."

Nikki bristled at the coach's conviction that he acted solely out of altruistic concern for his adopted son, a boy who was not even aware he was taking hormones. If he hadn't been exposed to the drug, he would be competing for an academic scholarship. Instead, he was being mourned.

"I'm sure you had the best intentions, but drugs can cause abnormal reactions, including mental disturbances. My concern is that the voices he was hearing may have been related to the drug."

"Kids get depressed like everyone else, that's all it was."

McConnachie was right: people see what they want to see, disguising reality in a cloak of self-interest, looking to others from the perspective of how they can benefit from the relationship. The coach witnessed his son's psychotic behavior along with auditory hallucinations, a side effect of the drug. He dismissed it as teenage angst, and his negligence resulted in the boy's suicide. If Angus had lived, the persistent elevation of growth hormone production would have caused acromegaly, its consequences unappreciated until his playing days were over. After he retired, the sport promoters would lose interest in him, and he would have to deal with the consequences of the disease by himself.

Instead of an illness to be treated, the pharmacological industry had spun acromegaly into an aberration to be cultivated. Biosense replicated the disease with synthetic drugs, and then foisted it onto naive athletes as a desirable condition. Impressionable kids, often devoid of interaction with their fathers, looked up to the coach as a replacement figure—please the coach and they were pleasing their father—but where would the coach be after the basketball careers of these kids ended? Most of them, if they're lucky, end up sitting on the bench of some college team, and even the college stars rarely ever make it into the pros. Some of Nikki's high school classmates had spent the majority of their lives in the gym, desperately trying to improve their athletic skills, glomming any drug heralded to improve their athletic performance, no matter the risks. Many sacrificed academic opportunities in exchange for careers in sport, guaranteed by overenthusiastic coaches, only to be discarded by their mentors when a better player emerged.

Coach Crowe manipulated these kids for his own personal gain, convincing his son that the drug was for his own good, to ensure his future. But the truth was that a successful basketball team meant improved career opportunities for the coach, the chance to upgrade to a higher level, a bigger school.

Nikki realized there was no point in continuing the conversation. "I'm sorry for your loss. I just wanted to let you know other team members might have access to the drug, but obviously that doesn't concern you."

"This drug is a major advance that's going to elevate sport to a new level. God wouldn't have made it available if he didn't want us to take it."

"Your conclusion may be premature."

"Time will tell. But I've seen what this drug can do first hand. If you followed our team in the papers, you'd have seen what I'm talking about."

He stood up, pumped her hand, and left. Nikki walked to the window and watched the coach toe his way towards the car with the boy following. She had forgotten to give him Jinny's message, but it didn't matter. Jinny would track him down. When she turned to leave, something glinted in the corner of the room. It was the cannister, the BrobaGen aerosol. Joy, in her rush, must have left it out of the bag. She picked it up, put it in her pocket, and left the hospital. She needed a cup of coffee, and she needed to think.

The cherry walls of the coffee bar were festooned with hunter green signs boasting a variety of coffees and optional flavorings inscribed in white lettering. Two uniformed employees stood behind a faux marble bar that showcased pyramids of muffins, coffee cakes and lemon squares on glass cake plates. One employee was taking orders while the other stood in front of a cappucino machine that hissed steam into his pitcher of milk. A woman on line in front of Nikki swayed to the classical music, her eyes closed, unaware the man behind the counter awaited her order.

"Next," the barista said, interrupting her with a verbal tap on the shoulder.

The woman opened her eyes, apologized for holding up the line, and ordered a grande cappucino. She then turned to Nikki, who was standing behind her.

"I'm sorry, I loved that opera. I guess I got carried away."

"I understand." How could anyone be overcome by the music in a coffee bar?

"You recognize it—act two of *Meditation* by Massenet?"

Nikki remained silent. "You know, when Thaïs gives up her corrupt ways to become the disciple of the holy monk Athanael," the woman said, attempting to jar Nikki's memory.

"I'm not really familiar with the piece."

"You should see it sometime. It's inspiring to know that no matter what mistakes we've made in the past, there's always hope for redemption." She stared at Nikki as if she was familiar with her past sins, and now was encouraging her to repent and follow the holy monk.

The cappucino arrived. Nikki was relieved when the woman picked up her order and walked out of the store.

"I'll have a caffe latte," Nikki said to the vendor.

"What size?"

"Small."

"No small," he said, pointing to the sign behind him.

The sizes listed on the green board ranged from "tall" to "grand," and there was a styrofoam bas-relief of cup samples on the wall with the store's unique size interpretation labeled underneath. Their equivalent to a small cup was called a "tall."

"A tall caffe latte."

The barista entered it into the computer, then presented her with a bill for five dollars before activating her request. After she had paid, she tried to justify the high cost of a cup of joe, attributing it to the supplied amenities—classical music, free periodicals, and the freedom to nurse her drink, uninterrupted by anxious waiters looking to turn over the tables. She picked up her cup along with a packet of sugar and a wooden stirring stick and walked to a counter by the window facing the street. A recently jettisoned *Wall Street Journal* offered itself. She sipped her coffee, gazing at the citizens passing by who were lunging towards their destinations with the determination of salmon swimming upstream. Nikki's tall caffe latte warmed her hands.

Jinny had administered BrobaGen, an experimental drug, to a minor without approval of the Institutional Review Board. But she had to give her credit—it was the ideal controlled study. She had compared BrobaGen to a placebo, tracking the effects of each on genetically identical twins, and now no one would be able to question the drug's efficacy. But unless the results of the twin study were publicized, there wouldn't be any benefit to Jinny, the members of the Lunar Club or Biosense. And the academic route, the usual means of revealing study results, was not available. Submission for publication in medical journals or request for presentation at medical meetings would be automatically rejected because the study had not been approved by the IRB. With Biosense's cooperation, Nikki figured they could bypass peer review and go right to the public by televising a video news release of Angus playing basketball, towering over his twin brother. The release of his autopsy results along with his elevated levels of growth hormone would confirm to scientific inquisitors that BrobaGen was the causative agent responsible for his growth spurt. But neither Biosense nor Jinny could take responsibility for an illegal or unethical experiment. They would have to play dumb, and claim they had discovered he had been taking BrobaGen without their approval, stolen from his mother's supply. A celebrity spokesperson, an NBA star, would be featured urging the public to ask their doctor about BrobaGen, informing them that the drug was only available with a physician's prescription. The ensuing demand by the public for BrobaGen would be met through the internet, and by physicians willing to humor their clients.

Gabrielle probably supplied Jinny with the aerosolized BrobaGen while the Biosense executives looked the other way. They knew they would never get approval to do a study with BrobaGen on minors. At least not until the study on cancer patients was completed, and it was proven not to spread disease. But if someone had accessed the drug without their knowledge, it was beyond their control.

A man about thirty years of age, his face gaunt from weight loss, was wheeled past the coffee bar window by his healthier companion of the same age. His escort leaned over so that they were cheek to cheek and whispered a secret, reinforced with an affectionate squeeze of his shoulder. Protease inhibitors had improved the quality of life for many people, converting AIDS into a chronic and controllable disease, and allowing sufferers to abandon wheelchairs and nursing homes until the final weeks of life. But all the progress gained from newer treatments could be immediately reversed if a terrorist ever got ahold of the BrobaGen-spiked AIDS virus. It would replicate so quickly that patients would die before the diagnosis was ever made, and New York would be the likely target because of its dense population. Talented people from around the world, the leaders in business, the arts and sciences, unknowingly exposed to the colorless and odorless gas, would be dead within six weeks of contact.

Nikki took another sip of her caffe latte and reminded herself the AIDS study was simply a research project on monkeys, and that it was premature to worry about biological terrorism. Every drug had a potential downside. Blood thinners, for example, when given in the proper dosage, had saved lives and limbs. But if given to the wrong patient or in too high a dose, the drug could cause serious side effects, even death. It was important not to condemn BrobaGen just because it could be harmful if used for the wrong indication—people with underlying tumors. It's not the gun, it's the person who pulls the trigger.

Maybe the coach was right—she was being too judgmental. What kind of life and opportunity did these twins really have? They were abandoned by their biological family, and struggled to survive in a foster home until they were adopted by the coach and his wife. Sports allowed them to develop pride, and to advance their academic careers via athletic scholarship. The other twin, the one who had received the placebo, was frustrated by his lack of height and wanted to be tall like his brother. Below average size had a negative connotation, one that society equated with failure, and even the coffee bar had avoided the term "small," upgrading it to "tall."

An elderly man walked by the window supported by a cane, his head bowed, unable to straighten up because of arthritis and the weakened musculature of aging. He shuffled by, each step a struggle. Two kids running brushed up against him, threatening his balance and causing him to stop and concentrate. He waited as if he were a sailor riding out a squall, and when calm had been restored, he continued his journey. She watched him pass wondering if she would be enfeebled with age, hoping she would never become dependent on others, too weak to wipe her own ass. The elderly, Nikki decided, could benefit from BrobaGen. People who didn't have cancer, but were confined to nursing homes because they were not strong enough to care for themselves. The drug, in combination with nutritional support and physical therapy, could increase their muscle mass, liberating those individuals from institutional care, and allowing them to remain players until the inevitable occurred. The nursing homes could then direct their efforts where they were needed most—individuals with Alzheimer's disease. BrobaGen, if used with judicious restraint, could prove to be a breakthrough drug providing the elderly with a better quality of life.

She had one reservation about doing research with Biosense: Mrs. Lamb's premature death. If BrobaGen was responsible for her metastases, then Nikki was being complicit with the drug company by stifling a protest in the interest of furthering her career. After the code was broken tomorrow, and the results presented at the lab meeting, she would know if Mrs. Lamb had received the drug. If those patients who had favorable prognoses developed metastatic disease prematurely after receiving BrobaGen, then both the FDA and the public would have to be notified. Giantism and acromegaly were diseases, not desirable conditions that the pharmaceutical industry should be trying to replicate. The aged, with their atrophied muscles and inability to function independently, were the group that could benefit from BrobaGen if properly screened. Mrs. Lamb's death may have been a sacrifice to help others, a wake-up call to Biosense to change its target audience to those people who are tumor-free but weakened with age. The median age of the population in industrialized nations was increasing, and the elderly were a growing market. Biosense needed to reconsider its priorities.

She finished her coffee, called her answering machine, and heard that same voice delivering another cryptic message: "Time is running out. It's your last chance to leave." It was easy for Nikki to attribute the first message to a wrong number. But not this time. Anyone telephoning her home was greeted by her voice identifying herself as Nikki, and if it was the wrong number, the caller would have hung up. Who could it be, and why were they trying to intimidate her? She didn't have any enemies, and no one she knew would make anonymous calls. It was probably that crazy bitch, Cynthia. Ever since Nikki had refused to join the Lunar Club, and particularly after she returned the shares, Cynthia had distanced herself. Nikki suspected Cynthia did not want her around because she couldn't control her. She knew Cynthia's type: insecure individuals who doled out money and political favors in order to win others over and gain their support. Cynthia had used that ploy with Jinny and the other Lunar Club members. Now they were beholden to her. Nikki had always thought Cynthia was strange, but certainly not sociopathic. The hospital administration considered her a dedicated and talented nurse practitioner, someone whom they respected. They deceived themselves—everyone except Carmen.

For now, Nikki decided it would be best to stay cool, act like nothing had happened. If she chose to leave the lab, she would do it on her own terms. No one was going to intimidate her.

Nikki walked into the conference room and sat down next to Jinny, who was preoccupied with last minute preparations prior to presenting the results of the BrobaGen study. Members of the research team meandered in while Nikki scanned the headlines on the front page of the *New York Times* between bites of her glazed donut.

"We going to hear the results of the BrobaGen study today?" Nikki asked Jinny, forcing her to look up from her laptop.

"As soon as the boss shows up."

Dr. Cogswell walked in a few minutes late as always, exchanging pleasantries with members of the team like a politician before a press conference, finally settling on his perch at the head of the table.

"I know you're all anxious to hear the preliminary results of the BrobaGen study, so why don't we end the anticipation and get on with it. Jinny?"

Jinny whispered to Nikki, "Shoulda held onto those shares," and then walked to the head of the room.

"Could we have the first slide?" Jinny said to Dr. Green, who always made the mistake of sitting next to the slide projector.

He turned on the projector light and advanced the carousel. An introductory slide appeared with the title of the study and its authors; Cogswell's name was listed first, as always, followed by the other members of the investigative team. The format of the presentation was familiar to Nikki, and adhered to the guidelines outlined by the program committee for the upcoming meeting in Hawaii. Each presenter had ten minutes to address the international assembly of oncologists, followed by a five-minute question and answer period. An invited discussant, a physician from another oncology center, asked the first question, and if time allowed others followed. This presentation was a practice run, an opportunity for the group to make suggestions and prepare for questions. Criticism of Cogswell's work at these meetings was limited because of fear of reprisal, his questioners aware they had to be discreet—their future depended on it. He never forgot who criticized his data, and he always made a point to retaliate by interfering with their advancement in the hierarchy of academic organizations.

Jinny began the presentation by defining the objectives of the study and describing the chemical make-up of BrobaGen. This was followed by the demographics of the patient population studied. She listed the type of cancer they had and their clinical course, but her critical slide was a chart comparing the weight of the patients before and after treatment. The patients who received BrobaGen experienced a marked weight gain as compared to the placebo group, and the difference between the two groups was statistically significant. A mild, non-specific increase in their measured immunological response also occurred in eighty percent of those that had received the drug, and only in one patient who had received the placebo. Dr. Cogswell looked on approvingly as she finished the presentation with her conclusion slide:

"In the patients studied so far…" It was a vintage Cogswell phrase, his disclaimer in the event that other investigators were unable to confirm his conclusions.

"…there was an average twenty percent weight gain in those patients treated with BrobaGen, as compared to those treated with the placebo. In addition, there was a non-specific improvement in immunological parameters of those receiving the study drug."

Although it was a small patient sampling, it was clear from the data presented that the cachexia of cancer could be reversed with BrobaGen, implying that improvement in outcome from metastatic breast cancer was achievable.

"Question."

"Yes, Dr. Green."

"The first question you're likely to be asked during the discussion period is the difference in the morbidity and mortality of the two groups. I noticed you didn't present that data, and its absence could raise a red flag."

"I didn't mention it because there wasn't any statistical difference in the two groups."

"Then it's better to say that, rather than make your audience think you're trying to hide the information," Dr. Green said, and Cogswell nodded.

"I did prepare a slide addressing that question, and I planned to pull it out if the discussion called for it. I can just weave it into the body of the talk. Dr. Green, can you show the slide at the back? I think it's number eleven."

Green advanced the carousel to the requested slide.

"Thank you. On this slide we can see that although the patients in both groups died from their disease, the treated group gained weight, and their immunological parameters improved. These patients, as a result of BrobaGen, will be able to tolerate aggressive chemo and radiation treatments, which ultimately will result in improved survival rates as compared to the untreated group."

It was an optimistic statement about future results without any data to support it, but Cogswell was pleased.

"Good. I think you handled that question well. No one can argue about the future."

George Lally stood up and applauded. "Bulletproof. Who can challenge those results?"

Nikki could argue with the results. She could point out that Mrs. Lamb had lost weight because of depression rather than cancer, which should have excluded her from the study, and that her cancer had a favorable prognosis before she had received BrobaGen. But there was no point. Jinny had undoubtedly covered her tracks and documented in the chart that Mrs. Lamb had lost weight in spite of maintaining her normal caloric intake. And Cogswell would argue she was a victim of a biologically aggressive tumor.

It remained unclear to Nikki whether other patients had favorable tumors prior to entering the study and deteriorated after receiving BrobaGen. Jinny claimed there was not a discernible trend.

Cogswell stood up, signaling the end of the meeting. "It just needs to be polished," he said. "We'll present it again next week with the suggested changes."

"Who's going to be the discussant?" Jinny asked.

"Judson Todd," Cogswell said. "We trained together. I told him we'd give him a copy of the completed paper before the meeting. I'm sure he'll reciprocate with the list of questions he plans to ask. Don't worry, there shouldn't be any surprises. Of course we don't know what questions the audience will ask, but they only have five minutes, and I have a feeling that Dr. Todd will fill the allotted time."

Many in the group chortled at their leader's manipulation of the outcome.

"Question."

"Yes, Dr. Green."

"Do you have any problem with us using this data in the NIH application that's due next month? I don't want to do anything prematurely."

"I'd include the abstract, but not go into any details until after it's been presented. I don't want people to have time to review our data and share it with anyone before we present the results."

"I can tell you there's going to be a lot of media interest. This is a major breakthrough," George said.

Nikki knew what he meant. Biosense was firing up the engines of their public relations juggernaut, and if there wasn't media interest, they would create it. The nightly news would air their video releases, and prescription writers would be standing by waiting for the calls.

George put his arm around Cogswell in a congratulatory embrace as the meeting ended.

"You outdid yourself with this study."

"We try."

Jinny walked out with Dr. Cogswell to have a word with him, leaving her laptop opened next to Nikki with a file visible on her screen entitled "physician profiles." The title piqued Nikki's interest. She leaned over, clicked on it, and an alpabetical listing of most of the oncologists, surgeons, and surgical residents appeared. She scrolled down to "M" and stopped at "Moriarty, Nikki." She clicked on her name, and the following description appeared:

"Nikki Moriarty: Ambitious, highly competent, and earnestly seeking a faculty position in oncology at the Manhattan University Medical Center. Resents the subtle and sometimes overt sexual bias that permeates the Department of Surgery. Out to prove that she's a better surgeon than her male colleagues.

"Weakness: Saddled with a $200,000 debt accrued during college and medical school, and anxious to eradicate it. Willing to make compromises to attain her goal.

"Personal: Parents divorced and has issue with trust. Heterosexual and has boyfriend who is anesthesiologist, relationship not serious. Hobbies include competitive sports and flute, but outside interests neglected because of inexorable desire to achieve her professional goals. Enjoys red and white burgundies.

"Approach:

1) Emphasize female camaraderie

2) Financial remuneration to assure loyalty

3) Compliment her performance and recommend her highly to Dr. Cogswell in her presence.

Conclusion: Anticipate total cooperation if above criteria met."

Nikki was both angry and disturbed. Angry about the invasion of her privacy and the documentation of her personal desires and goals. And disturbed by the accuracy of the assessment.

She was about to click on the profiles of Cogswell and McConnachie, but there wasn't enough time. Nikki shut down the laptop and closed it as Jinny approached, and handed it to her.

"I signed off for you. I thought you left without it."

"Thanks, that's my lifeline. I've got all the research data in there."

"You should download it onto a disk in case you misplace it."

"Yeah, but I'm paranoid that someone will take the disk and get a hold of the lab data before it's published. Easier to lose a disk than a laptop."

Jinny picked up her laptop and walked out.

Nikki knew she had to separate herself from both Jinny and Cynthia. Sooner rather than later. But she had to be careful. If she got fired, she would be buried by debt, and her father would gloat over her failure. And that wasn't going to happen.

Nikki hadn't seen Fred since her return from McConnachie's house on Sunday, and she needed to unload her thoughts and formulate a plan. Not that Fred was particularly insightful, but at least he was a sounding board. She found it helpful to articulate her options before making a decision. He answered his cell phone out of breath, his gasps accompanied by a background chant. It was lunchtime and Fred was at the gym, where he lifted weights and drank wheatgrass juice to improve his endurance. Physical conditioning, according to Fred, heightened the pleasure experience for both him and his partner, and also increased hormonal production, improving his sex drive.

"Fred, it's me. When're you going to be finished?"

"Not much longer. What's up?"

"I want to run something by you, but not over the phone."

"Where?"

"My apartment."

"I'll be there in fifteen minutes."

Her apartment was a small one-bedroom that was part of the housing complex reserved for the hospital residents and some of the faculty. It was one of the perquisites of the surgical training program—an apartment on the upper east side that was affordable because the rents were subsidized by the hospital. Comparable apartments for other New Yorkers were twice the price, and without the subsidy residents would be forced to find housing in the outer boroughs. It was unusual for Nikki to spend time in her apartment during daylight, but her laboratory rotation gave her the opportunity to eat lunch at home. The special at the deli was grilled chicken, and she ordered one on a kaiser roll with mayo. A "soda of your choice" was included with the price of the sandwich, and she picked out a diet cherry Coke. While she waited for Fred's arrival, she turned on the television and scanned the channels between bites of her lunch. Soap operas predominated, but she was unfamiliar with the story lines, and settled on a pop video of an unknown performer. The door bell rang three times, followed by Fred with his health shake in hand, wearing form-fitting Speedo shorts and a sleeveless top to maximize visibility of his honed muscles.

"So what's up?" He sipped his shake, looking at the biceps of his right arm that flexed as he moved the cup to his mouth.

After he swallowed, he stared at Nikki, trying to decipher if her call was a coded desire for a nooner, or if she really wanted to talk. She knew he was expecting a quickie, and she ignored his leer.

"I've been getting some weird messages on my answering machine."

"Like what?"

"Like, 'Leave while you can, it's your last chance.'"

Fred frowned. "What the fuck's that about?"

"I think it's Cynthia. She doesn't trust me because I returned the Biosense shares. That's the only thing I can think of."

"Crazy bitch." Fred shook his head and gulped his drink. "By the way, why the hell *did* you return those shares?"

"That's not the point. I had my reasons," Nikki said, realizing she was wasting her time talking to him. "Even if you think you know who's doing it, it's still upsetting."

"You should get a tap."

"All that'll do is give me the phone number of some pay telephone. I'll handle it."

"I know you will." Fred walked closer and put his hands on her shoulders. "I didn't mean to upset you about the Biosense shit."

Nikki nodded. "They just broke the code on the phase two study—BrobaGen increases muscle mass and reverses the catabolic effects of cancer."

"Then you're looking at a new shareholder."

Nikki pulled his hands off her. "Can't you stop thinking about yourself for a minute? You just don't get it."

"What?"

"Eventually some investigator is going to prove that it increases cancer. I'm convinced that it does, but that's not the only point. The research was flawed and misleading. I think they did the study just to get preliminary approval from the FDA, and then use it as a performance-enhancing drug for teenagers."

Fred nodded and walked over to the hall mirror, gulped another drink, and then returned.

"You know, you're right. Cancer isn't an issue in a younger population, and if it increases muscle mass–"

"It does increase muscle mass, and it increases size."

"How do you know?"

"I don't want to get into that right now. The point is that when I returned the shares, the shit hit the fan. Cynthia is trying to push me out, and I have to handle it the right way. If she undermines me with Cogswell, I can forget about ever getting a job here."

"If this drug really does the things you say it does, then it has an unlimited market."

"Exactly, but once someone shows it spreads cancer, it's dead in the water. That's why they're using the bait and switch—they get preliminary approval for use on cancer patients, then physicians can prescribe it at their discretion."

"I can tell you there's a lot of guys at the gym who'd like to give it a whirl. They're taking all sorts of crap to begin with. They always want to know my opinion about steroids and stuff."

"Fred, I'm asking you how to handle things."

He looked at the ceiling before answering. "I think you should buy more shares, because the stock is going to take off."

Nikki rolled her eyes. "You're not hearing me."

"I don't know, tell Cynthia you returned the shares because it was a conflict of interest, and you want her to back off."

"I wish it was that easy."

Nikki's beeper went off, and she interrupted the conversation to check her message.

"It's McConnachie."

She picked up the portable phone and began to dial his number while Fred kissed her on the neck and fondled her breasts from behind.

"Fred," she said, expecting him to stop.

"Let's do it while you're talking to McConnachie. He won't know."

She pulled away from him and turned on the speaker phone so she would have both hands free to defend herself.

"Dr. McConnachie's office."

"This is Dr. Moriarty, returning Dr. McConnachie's call."

"One moment please."

"Nikki, hi, I thought that you'd be interested in the M.E. report."

"What did they find?"

Fred began rubbing up against her again, forcing her to move away.

"Dr. Sorel just called and told me the final sign out was going to be a self-inflicted gunshot wound to the brain. The interesting part is the results of the radioimmunoassay—it documented elevated levels of the recombinant form of growth hormone, growth hormone releasing factor, insulin like growth factor, and the testosterone precursor, DHEA."

"In other words, BrobaGen."

"You were right. How's everything else?"

"Let me call you back, I'm in the middle of something."

"No problem, I just wanted to share that. Catch you later."

"Thanks."

Fred was kissing her on the neck as she disconnected the speaker phone.

"The busy researcher doesn't have time for Fred and Fred jr?"

"Fred, your breath smells like a hay loft."

"Wheatgrass juice, it has its downside."

"And the downside here is that I've got to get back to work. The upside is that you can save it for later."

"If that's how you feel. Mind if I use your shower?" he asked, removing his clothes before she answered.

Nikki turned off the television and headed for the door, and Fred stared naked into the wall mirror on the bathroom door.

"Does this BrobaGen come in a topical form?"

"Fred, what are you talking about?"

"I was just thinking that it might have another indication," he said, rubbing his penis, "even though, according to my men's group, size doesn't count."

"You should sit in on a women's group, you might change your mind. But I'll make sure to let the research team know they have a volunteer for topical BrobaGen."

"I'm serious. You know they're operating on people now to increase penile size—augmentation phalloplasty."

"I don't think your health care plan would cover it."

"I'm not interested in surgery, but if an ointment worked I'd try it. Not for me, I was just thinking of maximizing things for you."

"Good old, altruistic Fred. Bye Fred, lock up after you finish."

Nikki walked out the door and returned to the hospital. Jinny was sitting at her laptop when she walked into the lab, probably updating her physician profiles. Nikki went over to the nurses' station and waited for Cynthia to finish reprimanding one of the nurses for not having her patient ready for transfer out of the ICU. When there was a lull, Nikki interrupted.

"Cynthia, can I talk to you for a minute?"

"I always make time for you," she answered, making Nikki think that Fred had been right about Cynthia's intentions.

"My decision to return the shares wasn't easy."

"Easy or hard, it's a mistake."

"Maybe, but the last thing I need is someone suggesting an ethical impropriety on my part. I want an academic career, and if Cogswell ever found out I was a shareholder, he'd recommend someone else."

Cynthia smirked. "Don't you get it? We control Cogswell. He's totally dependent on us, he listens to us."

"I know, but he's not dependent on me."

"He wouldn't want to disappoint us."

"I appreciate that, but word around this place travels fast, and other staff members could cause problems."

"Let me tell you something about Cogswell." Cynthia walked Nikki by the arm to two empty chairs, and they sat down. "Who do you think pays for his world tours when he gives lectures?"

"Biosense probably pays him an honorarium."

Cynthia leaned over and patted Nikki on her thighs. "That's right, and that honorarium covers his whole tour and a lot more. And who do you think pays for his lab equipment and the salaries of his lab technicians?"

"Biosense."

"Right again. He wouldn't have a lab without Biosense. Do you really think he cares whether you own 200 shares in the company?"

Cynthia had a point. Cogswell was dependent on the largesse of Biosense for the support of his lab, and he was dependent on Cynthia and Jinny to keep things running smoothly.

"I guess not, but I can always buy stock later."

"You're not going to be able to afford it. I must say I'm disappointed, I thought you were smarter than that."

"Look, it's not a rejection of you guys, I just don't want anything on my record that might interfere with me obtaining an academic position later on."

"It's your life." Cynthia got up from her chair. Nikki stood face to face with her.

"You're right, and by the way, no one is going to pressure me to leave the lab."

Cynthia smiled, unwrapped a lollipop, and stuck it in her mouth. After a few licks, she leaned towards Nikki's ear and whispered, "It wasn't me, it wasn't me."

Cynthia walked out the door, and Nikki knew that things were going to get worse before they got better.

Cogswell's administrative assistant had scheduled Nikki to meet with the medical director of Biosense as part of her orientation, a meeting in which she had no interest. It was Cogswell's way of making sure everyone was on the same page, but at this point she wasn't even in the same book.

The appointment had been scheduled for 3:00 p.m., and when she arrived a secretary directed her to a sitting area. Nikki grabbed a *National Geographic* from a table. In the midst of her reading about tribes of New Guinea, a portly man appeared. He scanned Nikki, straining to look over his bifocals, careful not to linger at any particular anatomical site.

"You must be Dr. Moriarty," he said, as if his deduction was based on intuition rather than a prearranged appointment.

"And you're Dr. Waddle."

He walked over to her and enclosed her right hand between both of his, and shook it up and down, his downstroke coinciding with each syllable of his greeting, "Wel-come a-board."

He gave her hand a final squeeze, the signal to disengage.

Nikki flashed a smile. "Thanks."

"Heard lots of good things about you from Dr. Cogswell."

He pontificated with the authority of a U.S. Senator, and maintained an inexorable smile—two qualities that contributed to his efficacy as a fund raiser when he was Dean of the medical school.

"I worked with your father, a very capable man."

Nikki compressed her lips, which Waddle mistakenly interpreted as diffident admiration. She knew both he and her father had trained as psychiatrists at the same institution, and had spent most of their careers ministering to the needs of the socially well-connected.

"But I see you're forging your own pathway in surgery, which is admirable," he said, pausing to pout his lower lip. "I'm sure it hasn't been easy establishing yourself in the last male bastion of medicine."

"I've learned to adapt."

"Yes, you have. Well, you've come to the lab at the right time. Biosense has a few drugs in the pipeline ready for clinical trial, and of course," he said, looking both ways before lowering his voice, "we're very excited about the BrobaGen results."

"I suspect so."

"Since you're going to be involved in the next set of clinical trials, you should know—any questions, problems, Eric Waddle's available twenty-four, seven." He tilted his head and winked.

"That's good to know," Nikki said, glancing at her watch.

"No sweeping anything under the rug here. If there's a problem with one of our products, I want to know about it." He lowered his chin to his chest, staring at her over his bifocals before finishing his point. "You know what I mean?"

"I have a pretty good idea."

Her annoyance went unrecognized by Waddle. He possessed the same arrogance as her father, the attitude that their lives were highly evolved, both endlessly amused by the inferiority of those who did not share their insights into rational living.

"Were you able to appreciate the anabolic effect of our drug, BrobaGen, on some of those poor cancer patients?" he asked, taking credit for what he perceived as a major advance in the care and treatment of the terminally ill.

"Yes, but it's too bad the drug didn't improve survival. I guess it's like the saying, 'The operation was a success, but the patient died.'"

Waddle looked at the ceiling while reflecting solemnly on her cliché. "The operation was a success but...right, I see what you're saying, but there's a difference. Get these patients healthy with BrobaGen, and then we can hit them with a cocktail of chemotherapy that will annihilate those cancer cells. We're going to make inroads on survival, big time. Believe you me."

He completed his assessment of Nikki, poorly disguised as a welcome, and he appeared satisfied. Biosense had nothing to worry about; she was a team player.

"I've got to get to the Union Club. We've got a reception for our sales rep of the year, and boy did he earn it. Remind me to tell you the story behind that. You'll get a kick out of it."

"I'm sure I will."

He reached for her hand, and after enclosing it between both of his, he resumed pumping.

"I think you're going to do well here," he said, resorting to his plodding speech pattern denoting sincerity. "Welcome aboard, again." Nikki nodded, and placed her hand in her pocket so he couldn't grab it.

The Dean of the medical school was the paragon of academia, a person who espoused the ideals of the profession, and who placed patient care and the advancement of medicine through research above the desire to make money. Or at least that's what Nikki had thought. After only two years as Dean, Waddle had abandoned those principles for a high salaried position at Biosense, acting as a shill for a company that was first and foremost out to wrangle a profit. The company had commercialized the prestige of the Dean's office, and used it to access busy practitioners, offering them money in exchange for patients. After all, drugs had to be tested before they were disseminated to the general public, and as long as the investigators maintained their objectivity, everyone benefited. But Nikki now realized objectivity meant cooperation, and academic physicians learned early on in their careers that if they reported negative results, they would no longer be part of the Biosense team.

He grabbed his coat and opened the door, indicating Nikki should go first. Together they walked to the elevator bank, and after Nikki said goodbye she entered the stairwell to the ICU. When she arrived at the floor, she picked up the fragrance of Dr. Mueller, who was patting down the petrified strands on his head while he reminisced about one of his apocryphal cases.

She sat down at the nurses' station, waiting for McConnachie to finish rounds while she thought about her next move. It was self-destructive to take on the goliath, Biosense. But something had to be done. Maybe her feeling of obligation to intercede stemmed from possession of two x chromosomes responsible for a maternal instinct that compelled her to punish the misbehaving corporation. If she were a man there wouldn't be any expectation to risk career advancement over a principle; protecting his own interests was considered smart, not morally reprehensible.

How was she going to slay Goliath and still salvage her career? David had outmaneuvered Goliath, because the giant was a big target with limited agility, the consequences of an unrecognized growth hormone secreting tumor. And now she had to do the same.

McConnachie was raising his eyebrows and smiling at Nikki from the other side of the room, a covert "hello" that was intercepted by several members of the nursing staff. Nikki responded in kind, which encouraged him to approach.

"What's up?" he asked.

"I need to run something by you."

"You want to go to my office?"

"The waiting room's fine." Nikki led the way. The room was empty, and after he had crossed the threshold she closed the door behind them. "After you told me the post results, I've been thinking about how far to go with this."

"You returned the shares."

"Right, and Cynthia wasn't pleased," she said. "But that's another story. I just don't know if returning the shares is enough."

McConnachie hesitated to answer. She hoped he was going to tell her she was wrong, that she had done more than enough, and that it was ridiculous for her to sacrifice her career more than she had already done.

"You have to do what you think is right."

"I know," she said, closing her eyes and rubbing her forehead. He was not going to give her an out, and she understood why—she was the one who was going to have to live with the consequences. "Taking on Biosense is like David taking on Goliath. Come to think of it, if Biosense existed in Biblical times, they would've hired Goliath as their BrobaGen spokesperson."

McConnachie laughed, then walked closer, wrapping his arms around her.

She looked up at him, and he bowed toward her face, kissing her full on the lips. The jiggling door handle aborted their embrace and a housekeeper, preceded by a bucket and mop, entered the room. She nodded and began mopping the other side of the room. Nikki smiled at Luke, and they walked out of the room towards the elevators.

Nikki shared her plan. "For now, I'm going to try and do damage control, emphasize to Jinny and Cynthia that I'm still part of the team."

"I agree. It's better to keep them close until you decide the next step," he said. "Not to change the subject, but would you like to have dinner tomorrow night?"

"That'd be nice."

"There's a place on the west side, Greek, good food. We can talk some more about this stuff."

"I'll call you tomorrow to get the details," she said. "That'll be a good time to tell you about some other stuff I found out. You know, from the meeting with the coach and Angus's brother." He nodded, and they squeezed hands.

When she returned to the ICU she saw Jinny sitting at the nurses' station working on her laptop, and Nikki stopped in the employee lounge, poured a cup of coffee, and took it to her.

"I brought you a cup of coffee, you looked like you needed a break."

"Nikki," she said with a note of surprise. "Thank you."

"How's it going?" Nikki asked, while trying to read her smile.

"Good. I'm just going over some data."

"The study's going to stir up a lot of interest."

"That's why we were all so surprised to hear you returned the shares."

"Word travels fast. Call me paranoid, but I had this fear that the wrong person would find out, and my career would be compromised."

"You really are paranoid."

"I'll probably regret it when the stock bounces, but that's the way it goes. You aren't upset about it, are you?"

"Upset isn't the right word. Disappointed would better describe it."

"It's something I felt I had to do."

"I guess we're disappointed, because we wanted you to be part of us."

"I'm still part of the team," she said, looking at Jinny for confirmation.

Jinny smiled and turned to her computer.

Nikki was aware she hadn't made any progress. "I'll leave you alone, I know you're busy."

"Thanks for the coffee."

Nikki nodded and walked around the corner, almost bumping into George Lally.

"Just the person I wanted to talk to," George said.

"What's up?"

"Don't take this the wrong way, but if you're free tonight, I'd love to take you out to dinner. I know it's late notice, but I happen to have a reservation at the best French restaurant in the city, four stars."

She was about to say no, but checked herself. She didn't want to alienate anyone else on the Biosense team.

"What time?"

"Is eight o'clock good?"

"Fine."

"Why don't you stop by my apartment for a drink before dinner? It's only a few blocks from the restaurant. I'm on 76th and Third Avenue." George handed her his card with a scribbled note.

"Sounds good. I'll see you then."

Dinner with George was not at the top of her list of things to do, but it was a superb restaurant, and suffering, she thought, would be limited. And she had Luke to look forward to, just the two of them, without any interruption by hospital personnel. She couldn't wait to pick up where they had left off.

George Lally's Third Avenue apartment house was a white brick building devoid of charm. A freestanding sign in the lobby declared all visitors must be announced, and Nikki identified herself to the doorman and told him Mr. Lally was expecting her. He walked to the phone bank and buzzed George. After he hung up, he pointed to the elevators.

"It's 15D, elevator on the left."

She entered the elevator, pushed the fifteenth floor, and heard someone's footsteps followed by a plea to hold the door. She debated whether to push the open door button, but she didn't feel like making conversation with a stranger. As the doors closed, she was confronted with a cropped view of a woman, annoyed she had been ignored. Nikki fumbled for the buttons while apologizing to the petitioner, but the elevator began its ascent. It wasn't her fault, she'd tried, but the woman disagreed.

"Bitch," the woman hissed through the closed doors.

Nikki flipped her the finger, a gesture the woman couldn't see, and then looked to the right of the door, the usual site for the inspection certificate. It was missing, replaced by a sign advising anyone interested in the inspection record to contact the management office. How often, she wondered, did people read that sign, get off the elevator, and proceed to the management office to review the document before engaging the elevator again? When the doors opened she walked into a hallway that was lined with apartment doors, all alike except one that featured a protruding head.

"Glad you made it, come on in," the head said.

A small vestibule with parquet floors led into George's living room. She walked over to a paisley-covered couch and sat down.

"What's your poison?" he asked as he produced two wine glasses.

"Wine's fine."

"Will Chassagne Montrachet do?"

"Burgundies will always do," she said, and then remembered her profile on Jinny's laptop. Her listed weakness included Burgundies, and George just happened to have one opened and was ready to pour when she arrived.

"Before the evening starts I want to let you know I asked Eric Waddle to join us. He was stuck in the city at a meeting and didn't have anyone to eat with."

"No problem," she lied. That fop. If she had known he was going to be there she would've refused to come.

"Between you and me, I was disappointed he accepted my offer, but I felt obliged to ask."

"I understand." She gulped her wine and walked over to his bookshelf to get a closer look at his display of toy statues. Many of them were recognizable action heroes, except their musculature was exaggerated.

"You collect these?" she asked, hoping there was another explanation.

"Biosense is partnering with a toy company. They're the prototypes for a new line of superhero toys that'll be coming out."

"Why's a drug company getting involved with superhero toys?"

"It's confidential, but I know I can tell you. Performance-enhancing drugs are a huge market, and we think BrobaGen is going to be the answer," he said, picking up two statues from the shelf and holding one in each hand. "Meet G.I. Joe before and G.I. Joe after BrobaGen."

The smaller action hero was the currently available one. The bigger one with the rippling muscles was the BrobaGen-induced version. Biosense must know about Jinny's twin study. Why else invest in the production of a line of toys? They were already going after the youth market.

"You think it's a good idea to be promoting drug use amongst teenagers?"

"They take them anyway. More than a third of high school kids take steroids or some other drug."

When you have professional athletes bragging about taking a testosterone precursor, it wasn't surprising to Nikki that teenagers wanted to take the same thing. Kids don't understand the risks of steroids—heart attacks, strokes, liver disease—or they understand but don't care.

"How do you know that BrobaGen will work on kids?" she asked, challenging him to discuss the twins.

"Because it worked on the adult cancer patients, why not a younger population? When the results of Dr. Cogswell's study are public, I guarantee there'll be a demand to broaden its indications."

Young athletes don't think they're going to die; they consider themselves invincible. Even if BrobaGen was proven to increase the risk of diabetes, arthritis or even cancer, kids would still take it if they were convinced it could improve their athletic performance. Nikki excused herself to go to the bathroom, and he directed her down a hallway that had three doors, presumably two bedrooms and a bathroom.

"The door on the left," he said.

She walked in and closed the bathroom door. When she looked in the mirror, she pictured the evening news with a videotape of Angus Crowe towering over his twin. Another scene would show him playing basketball, and the coach testifying how Biosense had made his son a better athlete. BrobaGen use would spawn a generation of superior athletes, bigger and stronger than their drug-free predecessors, but an unhealthier one because of the increased incidence of psychosis, heart disease, and ultimately, unexplained tumors.

She opened his medicine chest. It bulged with an assortment of lifestyle drugs, products of all the major pharmaceutical houses, that conspired to forestall aging. His armamentarium included drugs heralded to prevent baldness, along with testosterone precursors and growth hormone tablets designed to improve sex drive, and an erectile dysfunction drug to assure increased desire resulted in increased performance. BrobaGen would be the next addition, because all employees of Biosense would be encouraged to take the drug in spite of the putative risks. It was similar to the tobacco executives who smoked out of loyalty to the company, even though they were aware of the health consequences.

Chronological age was no longer a valid measurement, replaced by physiological age. And drugs had become part of the anti-aging process, an accepted supplement for the Methuselah generation. Biosense was in on the ground floor with the next magic bullet.

When she returned to the living room, George suggested they hurry up and finish their wine. He didn't want to keep the boss waiting. They both emptied their glasses, and he held the door open.

"The plans for BrobaGen are confidential, but you're part of the team now," he said, patting her on the shoulder.

They rode the elevator down to the lobby, and Nikki was relieved when she didn't run into the woman who had appealed to her to hold the door. It was a three-block walk to the restaurant, and when they arrived the Maitre D' was standing at a podium reviewing the reservation book. George interrupted and identified himself.

"Yes, Mr. Lally. I believe Dr. Waddle is waiting for you at the table. This way please."

They snaked their way to table four, and they found Dr. Waddle perusing a menu while taking the remaining sip of his martini. After apologizing for starting without them, he stood up, shook hands with Nikki, and spoke in a feigned whisper.

"I hope I'm not interfering with anything by joining you two tonight." He looked over his bifocals at her and winked.

"Believe me, there's nothing to interfere with," Nikki said.

"Good, I feel better."

The waiter removed the extra plate and cutlery and handed the new arrivals their own menus.

"Dr. Waddle told me he had an interesting meeting with you today. He's glad to have you on the team," George said.

"Interesting" was a noncommittal term that could have either positive or negative connotations. Waddle's nod didn't elucidate its meaning. The wine list was handed to Dr. Waddle at his request, while George pointed out one of his boss's attributes.

"Dr. Waddle is a wine connoisseur. He possesses a very developed palate," he said, confiding in Nikki that she was in for a special evening.

"I don't know about connoisseur, but I find the best is just good enough," Waddle said. George laughed, looking at Nikki to see if she was impressed.

Nikki lowered her menu, flashed a smile, and returned to the food. The menu was replete with alluring selections, and she wrestled with three choices, finally deciding on the tuna. When the waiter returned to take the order, Waddle spoke first.

"We'll have the smoked salmon with potato pancake, crème fraiche and caviar for our appetizer, and the duck for our main course. In addition, this bottle of the Vosne Romanée."

"Very good," the waiter said as he collected the menus and wine list.

"I hope you don't mind my ordering for both of you, it's the specialty of the house."

"Mind? You're the main man when it comes to food," George said, the omega dog submitting to his boss, the alpha male.

"I'm sure the duck's quite good," Nikki said, turning to the waiter. "But I'd rather have the tuna, sushi rare, and a house salad as an appetizer."

The waiter wrote down her request, and George looked down at his plate.

"Whatever you want, but you don't know what you're missing," Waddle said, and then repeated her request to the waiter. "Waiter, she'll have—"

"The tuna instead of the duck, and a house salad, she just told me," the waiter said. He walked with the collected menus towards the kitchen.

"He seemed a bit testy," George said.

"Low self-esteem. If he were taller, he wouldn't have an attitude," Dr. Waddle said.

"If he has low self-esteem, I suspect it's related to other issues besides his height," Nikki said, surprised at the former Dean's naiveté.

"You're not alone. Most people don't appreciate the connection," he said.

"Lack of height didn't seem to be an impediment to your career," she said, while George laughed nervously. The diminutive Waddle made no attempt to disagree.

"You're right, I don't suffer from low self-esteem. But it took a lot of work to overcome it. It would've been a helluva lot easier if I could've taken a pill and avoided the whole traumatic period."

He was using his psychiatric credentials to suggest a societal obligation to correct below average height, and by the time the Biosense public relations machine had finished, it would be a curable disease. If they had a drug that prevented people from achieving their genetically predetermined height, Waddle would instead be arguing the negative health effects of being tall: people's growth had to be prevented because those saddled with above average height were prone to concussions from doorway lintels, and the added size was a strain on their hearts. Also, psychologically, they would suffer from the burden of success, and the humiliation of being the target of "tall" jokes. And of course we know what the Japanese say: "The nail that sticks out gets hammered."

The wine arrived, and Dr. Waddle directed the waiter to open it. He poured a small amount into Waddle's glass and watched him hold it to the light, swirl it, nose it, sip it, and pronounce it satisfactory. The waiter tilted the bottle towards Nikki's glass, but before she was able to numb her pain, he was ordered to desist.

"We would like to allow the wine to breathe before serving." Waddle spoke as if he was used to people listening to him, a consequence of being surrounded by sycophants who distorted his view of the world. He possessed the swagger of the incompetent—never in doubt, but frequently wrong.

The waiter complied, and placed the bottle in the middle of the table.

"Excuse me, but you can pour my wine now," Nikki said to the waiter in defiance of Waddle's directive.

The waiter filled her glass and Waddle appeared oblivious to her criticism, a character flaw of all incompetent people in positions of authority. George frisked his brain for a response in defense of his boss.

"You don't believe in letting wine breathe?" George asked, furrowing his brow.

"Yes, but leaving an uncorked bottle of wine on the table is an ineffective way to do it," she said, the waiter nodding out of view of

Waddle and Lally.

"Dr. Waddle has traveled the world—"

"Then, George, I'm sure he's aware of the study from the University of Bordeaux which showed that the narrow top of a wine bottle is inadequate to achieve sufficient aeration. The best place for wine to aerate is in the glass, or, even better, in my stomach." She swirled her glass before taking a sip.

While Waddle and Lally tried to cobble a retort, they watched the waiter fill their glasses.

"I'm familiar with the study, but I found it flawed, and that's why I haven't adopted its precepts," Waddle said, complacent with his parry.

"The boss has reasons for everything. He doesn't make decisions in a vacuum," George said, looking to see if Nikki was equally convinced.

It was best not to query Waddle about his perceived flaws in the study. It wasn't worth challenging his self-anointed expertise.

"To health," she said, raising her glass.

"To health," they droned, raising their glasses in response.

The food was served, and Nikki decided to probe the well-lubricated Dr. Waddle about his plans for BrobaGen.

"George tells me cancer patients are just the beginning for BrobaGen," she said.

George was forced to advise his boss about his recent disclosure. "I told her about its potential role as a performance-enhancing drug."

"That's a huge market, but I think there's an even bigger one," Waddle said, leaning towards Nikki and lowering his voice before revealing his target group. "I'm talking short people." He looked at her over his bifocals, steadying them between the thumb and index finger of his left hand.

"You mean pituitary dwarfs?"

"I mean every kid below average in size." He took a triumphant sip of his wine.

"You think increasing the height of short people will resolve their inherent psychological problems?" Nikki said, hoping in vain that by hearing her question he would recognize the absurdity of his plan.

"Not all psychological problems, but the most prevalent one: low self-esteem."

His intent was clear to Nikki. He was using his psychiatric credentials to justify BrobaGen for treatment of half the world's population, a pharmaceutical cure for a problem that didn't exist. BrobaGen was a drug in search of a disease.

"BrobaGen could help these people, people like our friend the waiter. Endless hours on the couch for treatment of low self-esteem will be replaced with a pill. It's going to do for low self-esteem what Prozac did for depression," he said, peremptorily pursing his lips.

He was on a quest to eliminate "small" like they had done in the coffee bar.

"If people bought into what you're saying, and everyone of below average height took BrobaGen and became taller, half the population would still be below average, it would just be a different half," Nikki said. She looked over at George, who had a dazed expression, as if she had just announced "checkmate" right after the chess game had begun.

"You'd be creating a 'seesaw syndrome,'" Nikki continued, "Those previously above average in size would now be below average."

"You're assuming everyone of below average height will take the drug, but that won't happen. It's not going to be cheap. Not everyone will be able to afford it," Waddle said, underscoring the weakness of her argument.

"So short people who are poor will be forced to leave the country," she said.

"I don't understand," Waddle said as he looked at George, who was equally confused.

"Short people who can't afford the drug would remain short."

"That's correct."

"If your theory about size and self-esteem is accurate, they would have no choice but to seek a psychological haven in a country that had smaller people—a mass migration of short Americans in search of Lilliput."

"I like your sense of humor. We need more of that at Biosense," Waddle said, cueing George to laugh.

Lampooning their scheme failed to open their eyes to its absurdity, and they were convinced that BrobaGen was going to benefit both mankind and themselves. The dinner ended abruptly at ten o'clock and they offered to drop her off, but she insisted on walking home. She had to be up early in the morning to attend Grand Rounds, and she needed time alone to sort out her thoughts.

She checked her answering machine when she got home, confident she had silenced Cynthia. Two people had called. The first was Fred checking in; the second was the same disguised voice. The message was, "Leave now, or face the consequences." Nikki kicked the machine, disconnecting it from the wall. That was it. Tomorrow she was getting caller I.D., and then she was going to have another talk with Cynthia.

Grand Rounds is held every Thursday at 7:30 A.M., and Nikki always attends. Each week a faculty member provides the audience with an unbiased review of a disease and its treatment, thereby concretizing for Nikki and her fellow residents the most effective therapeutic approach. Three months ago Dr. Bertrand Mueller, the director of medical education, had introduced a policy change, and ever since she had observed a decrease in quality of the lectures. He invited Biosense to procure speakers for the forum, alleviating himself of the responsibility, and the company embraced the opportunity. The physicians selected were awarded a substantial honorarium, and in return advocated the use of Biosense products over their competitors'. In addition, Dr. Mueller was compensated by the sponsor for his administrative efforts, and the audience received complimentary coffee, muffins, and drug samples. Turnout improved, and a predictable boost in physician prescriptions for Biosense products occurred, justifying the company's investment.

But today's lecture didn't have a sponsor. McConnachie was scheduled to talk on Humanism and Medicine, a subject too ambiguous for product identification and promotion. The audience was small, deterred by both the unavailability of free breakfast, and a topic that the residents would not be tested on. The people who attended were the few who were interested in the subject. The ones who could benefit the most were not to be bothered.

Nikki settled into a seat on the aisle of the middle row, and as McConnachie showed his first slide she was distracted by an aura, a recognizable fragrance heralding Dr. Mueller. When she looked up, his paunch hovered over her arm. He nodded "hello," oblivious to the rows of empty seats, and waited for her to move her legs. He rocked in next to her, his attendance a consequence of his role as director of medical education rather than interest in the topic.

McConnachie pointed with a laser to the projected slide that summarized a recent poll: only sixty percent of people thought of the medical profession as prestigious, a decline from previous generations. It was disturbing to Nikki that her predecessors, deprived of the technical resources available today to diagnose and treat disease, were held in greater esteem.

"What's the reason for the decline in our public approval?" he asked. No one raised their hand. "A decline has occurred at a time when the life expectancy of people in industrialized nations has achieved new milestones due to improvements in both prevention and treatment of disease."

Mueller turned to Nikki to share his insight. "The answer is lousy public relations. The world needs to be reminded it's lucky to have us."

McConnachie had a different view. "The reason for the decline in public opinion is that we have put our interests above those of our patients. It's not the dedicated majority of physicians who have alienated the public, but some of us in University hospitals who have betrayed our patients' trust, viewing them as resources for collecting experimental data, a means to advance our academic careers."

Mueller nodded. He didn't participate in research, and therefore anointed himself amongst those physicians dedicated to their patients. His elbow nudged Nikki's arm, and when she looked up he was smirking, his eyebrows raised, nodding his head in the direction of Cogswell. Dr. Cogswell was massaging his forehead as if he were trying to erase McConnachie's words from his mind.

McConnachie persisted, suggesting that academic medicine was plagued by applied scientists concerned about disease, but not the patient. It was a rut easy to slip into, one she had witnessed and occasionally participated in during her training. Her enthusiasm for the opportunity to exercise her craft and hone her skills on the "gallbladder in room 323" or "the colon in room 304," took away the individuality of the patient and ignored his fear and concerns.

Nikki gazed over at one of the interns who was nodding out, saliva pooling in the dependent corner of his mouth and threatening to overflow onto his chin.

"Diagnostic skills," McConnachie said, "have withered from disuse, replaced by scanning machines and laboratory tests that have further separated the physician from the patient."

Mueller tapped his fingers on his armrest and then leaned towards Nikki, whispering, "The hepatitis addled his brain. What's he saying, we should give up technology and go back to sitting at the bedside, holding the patient's hand?"

Mueller, you're an idiot, Nikki thought, before responding. "McConnachie isn't suggesting we ignore technical resources, he's just saying they need to be complemented with careful observation and skilled diagnosis." Mueller disregarded her comment, looking around the auditorium at the reaction of others.

Nikki agreed with McConnachie that physicians, enamored with their knowledge, didn't listen to their patients as well as their predecessors, relying instead on objective tests, further alienating their patients. Medicine had achieved its greatest success in treating disease, yet in spite of improved survival rates, integrative medicine was thriving because patients were seeking alternative approaches that emphasized the importance of the individual.

McConnachie exhorted his audience not to neglect the art of surgery. "Look at the patient and cultivate your power of observation. Let's not ignore the legacy of fellow surgeon, Joseph Bell, who was the prototype for the greatest observer of all time: Sherlock Holmes."

Mueller continued his *sotto voce* commentary. "Sherlock was a drug addicted misogynist who was probably getting it on with Dr. Watson—not a great role model."

It was obvious to Nikki that Mueller had never read her favorite Holmes adventure, "The Scandal in Bohemia," the story introducing

Irene Adler, a brilliant and beautiful woman, and the only person who had outwitted Sherlock. Prior to her appearance, he had a perjorative view of women and considered them an impediment to his unique reasoning skills. But Adler changed that and fostered a new respect for the opposite sex. He referred to her as "the woman," and kept a picture of her in his room. Although a fictional character, her ability and self-confidence empowered Nikki to confront the occasional male colleague who disparaged women in surgery as interlopers—visual distractions who should be pursuing a "female" specialty, not surgery. Irene Adler singlehandedly changed Sherlock's view of women by her intelligence and tenacity, and Nikki planned to do the same with her male critics.

The intern had now entered an R.E.M. sleep pattern accompanied by snoring, particularly noticeable during pauses in McConnachie's talk. The resident sitting behind him kneed the back of the intern's chair. He responded by wiping saliva from his chin, nodding in agreement with the speaker, and closing his eyes.

McConnachie informed the audience that Sherlock's last name was derived from another physician and writer of that time, Oliver Wendell Holmes. He was also an excellent observer, and identified the cause of puerperal fever, a lethal infection that occurred in women during childbirth. He noted that the disease appeared most commonly in women whose physician had been working in the dissecting room right before entering the delivery suite. They were transferring the infection present in the cadaver and spreading it to the women until Holmes insisted that physicians change their clothes and wash their hands before entering the delivery suite. A marked decrease in the number of deaths occurred as a result of this simple precaution, and his observation marked the beginning of antisepsis.

Nikki was familiar with Dr. Holmes because he was one of the first physicians in America to advocate the admission of women into medical school. He appreciated their valuable contributions, and she laughed when she had read he believed the ideal physician would be someone who was able to combine both male and female qualities: a well-trained hermaphrodite.

"Dr. Holmes had an open mind, and he challenged authority, never accepting teachings merely out of tradition," McConnachie said. "And Dr. Holmes appreciated the benefit of physicians from diverse backgrounds, each possessing their own special qualities and cultural differences, but united together in the art and science of medicine."

Mueller elbowed Nikki's arm. "Now he's advocating affirmative action. Why doesn't he just come out and say it?"

It was important to Nikki not to negate her background, but incorporate it into her practice. Role models in surgery voicing the female perspective were rare, and it was a void that needed to be filled. Her colleagues often resorted to mimicking their male counterpart in order to be accepted, bowing to corporate loyalty and group ego at the expense of the true self. Women in surgery were like the new immigrants, but rather than being proud of their special qualities, they suppressed them, desperately trying to fit in, and by doing so losing their identity along the way.

McConnachie said, "Don't become slaves to routine, but open your minds to new possibilities and analyze them objectively. Not from the point of view of how a treatment is going to benefit you, but how it's going to benefit the patient."

She recognized parts of his talk as an exegesis of his syncretized philosophy, TransZenCatholicism. Mueller shook his head in disbelief before querying Nikki.

"What's wrong with routine? It's better to make it up as we go along?"

Ignoring him, Nikki realized what McConnachie had said applied not only to clinical practice, but to research also. Everyone was looking at BrobaGen from the perspective of how it was going to benefit themselves rather than the patient: personal profit, notoriety, career advancement or a combination of all three, and she had been guilty of the same ambition. Too often the best interests of the researcher were paramount, and the laboratory was viewed as an opportunity to generate papers and bolster a C.V. rather than to study a problem and share the information with the intent of improving patient care. It was an attitude encouraged by medical schools preoccupied with procuring a faculty of academically productive people, their value equated with the quantity of articles they published in peer review journals, not their ability to care for patients. Nikki referred to it as a policy of "publish while the patient perishes."

McConnachie urged the inclusion of humanism in the curriculum of medical education, because it taught the importance of each life, and the need to understand and treat each patient with more understanding and compassion.

He said, "A familiarity with the humanities, including literature, philosophy and history, doesn't guarantee a more compassionate understanding of the individual, but it makes it more likely."

Mueller asked Nikki, "How's knowledge of the humanities going to help you when a patient is bleeding to death?"

He had a point, Nikki thought. Mueller had more experience than anyone at watching patients bleed to death, and he was right; knowledge of literature wouldn't overcome his technical incompetence.

McConnachie continued, "Members of the academic community are supposed to exemplify the highest qualities of the medical profession, but instead of protecting the patients, we have abdicated both them and our teaching responsibilities by creating a culture of dependence on the pharmaceutical companies."

Nikki nodded, and Mueller shifted in his seat. McConnachie was repeating publicly what he had told the chairman of surgery in private, and she could see that both Mueller and Cogswell were concerned about what he was going to say next.

"The speakers and topics presented at this conference are chosen by drug companies, and indirectly so is the content. We deceive ourselves, myself included, believing we're not influenced by the lab support and honoraria we receive from private industry."

McConnachie concluded that the drug industry's objective is to increase sales, and that many academic physicians had partnered with them, convinced they're immune to their influence just as politicians believe they're immune from temptation to create favorable legislation for their donors.

Nikki admired McConnachie's willingness to admit mistakes of the past and challenge his colleagues to see the truth. It was long overdue. His illness had allowed him time to be with himself, examine his life, and he recognized the need for change.

His audience was stimulated by McConnachie's controversial comments. He concluded his talk and asked if there were any questions.

Mueller, the invertebrate, spoke under his breath. "That talk was irresponsible. Without a standard of care—an agreed upon routine— he's advocating chaos. And on top of that he criticizes Biosense, our support system."

"Stop mewling and raise your hand. Voice your objection like a man," Nikki said, tired of his whispered critique.

Mueller's face reddened, but he accepted the challenge. He couched his question with one of his smarmy introductions.

"Luke, I enjoyed your talk. It was refreshing, and I think everyone here is in agreement with the many points you raised," Mueller said, as Nikki's nostrils flared. "I have just one concern. Some of the younger residents might leave here thinking they're supposed to ignore the standard of care, and do their own thing. Now I know you're not advocating that, but could you set the record straight for the others?"

"I say this somewhat facetiously, Bert, but the so-called 'standard of care' is not a standard, but rather a compromise of committee members."

Mueller sighed as McConnachie explained his heretical view.

"That which had been designated the 'standard of care' twenty years ago, is scoffed at today, and today's 'standard of care' will be dismissed as quackery in another twenty years."

He referred to Dr. Holmes, who had advocated handwashing, and also Holmes's contemporary, Dr. Semmelweis, who proved that the mortality rate of expectant mothers was dramatically lowered by that one simple precaution, and yet they were both ridiculed because it was not accepted procedure—not the "standard of care." McConnachie conceded it was essential for the residents to learn the accepted surgical teachings. But at the same time they had to learn the art of surgery—the subtleties, what's not written.

McConnachie concluded, "Physicians who care about their patients often individualize their treatment, treatment which differs from the accepted routine but is based on sound scientific principles. This doesn't mean that because something is new or different, it is, therefore, good; but it doesn't mean that it isn't. It's important to keep an open mind."

"Thank you," Mueller said, and then mumbled to Nikki, "He lost it."

McConnachie scanned the auditorium for further questions, and Cogswell stood up.

"I would be remiss if I neglected to take issue with your disparaging remarks about the pharmaceutical industry. We ought to be thanking the drug companies, not criticizing them."

Mueller nodded while looking around the auditorium, trying to engage others with his stare to support Cogswell's view. Nikki saw Cynthia standing in the back, nodding along with him.

Cogswell continued his defense. "My laboratory has a cooperative relationship with Biosense, and together we've been able to bring the laboratory to the bedside, impacting many lives." Nikki was tempted to offer Mrs. Lamb as an example of their impact.

"The fact that this conference is generously supported by Biosense deserves our praise and gratitude, because we all benefit from hearing about the latest treatment advances from leading physicians in the tri-state area. Let's not forget that physicians share the same goal with Biosense—saving lives." Cut the bullshit and ask a question, Nikki thought, but he continued his rebuke.

"I don't have to remind you, Dr. McConnachie, of all people, that the treatment of diseases, diseases like hepatitis, would not have improved without their commitment to research. And I'm sure you can relate to that." Cogswell sat down, confident he had silenced McConnachie.

"Thank you for your comments. You're right. Drug companies have contributed to improved world health. But I think it's important to remember their primary goal is to sell drugs, and ours is to care for patients. Academic institutions like MUMC set the example for others, and we have to be vigilant about undue influence from the business sector that can compromise our objectivity." Cogswell had heard enough, and climbed the stairs toward the exit as McConnachie finished. "I agree research is essential in order to improve care, but patients must be fully informed of the inherent risks. And I'm sure, Dr. Cogswell, you can relate to that." Cogswell's face flushed before exiting the door, unwilling to continue the public confrontation.

There were no further questions, and after scattered applause, the audience got up and filed out. Nikki waited to intercept McConnachie because she wanted to congratulate him and confirm the details about dinner on Friday night, but a resident had sequestered him. After another few minutes, she decided she would call him later and left the auditorium.

His words inspired Nikki. It was as if someone had held up a mirror, and she was seeing for the first time who she was. She had been fixated on her goal of obtaining a staff position in oncology and had ignored several disturbing events out of fear of compromising her career. The premature death of Mrs. Lamb, the planned cardiac arrest of Mr. Washington, the unauthorized experimentation on the kid were all witnessed by her and tolerated. She had been paralyzed by fear of reprisal. Now it was time to act on her convictions. Divestiture of the Biosense shares was not enough. It was time to remove the veil of her own self-interest, and look at the world with what McConnachie called a "peeled eye." No more silently standing by while statistical outcomes were manipulated, and children were subjected to clandestine experiments. She was tired of playing the game, tired of trying to blend in rather than speaking her mind, and tired of a physical relationship lacking in emotional growth.

Spouses of surgeons were often labeled by their partners as obstacles who interfered with their burden of doing good, harpies who sapped their energy, and she had adopted that same pejorative view of relationship. She had become independent of the need for companionship, dating people she could dominate rather than an equal partner, someone who could complement her, someone like Luke. Her relationship with Fred was celibacy without abstinence, and it needed to change.

When she arrived at her apartment, she sat down at her desk and drafted a letter to the program committee of the International Society of Oncology, but she was interrupted by her beeper. It was Cogswell's office. When she returned the call, his secretary told her she was expected in his office in fifteen minutes. It did not sound like a social call.

The passageway to Dr. Cogswell's office was decorated with photographs of himself in the company of entertainers, sports figures, and politicians, interrupted by a few framed citations for research. His secretary assumed an air of self-importance predicated on the belief that his success was the product of her computer skills. Nikki introduced herself, interrupting her typing. The secretary appeared annoyed, as if the rhythm of her thought had been violated.

"I have a meeting with Dr. Cogswell."

"Have a seat," she said, as if the meeting depended on her approval.

She returned to her typing and made no effort to contact Cogswell. After a few minutes had passed, she picked up the phone.

"Dr. Cogswell, Dr. Moriarty is here."

She returned the phone to its cradle and began typing for another twenty-five seconds before speaking.

"You may go in now."

When Nikki entered his inner office, Cogswell was sitting at an oval cherry desk perched on a six-inch platform, a replica of the table used during the final negotiations to end the Viet Nam war. The leather-trimmed blotter was complemented by a matching leather pencil holder containing four Montblanc pens of two different sizes. His folded hands exposed gold cufflinks and a gold Rolex watch. Different camouflage than his hunting outfit, Nikki thought, but camouflage just the same. He looked down from his aerie and peered over his glasses as if he was not sure who had entered, before asking her to sit down.

"Nikki, how's it going?"

"Okay, I guess."

"You like it here?"

"Yes."

"That's good. If you like it here, you'll have a productive time, and we all benefit from that. A win-win situation."

They were just the introductory remarks, and Nikki knew he had something more ominous to say when he leaned towards her.

"I have to tell you," he said, speaking in a slowed cadence, "I've been disturbed by some recent reports I heard from my staff."

What reports? Complaints that she returned the Biosense shares? If anything, she should be commended and not criticized. Maybe the so-called recent reports had nothing to do with her, and he was just venting after his confrontation with McConnachie during grand rounds.

He looked down at his desk, collecting his thoughts before refocusing on Nikki. "Your first couple of days, all I heard were positive things. But that's changed."

Nikki knew what had changed—Jinny and Cynthia were out to get her ever since she returned the shares. Both were afraid she would expose their investment group and accuse them of insider trading, and they had to undermine her credibility. They had attacked first, and now anything she said against them would be dismissed as vengeful, the verbal meandering of a disgruntled employee.

"I'm surprised. The only thing I can think of was a minor disagreement with Cynthia about a personal matter."

He compressed his hands together in a position of prayer, his joined index fingers resting on his lips. "I've been told that you're not a team player."

"I disagree."

His hands parted, tapping the desk, a conductor seeking the attention of the orchestra.

"Let's understand each other. I've worked with this team for several years, and we've been quite successful. If I have to choose sides, it's going to be with them."

"I understand," Nikki said, knowing it was useless to argue.

Cogswell protected his lieutenants, and the facts never interfered with that obligation. She thought of pointing out the medical examiner's finding of BrobaGen in Angus's blood, but Cogswell only cared about his cancer studies. He didn't want to hear that Jinny gave BrobaGen to a minor; it didn't concern him. Even if it did, Jinny and Cynthia would deny their role, claiming that the kid had stolen his mother's medication.

"I hope I've made myself clear." He stood up, and Nikki knew there was nothing else to say.

She nodded, walked towards the door, and stopped. "Can I ask you an unrelated question?"

"Go ahead."

"I was curious about the results from the pathologist, his review of Mrs. Lamb's biopsy slides."

"Nothing different, we agreed she had a biologically aggressive tumor. Anything else?"

"No."

"Remember what I said," Cogswell warned before he gave her a perfunctory nod, and escorted her out of the office.

She decided not to wait for the elevator and walked down the stairs to the first floor and out the main entrance. If she contacted the program committee and requested they withdraw the abstract, it would guarantee the end of her career in oncology. If she didn't, BrobaGen would be foisted onto the public, and it would be years before the full repercussions of the drug were realized. She returned to her apartment, sat at her desk and revised her letter, introducing herself to the chairman of the program committee as a member of the BrobaGen research team. She wrote:

"Recent evidence suggests that the study drug increases the doubling time of cancer cells and we are, therefore, requesting withdrawal of our abstract until further studies are completed." No, that was no good. An admission like that would trigger a state investigation, and then the burden would be on her to prove her claim, an impossible task without more data. Better to say something generic:

"The conclusions of our pilot study were premature, and we request withdrawal of our abstract until we are able to confirm our results with a larger patient sampling." That would work. Cogswell would have to admit the numbers were small and agree with the postponement of his presentation.

The apartment buzzer rang three times, followed by the sound of a key turning the lock. When the door opened, Fred appeared.

"I knew I saw you going into the building."

"I'm busy, Fred. I've got to finish a letter to the oncology society."

"Why them?"

"Fred, I don't want to explain this again. I told you I think the drug increases the spread of cancer, and if this abstract is presented, it could end up with conditional approval from the FDA."

"And the stock will bounce. That's why I bought 200 shares."

"If you did, you're an asshole."

"Does Cogswell know you're doing this?"

"What do you think?"

"You send it, you might as well bend over and kiss your ass goodbye. Forget about practicing in this town."

"Sometimes you have to do what's right, not what's convenient."

"What's that, more Zen shit from the holier-than-thou McConnachie?"

"Look, Fred, you're not talking me out of this."

"Could you at least wait until there's an uptick in the shares? It's down a point since I bought it."

"No, Fred, I'd suggest you unload them now."

"You sure I can't get you to reconsider," he said, massaging her shoulders.

"Take your hands off me, and go do your play-sure research with someone else. I'm sure you'll find a lot of willing candidates at the gym."

"You've lost it."

"Fine, I lost it. I think it's best we go our separate ways."

Fred stomped out the door, slamming it behind him. Nikki felt a sense of relief. She was tired of his preoccupation with pleasure and his lack of support for what she was going through. He judged everything based solely on how it affected him. If he benefited then it was positive, if he didn't it was negative—Fred's situational ethics. She left the apartment after she was sure he wasn't around, and walked to Central Park. When she entered the 72nd Street entrance, she descended a hill overlooking the model boat pond and sat down on a bench near the Alice in Wonderland statue. A man wearing a double breasted blue blazer, white duck pants, topsider shoes, and a captain's hat had just launched a five foot replica of a yawl. The boat, unburdened by crew, sailed to the buoy located in the center of the pond, powered by the wind, and guided by radio waves. It came about, hugging the buoy, and a collision with the stone wall was avoided by a sharp turn to port combined with gentle prodding from the owner's rubber-tipped stick nudging it to a halt. After several more excursions, he removed his boat from the water. Nikki thought about her letter.

Fred was correct about one thing—her oncology career in New York was over. McConnachie said you create your own reality, and maybe she was purposely sabotaging her career because, subconsciously, she didn't want to be an oncological surgeon. What other reason could there be for a fledgling resident to take on an academic power broker like Cogswell? It was professional suicide. But, she decided, it was not fear of success that caused her to act. It was Mrs. Lamb, and people like her. They had put their faith in Cogswell and his subordinates, agreeing to participate in a study they were told would advance their care, and the care of all cancer patients. And she was also speaking out for innocent kids, the prospective addicts of BrobaGen, who would be inspired by the video of Angus and try to morph themselves into America's next superstars. Unless she interceded, it would take years before the deleterious effects of the drug were clearly defined, and meanwhile the pundits would dismiss the increase in teenage suicide as copycat tragedies, a product of the vagaries of youth.

She walked out of the park and returned home to finish her email. Maybe she would invest in a model boat. She probably was going to have plenty of time to sail it.

Cynthia identified herself to the driver of the car service provided by Biosense, and slid into the back seat.

"I hope you know where we're going, because I don't," Cynthia said, perched on the edge of her seat. The driver nodded, looking at her through the rearview mirror.

"Brooklyn, the Green-Wood Cemetery."

Cynthia sat back, vexed at Waddle's geographical selection for his "important meeting." When he discussed business with physicians, he invited them to lunch at the Four Seasons instead of arranging a clandestine rendez-vous at a graveyard. But it was consistent with the Biosense caste system: physicians revered at the top, and other health care professionals relegated to second class status.

They approached the exit for the Brooklyn Bridge and the traffic slowed, a result of both construction and vehicular avoidance of the alternate route—the Brooklyn Battery tunnel and its burdensome toll. Cloying fumes dissipated after the cab balked beyond the entrance ramp. The tires grazing the road produced a gentle drone that hummed memories of her youth, memories she wanted to forget. The thrill of riding the Coney Island Ferris Wheel at the age of five was expunged by the revolving view of her mother vanishing into the crowd and abandoning Cynthia to a foster home for over three months. When her mother reclaimed her, she attributed her absence to an unexpected illness that prevented her from seeing her daughter sooner. It was years later that Cynthia realized her mother's recurring illness was produced by alcohol and prescription drug abuse, a combination that eventually killed her.

A rattle of passing subway cars interrupted her reverie. After they passed, she watched a Moran tugboat nudge an indifferent tanker up the East River. Her driver continued onto Flatbush Avenue and turned right at Third until he reached the front of the Green-Wood Cemetery. The Gothic archway hovered over its entranceway, a replica of a medieval cathedral wall that guarded an estate of manicured lawns interrupted by crops of tombstones and mausoleums reserved for those who preferred above ground putrefaction.

Cynthia leaned towards the driver. "Only in America. I'm sure your country doesn't waste real estate like this."

"We also have cemeteries."

"I thought you people believed in cremation."

"Hindus, like myself, cremate the dead. But in Guyana, there're people of all denominations."

"I was thinking India."

"In India, Hindus burn the corpse on wood pyres and the ashes are scattered on the Ganges."

"That's how I want to go, but I don't care about my ashes. You never know if they're yours anyway."

The driver stopped at the front office to get directions to the gravesite. Cynthia walked over to a table outside the building and picked up a brochure containing the cemetery's schedule of charges. By far the cheapest option was cremation, and it had the added benefit of bypassing the gruesome consumption of the corpse by macro and microscopic organisms. The use of the furnace cost only $260, and for an additional $50, a chapel was provided. But a prayer service wouldn't be necessary—mourners were not expected.

The driver returned to the car and they drove for a couple of miles through the 478-acre estate. It was an invaluable piece of property, close to Manhattan, but committed to the dead. If she were a developer, she would offer money to the families of the deceased in exchange for the rights to their burial plots. The price would include disinterment and cremation of any remains which would be respectfully placed in a decoratve urn emblazoned with her company's logo, and submitted to the bereaving investors for either scattering or for living room display. After she had procured twenty to twenty-five adjacent sites, she calculated she would have enough land to build her first luxury high-rise.

"This is it," the driver said, parking along the curb.

Cynthia recognized the pear-shaped outline of Waddle supported by a stone bench. She walked up behind him, tapped him on the shoulder, and asked, "What's up?"

He turned towards her, held up his hand for silence, and a man wearing reflective sunglasses approached.

"May I?" the man asked, frisking her before she answered. When he finished, he nodded to Waddle.

"I apologize for that intrusion," Waddle said, "but I find the habit of covert tape recording distasteful."

"Don't apologize, that's the most action I've had all week."

Waddle smiled and patted the bench while his associate returned to his car.

"Been sitting in the car too long. I'd rather stand," Cynthia said, stretching her arms over her head.

Waddle nodded, placed a hand on each thigh, leaned forward, and listed into an upright position. He looked at her eye to chin.

"When was the last time we met alone?"

"Over a year ago on the Staten Island Ferry. At least there you could get a cup of coffee, here the only thing you can get is a séance."

"Privacy has always been my first priority, and I think you know why."

Is there a better place than the Staten Island Ferry to hand someone a suitcase with $250,000? The commuters mind their own business, and even if they were seen together, he could claim it was coincidental. The man was a fop, but he wasn't stupid.

"You made a good investment," Cynthia said.

"I should say so. The Lunar Club portfolio is now worth over a million dollars. I find that a tidy profit keeps investors happy, and I have to thank you for your leadership, and also for not disclosing the source of the donation."

It not only keeps the investors happy, Cynthia thought, but it guarantees positive results. The research team knows that if the BrobaGen study is successful, they stand to make tens of thousands of dollars, and enthusiasm for money obscures objectivity. It was a well-thought-out plan, and Biosense was its greatest beneficiary.

"You paid me well for my services. So why are we here today? I don't see any more suitcases of money."

"We're here to discuss a way to protect our mutual interests."

The only interest she shared with Waddle was making money off Biosense. Otherwise, for all she cared, he could drop dead.

"Biosense needs protection?"

"The results of the BrobaGen study are going to get Wall Street's attention, and trigger a 'strong buy' rating for the Biosense stock. I want to keep it that way, and I'm sure you do too."

"Let me guess, you're worried about Nikki Moriarty."

"Precisely. I anticipated that she was going to be a problem as soon as she started asking questions about the BrobaGen effect on cancer, but our friend Cogswell poohpoohed my concerns."

Poohpoohed? Who talks like that, Cynthia wondered. He's such an asshole.

"Cogswell's dangerous. He thinks he's got everyone figured out," she said.

"He has his faults, but he can be useful."

"After Nikki returned our gift, I made a few anonymous telephone threats, you know, trying to get her to quit."

Waddle shook his head. "Not the personality type to back off. If you'd asked me first, I would've saved you the trouble."

Cynthia looked down on his scalp, counting the transplanted stalks of hair reminiscent of a failed corn harvest. If he was such a genius, why didn't he solve the problem himself?

"I don't think she'll do anything crazy, too concerned about her career."

"I beg to differ. She just tried to withdraw the BrobaGen abstract from the upcoming oncology meeting."

Cynthia shook her head. "Fucking bitch."

"Not to worry, she e-mailed the wrong member of the program committee, someone we do business with," Waddle said, giving Cynthia a wink before returning to the bench. "The BrobaGen presentation is still on."

"That won't be the end of her, she knows about the twin study."

"Jinny told me, but we have that covered—the kid took his mother's medication."

Cynthia nodded. She hated when Jinny went to Waddle or Cogswell without consulting her first, but she would deal with her later.

"That bitch Moriarty has to disappear," she said.

"That's why we're here. We need to formulate a plan."

"Buying her off isn't going to work."

Waddle nodded. Cynthia walked towards a tombstone, waiting to hear his proposal. His silence made her uncomfortable; it reminded her of when her therapist remained silent during the session, waiting for her to produce the solution to her problems. He got paid the big bucks, let him come up with the answers. She had a vested interest in Biosense, but she was not going to put her ass on the line for either Waddle or his company.

Cynthia read the inscription on the tombstone. "Who was this guy anyway, William Stewart Halsted, M.D., 1852-1922, some relative of yours?"

"No, a famous physician. He was the father of modern surgery, established the first surgical training program in the United States, in addition to making a lot of contributions to operative techniques."

"Hold the history lesson for McConnachie and Moriarty. I'm tired of hearing about the dead male heroes of medicine."

"I think you'd be interested in this one."

"And why's that?"

"He was a cocaine addict. Happened after he did experimental work on its use as a local anesthetic. Not an uncommon problem at the time; it was before the drug was restricted. Even my mentor, Sigmund Freud, was addicted."

"Anyone who thinks your personality is based on how you sat on the toilet as a kid must've been on something."

Waddle smiled. "You have the talent to reduce complex issues to their essence."

"Anyway, how's a discussion of celebrity drug addicts from the past going to resolve our problem?"

"It's not, but it shows that high achievers like Halsted and Freud, and even the fictional Sherlock Holmes, were able to accomplish great things in spite of their habit. I'm sure you can relate to that," he said, peering over his bifocals.

Cynthia was tempted to rip them off his fat face and crush them under her heel. "I beg your pardon."

"Come, come, Cynthia, you're in good company," Waddle said, waving his arm towards Halsted's grave.

She turned her back to him. "I don't know what you're talking about."

"Au contraire, my dear, we had a very informative discourse with your supplier. Quite the entrepreneur, he charged us dearly for the information."

"You prick, you had me followed."

"Such harsh language. I have no intention of disclosing our little secret. We all have peccadilloes. Mine, alcohol and gambling, just happen to be legal. I only gather information to help me formulate my character profiles."

"And what do you do with these 'character profiles'?"

"I make decisions based upon them. For example, if I were asked to investigate the missing ampules of narcotics from the ICU, a problem as you know that has perplexed the nursing administration, I would reference my character profiles of ICU employees to solve the mystery. Most likely it was someone supplementing their drug habit. Cocaine can be costly."

Cynthia knew they couldn't prove she had stolen hospital drugs, but her career would be over if they discovered she was a user. She had to be cooperative; now was not the time to take on Waddle.

"Let's cut the bullshit. What's your plan?"

"I wouldn't be so presumptuous as to tell you how to perform your craft." He looked up at the sky, holding a lapel in each hand before continuing. "Bottom line—Nikki has to go, and it has to look like an accident."

Cynthia never thought this pismire was capable of planning a murder. A respected psychiatrist and former Dean, hiding behind his credentials, deceiving others into thinking of him as a humanitarian instead of a ruthless bastard. Like all cowards, he manipulated others to do his dirty work using words and gifts, but she wasn't stupid. If something went wrong, she would be left holding the bag.

"You're talking murder, and that's windows. I don't do windows."

"Ah, but you do. Certainly, you haven't forgotten that year you spent in a reform school upstate for stabbing a young black girl to death?"

"She attacked me first," Cynthia said. "How'd you find that out anyway? I was a juvenile and those records are sealed."

"For the right price, there's no such thing as sealed information."

Biosense had former FBI agents and former police detectives on their payroll, and they knew how to work the system. Cynthia was aware Biosense used personal information in conjunction with monetary gifts to influence politicians and procure extensions on their drug patents. A delay by Congress in allowing the production of generic equivalents translated into billions of dollars in profit, and the pharmaceutical industrial complex was not going to allow a few individuals to interfere. She stretched her neck, turning it from side to side.

"What stops me from going to the police and telling them you tried to hire me to kill Moriarty?"

"I'm sure the tabloids would find it entertaining for a day or two, but there's no proof to support your claim. Ultimately, who's a judge and jury going to believe, a drug addict with a record of manslaughter, or the former dean of an Ivy League medical school?"

He was right, and she knew it.

"Even if I get rid of Nikki, you still have McConnachie to deal with, and he's not going to be bought off either."

"My sources tell me he doesn't know about the twin study, at least not yet. That's why the sooner we take care of her the better."

Waddle explained how he had already begun a whispering campaign against McConnachie, disseminating damaging rumors to the hospital gossipmongers about his divorce, and suggesting that his time off from work was not just because of hepatitis, but rather the result of a mental breakdown. It was a campaign to undermine his credibility and provide the chairman of surgery, a paid consultant of Biosense, with reasons not to renew his contract. Waddle claimed it was all in the best interests of the patients.

Cynthia thought of another weakness in his plan. "I don't trust Jinny, especially when the shit hits the fan."

"I like your instincts. I don't trust her either. But I can tell you that when Nikki is silenced, Jinny will get the message."

There was no point in getting angry. The only thing left to do was cut the best deal for herself.

"What kind of compensation are you talking?"

"If you accomplish our goal, you'll be well taken care of."

"How well?"

"Let's just say you'll have enough money to buy an endless supply of leaves from the erythroxylon shrub."

She didn't like his vague promises, but she wasn't in a position to negotiate. It was a tempting thought to just whack Waddle now and put an end to his blackmail. When they found his body, they would attribute it to a heart attack suffered while mourning the loss of a loved one. But there was the guy with the mirrored sunglasses.

He held out his hand and began pumping Cynthia's while reminding her to make sure it looked like an accident. What a brilliant suggestion, she thought, make it look like an accident. She wriggled her hand free and entered the back of the waiting car.

"Back to Manhattan?" the driver asked.

"Back to Manhattan," she said, looking at the side of the driver's head. "Let me ask you something, what exactly does reincarnation mean?"

"The spirit of the dead returns in another form."

Cynthia nodded. "That's what I thought."

Maybe she was Freud or Halsted in a previous life, someone who did good in spite of their handicap. She was not really killing Nikki, she was just enabling her to return in another form. She was doing her a favor.

Nikki retrieved her beeper from her jacket pocket. It was the legal affairs office and they wanted to speak with her, which meant only one thing—someone was suing. All the surgical operations that she had participated in flashed through her mind, but she couldn't recall any egregious errors like amputating the wrong limb or leaving a clamp inside someone's abdomen. It didn't matter. Colleagues had been sued simply because a patient had a poor outcome, even though there was no deviation from the "standard of care."

Abdominal cramps, the consequence of thinking about a lawsuit, forced her to take refuge in the bathroom and delay returning the call. When she finished, she took a deep breath and dialed the number. Her voice sounded different, almost unrecognizable, as if she was in the room listening to someone else talking. The secretary informed her the hospital lawyer wanted to arrange a meeting about a former patient, a Mrs. Lamb.

After everything she had done for her: saving her life, and agreeing to act as her health care proxy. No good deed goes unpunished, Nikki thought. A family member must have surfaced looking to capitalize on her death, someone claiming they had not been informed of their loved one's hospitalization until after she was dead. It was similar to that patient who had been buried in Potter's Field, the burial ground for unclaimed bodies. A family member sued because of emotional stress suffered as a result of the hospital not informing the family of their relative's death, preventing them from providing a proper burial. Mrs. Lamb's estate was probably accusing her of failure to apprise the family of the patient's condition. But how could they? There were no known family members during her first hospitalization, no one available, not even a husband. But the prospect of remuneration attracted long lost relatives, people convinced that because of shared DNA they were deserving of the deceased's accumulated wealth. The prospect of inheritance created a magnetic pull that defied the laws of Newtonian physics.

At least she had malpractice insurance, but that wouldn't cover her for punitive damages. All she had done was help a patient carry out her wishes outlined in her living will. She had been officially designated the surrogate, and she had stopped life support only when further treatment was medically futile. Hopefully, the neurologist had written a detailed note in the chart documenting that she had met brain death criteria. If he hadn't, they could claim she had pulled the plug prematurely and charge her with manslaughter. Why did she ever agree to get involved in the first place? Her fate would be in the hands of an assigned lawyer from the liability company, an individual lacking ambition and who gracefully accepts defeat. The counselor for the plaintiff, a shark hired on a contingency fee basis, would leave no stone unturned, knowing he had to win the case in order to get paid. After it's over, she'd be labeled as the surgeon who killed a patient. And not only that, she didn't even have the decency to notify the family the patient was dead.

Nikki hurried to the lawyer's office located on the first floor of a building adjacent to the hospital, and when she arrived a woman was standing in the room, confused by her arrival.

"I'm trying to remember why I called you. My secretary just went to lunch."

"Something about Mrs. Lamb, she had asked me to be her health care proxy."

"Right, have a seat."

Nikki sat in a captain's chair in front of the desk, while the lawyer shuffled through papers.

She felt the need to defend herself while the lawyer continued her search. "Just so you're aware, I definitely asked Mrs. Lamb if she had any family or friends, and she denied it. Otherwise I would've contacted them."

The lawyer looked up, nodded, and then continued her search.

"Here's what I was looking for, Mrs. Lamb's last will and testament. She left $100,000 to be used for research at your discretion."

"You're kidding."

"I don't kid. She must've really liked you."

Nikki sat up in her chair. She had thought Mrs. Lamb destitute. Now she was named in her will. The lawyer handed her the papers to read, and it stated the money had been left for "research, with the understanding that Dr. Moriarty, and her team, provide clear communication with patients, and assure that they are completely informed of the indications and potential complications of the proposed treatment."

She must've known she had been deceived by Jinny, and herded into a study that spread cancer rather than cured it. Mrs. Lamb recognized her precipitous decline was a consequence of BrobaGen, and her stipulated donation to research was a posthumous protest of the system, a system distorted by ambition and personal aggrandizement, and one that needed change. She didn't deserve Mrs. Lamb's confidence. It humbled her. Nikki had surmised that both data and patients had been manipulated, but she'd ignored her suspicions, not wanting to jeopardize her career. The combination of Mrs. Lamb's death, Mr. Washington's arrest, and Angus's death should have awakened her to act. If she hadn't glimpsed the profile of herself on Jinny's laptop, and listened to McConnachie's lecture, she may never have interceded.

The hospital lawyer informed her an account would be established in the department of surgery under Nikki's name, and that she would be required to have the chairman of surgery approve and co-sign any withdrawal of money. It was a safety precaution that protected her from allegations of misappropriation of funds.

While the lawyer continued to explain the ground rules, Nikki was planning her research project. She would have enough money to hire a lab techncian for the duration of the two-year period, and also cover the costs of housing and feeding the experimental animals. Collaboration with Dr. Green would probably be the most productive partnership, and since she was self-supportive, there wouldn't be any drain on his resources. No more kowtowing to company executives or academic pundits. All her energy could now be directed towards the pursuit of honest and reproducible research.

When the lawyer had finished, Nikki thanked her before walking over to Dr. Green's lab to discuss a research proposal, one that would document the mitogenic effect of BrobaGen. His animal lab housed a variety of genetically engineered mice, mutant rodents programmed to develop specific types of tumors, the perfect animal model to study the effect of BrobaGen on tumor growth. She walked down a laboratory hallway and looked through a windowed door. Inside there were shelves lined with transparent plastic cages, each one containing a handicapped mouse.

Dr. Green's door was closed. Nikki knocked, turned the doorknob, and walked inside. The overhead light reflected off his bald head as he sat at a table with his hands and forearms extended under a partially closed glass hood. His beard brushed the outside of the window while he injected a solution into the abdomen of a mouse.

"Dr. Green," she said, wondering if she should raise her hand and say question in order to get his attention.

He finished the injection, placed the mouse back in its cage, and turned in the direction of the voice.

"Nikki, what's up?"

"I have a proposal for you."

"I'm listening."

"Would you be willing to collaborate on a project with me, a study of tumor growth in mice, probably around fifty?"

"You're talking big bucks," he said, tugging on his beard.

"A research fund was just established in my name, and it'll cover the costs, including a salary line for a technician."

"Will it cover $75,000?"

"With some left over."

Dr. Green sat back down. "How did you come up with that kind of funding?"

"Remember Mrs. Lamb, one of the study patients? I was her health care proxy."

"Right, you were concerned about how quickly she went down the tubes."

"She left me $100,000 in her will specifically for research."

"Not too shabby."

"So what do you think?"

Dr. Green stood up, palmed his bald head, and offered Nikki a cup of coffee while he poured one for himself. She declined.

"I'll tell you what I think: you've got the gold, you make the rules," he said, and smiled. "What exactly do you want to do?"

"Half the DNA-specific mice get injected with BrobaGen, the other half with a placebo. I want to see what BrobaGen does to tumor growth."

"Been there, done it."

Her brow furrowed. "Was it published? I never saw any references about it."

"That's because it was relegated to the department of negative results."

"You mean you didn't see any difference between the two groups?"

"Let's just say the results were not favorable for BrobaGen, and Cogswell didn't want to submit it for publication."

"So the Institutional Review Board approved the human study unaware of your animal results."

"Not exactly." He paused to sip his coffee. "I didn't feel comfortable sequestering the data, so I submitted the results. But it didn't matter, the IRB approved it anyway."

"How could they ignore your findings?"

"Because BrobaGen also increased muscle mass and weight, and that's what they focused on."

He reminded Nikki that the Institutional Review Board was comprised of people who were not compensated for their time, and they wanted to review the protocols as quickly as possible. They were also pressured by the hospital administration not to roadblock studies, because every approved study provided the institution with thousands of dollars from the sponsoring drug company to cover their so-called administrative costs. Cogswell threatened to fire him for submitting data to the IRB without his permission, but he relented after he had received approval for the pilot study of five patients. He was able to show an increase in weight and muscle mass in the volunteers, and based on those results he was granted approval for the just completed phase two study of twenty cancer patients.

Nikki reviewed the data from the pilot study on the five volunteers, all college kids, who were paid $2500 for agreeing to submit to an array of laboratory tests after receiving injections of BrobaGen. Over the six month period, none of the volunteers had any untoward reactions, and they all had increased weight and muscle mass.

"With the increased numbers of patients in the phase two study, I was concerned some were going to show signs of increased tumor growth from BrobaGen. Fortunately, it didn't happen."

"It didn't happen if you believe Jinny's results."

Green's eyes gleamed. "I hear you."

Nikki continued to read the results of the pilot study and discovered there were originally six patients, not five. One of the volunteers had been dropped from the results because he experienced auditory hallucinations and was admitted to Payne Whitney for treatment.

"This sixth patient should've been included as a complication of the therapy," Nikki said.

"I agree, but Cogswell saw it different. He said the patient should never have been admitted into the study, because he had a pre-existing psych history."

"Even if that was true, he was started in the study and had a complication. You can't ignore that."

"You're right, he should've been included. But you know Cogswell, he didn't want to hear it."

He went over to a file, unlocked it, removed the original IRB application for the phase two study, and handed it to her. She scanned the papers and didn't see any reference to either the animal study or to the volunteer who had been dropped because of a complication. The body of the application focused on the five college volunteers. It emphasized their weight gain, secondary to BrobaGen, to assure that Cogswell would receive approval to use it on cancer patients. Dr. Green had submitted evidence to the IRB showing that BrobaGen was associated with significant risks, but they had ignored his warning.

"You mind if I keep the IRB application overnight? I want to look it over in detail."

"Take your time, we can go over your questions tomorrow."

Nikki thanked him and walked towards the door

"I've got to give this more thought, but I'm sure I'll come up with another project."

"I'll be here."

Nikki left the lab, thinking about the research records. The deleterious effects of BrobaGen had been documented and suppressed by Cogswell, and now Biosense was poised to damage thousands of others. She was relieved that her e-mail was in the hands of the program committee, and that the anticipated rejection of Cogswell's BrobaGen abstract would prevent its further use—at least for now.

"Don't you know I can destroy your career?" It was the first time Nikki had ever heard Cogswell raise his voice. "Who the hell are you to try and withdraw one of my abstracts? An abstract, I might add, you had nothing to do with."

Nikki should have known they wouldn't just cancel the abstract without discussing it with Cogswell first. He probably convinced his cronies on the program committee that she was an incompetent who had been fired, and in revenge, she was trying to sabotage his lab. No one was going to believe a cipher like her over Dr. Cogswell, the former president of their organization.

He pointed at her, wagging his finger. "You tarnished my reputation, and I can assure you there'll be repercussions. To begin with, you're no longer a member of this research team, and I'd plan on never practicing oncology in New York."

She had to say something, but if she repeated what Dr. Green had told her, he would get fired too.

"If you're concerned about your reputation, then you should be concerned about the teenager who died after being treated with

BrobaGen. It happened on your watch, and I can tell you there's going to be a lot of other premature deaths if your abstract is ever presented."

"There were no deaths in my pilot study."

"I'm referring to a pair of twins in an unapproved study performed by members of your staff."

"I don't know what you're talking about, but you'd better be careful what you say or else you'll find yourself in court," he said, standing up and ending any further discussion.

He either didn't know about the twins or was feigning ignorance, but there was no point in persisting. She left his office upset that she would never achieve her goal, an academic appointment on staff at the medical center, but at the same time relieved she would no longer be associated with his group.

Cogswell was probably on the phone telling Jinny and Cynthia that Nikki's allegations were ludicrous, the product of a disturbed mind, and both would reinforce his assessment. Before long everyone would know she had been fired for attempting to withdraw Cogswell's abstract, and that she had accused him of participating in an experiment on twins. If she wanted to stay in New York she would have to pursue another sub-specialty. But it wasn't that bad, she thought, as long as she was still doing some kind of surgery.

She had to find McConnachie and tell him what was going on. All she could think of was being in his arms, hearing his supportive words, telling her everything would be all right. She entered the elevator and someone interjected a hand between the closing doors, causing them to retract. It was Cynthia. She twirled a candy stick protruding from her mouth.

"I didn't see you coming," Nikki said.

"No problem, it's just my hand," she said, after removing her lollipop from her mouth. She reached into her pocket and produced another one which she handed to Nikki.

The doors reclosed, and the elevator ascended. They both looked up at the illuminating floor numbers, and Nikki unwrapped her lollipop. Now was a good time to accost Cynthia about her continuing threats, but Cynthia spoke first.

"What's this shit about you not working with us anymore?" Cynthia asked, scrunching her nose, wrinkling her forehead.

"Cogswell, that prick, just told us."

"I guess there's nothing else to say, except that I had the shortest research career in the history of the program," Nikki said, between sucks of her lollipop.

"I really wanted you to be part of the team. That's why I tried to make you look good in front of him."

"You mean Mr. Washington's arrest?"

"If that's what you want to call it."

"What would you call it?"

Before Cynthia answered, the elevator jerked to a stop between floors and she turned around and faced the panel of buttons.

"I don't know if I leaned against something," she said.

"I've had problems with these elevators before," Nikki said, reaching around Cynthia and pushing the alarm button, which was mute. "I can't believe they still haven't fixed it."

"I'll call security on my cell," Cynthia said, while Nikki scanned the side panel for an inspection certificate, but there was just a sign that said it was kept in the security office.

"I think I need something to drink. I'm feeling a little woozy." Nikki dropped her lollipop to the floor.

"Poor baby, it's been a very emotional day," Cynthia said, pretending to reach in her pocket for her cell phone.

Nikki bent over to pick up her lollipop and she felt unsteady. She stabilized herself with both hands on her knees. A sharp pain, a hornet's sting, caused her to reach for her left thigh, where she encountered Cynthia's hand. When she looked at what was going on, she saw her removing an emptied syringe from her thigh.

"What the fuck did you give me?"

Cynthia ignored her while she collected the drug paraphernalia and dropped it into a plastic bag. Nikki fell towards the button panel and tried to release the stop button, but Cynthia pushed her away.

"Just take it easy."

"What did you give me?"

"The same thing that was in your lollipop, something to relax."

"You goddamn bitch, what the fuck do you think you're doing?"

"I wanted to help you, but you just wouldn't cooperate."

Nikki steadied herself against the elevator wall, trying to collect her thoughts while Cynthia positioned herself in front of the panel of buttons. She should have recognized the Fentanyl lollipop; it was just like the one given to pediatric patients in preparation for surgery to calm them prior to receiving deeper anesthesia. Fred had taken several home and sucked on them as part of his pleasure research while she ended up babysitting him, making sure he didn't stop breathing.

She had to do something fast, but the lollipop had put her at a disadvantage, and it was only going to get worse when the injection kicked in. She had to focus if she was going to survive, and Cynthia stood between her and the stop button. From the kneeling position, she reached over and grabbed Cynthia's right ankle and stood up. She held on to it as Cynthia tried to free her leg from her grip, but Nikki kept her off balance, forcing her to hop away from the buttons. She elevated Cynthia's leg above her head until Cynthia lost her balance and fell to the ground. Nikki's vision was becoming blurry, but she was able to identify the stop button and release it. The elevator resumed its ascent as Cynthia rushed her, but with her last bit of strength Nikki kicked her in the abdomen and dropped her to her knees. The doors opened, and Nikki stumbled down the hallway trying to make it to McConnachie's office. Her struggle had increased her cardiac output, hastening the absorption of the Fentanyl, and everything moved in slow motion. Her lethargy increased, and soon she would no longer be able to breathe—dead from internal suffocation. She needed an injection of Narcan to reverse the effects of the narcotic, and McConnachie was the only one she trusted. Her head spun as she staggered into his office, as if she were supporting a 200 lb weight on her back.

The secretary put down her emery board. "Do you have an appointment?"

Nikki kept going past her desk and into McConnachie's inner office and collapsed at his feet. He knelt down next to her, and when he saw her breathing had become labored, told the secretary to call the cardiac arrest team. Her pulse felt thready, and he knew she was about to code, but he didn't know why.

"Fen-ta-nyl," she mumbled, and she felt McConnachie press his lips against hers and begin mouth to mouth resuscitation before she lapsed into unconsciousness.

Nikki awoke in the ICU, her throat splinted by an endotracheal tube. A ventilator controlled her breathing, and attempts at communication were restricted to eye movement. At least she was alive and not brain dead, but she wanted her nurse to remove the endotracheal tube so she could tell her about Cynthia. She heard someone in the room but couldn't lift her head to see who it was. Her arms and legs were too weak to move. But she knew she could get her attention by bucking the respirator—expiring when the machine was trying to deliver a breath—and triggering the alarm. It worked; an irritating buzzer sounded, and the nurse turned off the alarm and walked over to the bedside.

"It looks like we better give you something to calm down, we don't want you pulling out your E.T. tube now, do we?" The voice was familiar, but in an unsettling way. Nikki had an urge to escape, like white tailed deer cognizant of a predator. She reminded herself it was her nurse, her protector from the indifference of hospital technology. No reason to be alarmed. But now she understood the reason for her sense of impending doom. It was Cynthia.

Someone had to stop her. Where was Carmen Gonzalez? She knew that Cynthia wasn't supposed to be left alone in the room with any of the patients. Another injection of Fentanyl and Nikki knew she would stop breathing again. But unlike before, she had the ventilator to take over and breathe for her. A warm flush journeyed up her forearm; her muscles became flaccid, and her eyelids closed, refusing to reopen. She could hear and feel, but she couldn't move. Another Fentanyl injection, but something didn't make sense: Her mentation was clear, not fuzzy like before. Cynthia had injected something else. Another person entered the room and spoke, a voice that sounded like Carmen's.

"What did you just give her? I'll record it on her flow sheet."

"Nothing to record. I was flushing her I.V., it was backed up."

Lying bitch. Don't believe her, Carmen. Nikki felt someone lifting her eyelid and inserting drops.

"A few drops of saline to keep your eyes moist, sweetheart," Cynthia said, and then kissed Nikki's forehead.

"Cynthia, hasn't she woken up from the Narcan yet?" another voice asked that had just entered the room.

"I'm afraid not, Dr. McConnachie."

Not waking up? What the fuck is she talking about? Luke, don't tell me you believe her too. She must have injected vecuronium, a paralyzing agent that made me dependent on the ventilator and unable to tell anyone what happened.

McConnachie sounded confused. "Was she responsive at all? I thought I heard her ventilator alarm go off."

"It went off when I disconnected the ventilator from her E.T. tube so I could suction her. I'm afraid there's no sign of breathing on her own."

Nikki tried to show she was lying by fighting the ventilator to set off the alarm again, but her body wouldn't respond.

"You didn't notice any spontaneous movements?" McConnachie asked.

"Nothing purposeful," Cynthia said. Her voice deteriorated into a childlike tone. "Dr. McConnachie, we know how much you tried, but it's hard for anyone to adequately ventilate a patient with mouth to mouth. I hope she wasn't intubated too late, but her pupils are fixed and dilated."

No fucking way—it's physiologically impossible for me to be aware of what's going on, and have fixed and dilated pupils.

"That's hard to believe. We had her intubated within a couple of minutes of her arrest, and she had a pulse while I was resuscitating her before the cardiac team arrived."

"I wish I was wrong," Cynthia said.

Nikki was relieved when she heard McConnachie pick up the ophthalmoscope that hung on the wall, impatient for him to prove Cynthia wrong. He pulled up her right eyelid and flashed light over the exposed pupil, and then over the left, not once, but twice, and then a third time.

"I agree," he said, distressed by his confirmation of the previous examiner's finding. He knew that the prognosis was grim.

"Maybe her pupils are dilated from the atropine she got during her arrest. It'll wear off," Carmen said.

Thank God for Carmen. She's the only one who made sense. The pupillary dilation was a red herring, caused by the atropine injection and not a lack of oxygen to my brain.

"From your mouth to the goddess's ears," Cynthia said.

"Excuse me?" Carmen asked.

"Nothing, I was just saying I hope you're right."

They didn't understand the goddess reference, because they didn't know that she was a fucking witch, pretending to support and empower her female colleagues. Nikki regretted she hadn't told McConnachie about their female empowerment group, the Lunar club. If he was aware of it, maybe he would be more suspect of Cynthia.

Another voice spoke to McConnachie. Nikki was sure it was Jinny.

"Dr. McConnachie, we were removing Nikki's valuables from her pockets for safe keeping, and we found this—an empty syringe of Fentanyl," Jinny said.

"It's always the ones you least expect," Cynthia added.

Nikki silently screamed at McConnachie not to believe her. It was staged just like Mr. Washington's arrest—they wanted everyone to think she had overdosed and caused her own death. The vecuronium was going to wear off, but not before they all went to lunch and left her alone with Cynthia. Four minutes without anyone else in the room was all Cynthia needed to end the debate. Four minutes without oxygen and Nikki knew she would be brain dead.

The door opened and she heard Fred ask McConnachie how she was doing, but before he answered McConnachie told him he wanted to speak with him outside. Fred knew she didn't take drugs, but after kicking him out of her apartment she was unsure if he would still defend her. Cynthia was talking to someone else, sounded like George Lally, telling him it looked like a drug overdose. McConnachie returned and addressed the others in the room.

"It's probably best to transfer her to the Neuro ICU, since it doesn't look like she's going to have a quick recovery."

At least in the Neuro ICU Cynthia would lose jurisdiction over her care, and it would be harder for her to interfere with her recovery.

"I agree. We can have her ready after lunch," Cynthia said.

Not after lunch, now! After lunch will be too late, and by the time I arrive in the Neuro ICU, I'll be brain dead, prepared for organ donation.

She felt someone grab her flaccid hand.

"I can't believe it, I just can't believe it," Fred mumbled, rubbing her hand between his. Nikki felt like she was observing her own funeral, hearing the mourners but unable to see them.

Jinny consoled him. "You couldn't see it coming, none of us could."

Cynthia agreed. "There are some secrets people don't share, not even with their most intimate friends."

McConnachie told Cynthia it would be best to restrict visitors until they were sure which way things were going. Cynthia nodded. She knew that without visitors, the likelihood of being alone with Nikki before her transfer increased.

The neurology resident arrived and Cynthia assured him Nikki hadn't received any medication that could interfere with the accuracy of his exam except for the possibility of atropine during her arrest. McConnachie asked Carmen for the cardiac arrest sheet so he could confirm whether she had received atropine, and Nikki heard the riffle of papers.

Cynthia spoke to Carmen. "I'll be back in ten minutes, I'm just going to get a quick bite, and then I'll cover for you so you can eat before we get her ready for transfer."

"Take your time," Carmen said.

Nikki hoped Carmen was smart enough not to leave her alone with Cynthia. She should know better. After all, she was the first one to suspect her.

The resident had reviewed Nikki's chart, finished his preliminary exam, and shared his impression: She was in a permanent vegetative state.

He reserved his final diagnosis until he reevaluated the patient with his attending later in the day, and he also wanted to make sure the atropine had worn off.

"She didn't receive atropine," McConnachie said, massaging his forehead with his right hand. "No record of it on the arrest sheet."

"If there's no atropine on board, then it pretty much confirms my initial impression," the neurologist said.

The neurologist approved her transfer to the Neuro ICU and ordered an EEG. He asked Carmen to place a liter of saline on ice, so that when they returned to do their follow-up exam they could try and elicit a vestibulo-ocular reflex. But Nikki knew by then she wouldn't have any reflexes.

"Maybe the atropine was given, but not recorded," Carmen said, trying to maintain some hope for recovery while she applied a moisturizer to Nikki's hands and arms.

Carmen was right. If my eyes were fixed and dilated from lack of oxygen, I wouldn't be aware of my surroundings. When is McConnachie, the advocate of keen observation and deductive reasoning, going to realize Cynthia is killing me?

"And she received no medications today?" McConnachie asked once again.

"Just the I.V. flush to clear her line, and the eye drops," Carmen said.

"What eye drops?"

"You know, duratears—Cynthia said her eyes were dried out."

"Dried out? Her lids have been closed, and her corneas protected. There's no reason she'd need drops," he said, lifting her eyelids to reexamine her pupils.

They remained fixed and dilated, but they were moist. He reclosed her lids and stayed silent, which was a good sign, she thought. Maybe he was starting to get suspicious. He was probably looking at Nikki's urine output like he did with every patient when he was perplexed, lifting the tubing, milking its contents and directing the fluid into the collecting bag.

"I don't understand," he said, "she always had a pulse. Granted, it was weak, but it was there."

"So you don't think she had a full cardiac arrest?" Carmen asked.

"No, it was respiratory. And I was giving her mouth to mouth right up until she was intubated. The fixed and dilated pupils don't make sense," he said, as he reviewed Nikki's lab data once again.

"Dr. McConnachie, did you turn off the alarm on the ventilator?" Carmen asked.

"I didn't touch it."

"Someone did," she said, turning it back on.

"It's good you picked that up," Cynthia said, returning from lunch. She hung her jacket on the hook on the outside of the door before coming to the bedside. "I bet that damn respiratory therapist forgot to turn it back on after he checked the ventilator."

That's it, Cynthia, blame everyone but yourself. I know you turned it off, because you didn't want me triggering the alarm and convincing the others I could breathe on my own.

Cynthia suggested that Carmen and McConnachie take a break, because she had just made a fresh pot of coffee.

"I could use a cup. Carmen, you need a break too," McConnachie said, not willing to take no for an answer.

"Enjoy, guys."

Enjoy, my ass. The dumb shits, they're leaving me alone with my executioner. By now Dr. Joseph Bell would have deduced what was going on and exposed Cynthia, instead of wasting time like McConnachie, drinking coffee in the nurses' lounge and dropping aphorisms.

After they left the room, she heard Cynthia flick the alarm switch off again, then disconnect the ventilator tubing that had been linked to her endotracheal tube. Nikki knew if she didn't start breathing on her own, she would die. But she was paralyzed, her body ignoring her mind. A few minutes more without oxygen, and the neurology resident would be right—she would be in a permanent vegetative state.

"You should've listened. I was just trying to help." Cynthia stroked Nikki's cheek. "We could've guaranteed your career, but you had to go and ruin everything."

The carbon dioxide building up in her blood from lack of venti-lation would normally trigger her respiratory center to initiate a breath, but her paralyzed body couldn't respond. Her thinking was becoming more and more confused, and soon she would be disori-ented, followed by coma, and then brain death. Two more minutes, and it would be irreversible.

A suction catheter was inserted by Cynthia into the unattached E.T. tube, a cautionary measure in case someone walked in unexpect-edly and saw Nikki disconnected from the ventilator. If that hap-pened, Cynthia would make her usual claim that the patient had developed a mucus plug and that she was trying to dislodge it with the catheter—it was the "standard of care."

Her oxygen level was decreasing. In another minute she would morph into a giant legume, relegated to custodial care. She hadn't prepared a living will because she wasn't expecting to be murdered, and without specific direction to the contrary, her fellow physicians would be reluctant to terminate her. She prayed her father wouldn't show up like he had when her mother was dying, insisting that ev-erything be done, only to prolong the inevitable. It would be best if she had a cardiac arrest and died before she could be resuscitated, but Cynthia was not going to let that happen. She wanted Nikki alive, but brain dead. If Nikki's heart stopped, Cynthia would give her 100% oxygen, and even cardiovert her if necessary. Her young heart would respond, and she would be successfully resuscitated, but permanently unresponsive. Another "save" for Cynthia.

She entered a dream-like state interrupted by McConnachie's muddled voice, and the sound of Cynthia yelling.

"Dr. McConnachie, what are you doing? I was suctioning her," Cynthia screamed, while he pulled out the catheter and attached an ambu bag to the E.T. tube. Nikki could tell he was bagging her.

"Her heart rate is forty," he said, increasing his rate of ventilation and using one hundred percent oxygen to correct her bradycardia. "Pull the emergency alarm."

Nikki felt like she was in suspended animation, hovering between life and death. She became more aware of her surroundings, presum-ably because her carbon dioxide levels were returning to normal, and her oxygenation was improving. If she had only told McConnachie that Cynthia had staged Washington's arrest, he would know the psychotic bitch was lying again about the mucus plug. He had arrived just in time. A successful resuscitation and it would be all over for Cynthia.

"Damn it, I told you to call for help." He reached over Nikki and pulled the alarm himself.

Carmen, Jinny, and two male nurses responded to the alarm, and found Cynthia disheveled and crying for help. "I pulled the alarm, he's crazy, look what he did to me."

Jinny picked up on Cynthia's lead. "Who the hell does he think he is?"

"Let's take care of the patient first," McConnachie said, while continuing to bag her. "Her pulse was forty, and I got it up to sixty, but it's deteriorating again."

Cynthia blubbered on her knees. "He doesn't know what he's doing—it was a nursing problem. I was trying to suction out a plug, and he attacked me."

Nikki could feel herself slipping, becoming more confused just like before. Something had changed.

Carmen recognized the problem. "There's no oxygen attached to the ambu bag." She reattached the oxygen line Cynthia had disconnected.

Dr. Cogswell, who had been apprised of McConnachie's errratic behavior by one of the other nurses, entered the room with a security guard. He asked McConnachie to leave, accusing him of interfering with patient care and assaulting a nurse. McConnachie ignored his request and remained fixated on the cardiac monitor, watching Nikki's pulse return to normal.

"Dr. McConnachie, you overreacted," Cogswell said, trying to regain his attention.

"If I didn't overreact, she'd be dead."

McConnachie reattached her E.T. tube to the ventilator and told Carmen to keep her on 100% oxygen and a respiratory rate of sixteen.

"Mac, if you don't leave, I'm going to ask security to forceably remove you," Cogswell said, and the security officer straightened his back, shifting his size seven shoes.

"Not until I'm sure she's stable."

"She's starting to wake up, she just moved her hand," Carmen said.

"Call neurology back and tell them to reexamine her. She's not brain dead," McConnachie said.

"Mac, I'm serious, we can handle things from here. You're going to have to leave."

"I'll leave as long as everyone else leaves, and just Carmen stays with the patient."

"Fine. Everyone leaves except Carmen," Cogswell said, unaware he had just thwarted Cynthia.

Cynthia asked if she could stay, insisting that Nikki was her responsibility. But McConnachie said if she stayed, then he stayed. Cogswell had no choice but to refuse Cynthia's request in order to keep things calm, and he spurred everyone out of the room. Carmen remained and drew a blood gas, and then checked Nikki's vital signs, recording the results on her flow sheet. She asked Nikki to squeeze her hand, and she responded, compressing her hand three times.

McConnachie and Cogswell returned a few minutes later with the neurologist, who examined her pupils, checked her reflexes, and confirmed she was responding appropriately to commands.

"Looks like you were right, Dr. McConnachie. We were fooled by a combination of drugs."

"Let's not jump to conclusions just yet," Cogswell said, knowing if it was true, there would be serious fallout.

The neurologist finished his exam, and they all left together. Nikki opened her eyes and lifted her head from the pillow. Carmen reassured her and told her to save her strength.

"I know when we get that tube out, you're going to have a lot to tell us."

Two hours later Carmen extubated Nikki in the presence of both Fred and McConnachie. After she finished coughing, Fred caressed her hand and apologized.

"I'm sorry, I didn't realize what you were going through, but promise me you're through with drugs."

Nikki jerked her hand away from his and shook her head in disgust.

"You're such a fool—just leave the room," she said hoarsely.

Fred turned to McConnachie and Carmen for support. They both remained silent. He stood up and left.

"It was Cynthia," she said, after Fred exited. "She stopped the elevator between floors and injected me with Fentanyl. Tried to make it look like I o.d.'d."

"It almost worked," McConnachie said.

"Thanks to you guys it didn't, but I gotta tell you, I thought she was going to finish me off when you left me alone with her."

"We were a little slow. I didn't suspect her at first," McConnachie said.

"What changed your mind?"

"For one thing, she was too cool. I know imperturbability is a desirable trait for a surgeon, but that doesn't mean you don't care what's happening to a patient, especially a patient who's also a co-worker. But it was what Carmen said that really woke me up."

"Carmen, you told him about Mr. Washington?"

"Not only Washington, but the other patients Cynthia injected so she could look like a hero."

"That's why I couldn't believe it when you left me alone with that fucking psychopath."

"I know, I'm sorry, but you were on the ventilator, and I figured even if she gave you Fentanyl, you'd still be all right. I didn't expect her to paralyze you and disconnect the ventilator."

Nikki reached out and Carmen took her hand and squeezed it. McConnachie explained his epiphany. "After Carmen told me about the staged arrests, it clicked that Cynthia also injected you with Fentanyl."

"How did you figure out the Vecuronium?"

"Carmen and I kept going over your meds, and all we came up with were the eye drops, and the saline flush for the I.V. We decided to check the medication sheet for the unit, and see if Cynthia signed out any other drugs."

Carmen added, "Besides the ten cc's of Fentanyl at 8 a.m. for Mrs. Cummings, she also signed out Vecuronium four hours later for the same patient. According to her nurse, Mrs. Cummings never received the medication."

Nikki closed her eyes and nodded. Everything made sense. "Sign out drugs for one patient, and give it to another, just like she did with Mr. Washington."

"Exactly," Carmen said.

"The Fentanyl was supposed to kill me, and then they'd find the needle and syringe in my pocket. A typical o.d."

"But you screwed everything up by living," Carmen said, squeezing Nikki's hand and smiling. "When you didn't cooperate on the elevator, you forced her to go to plan B—paralyze you with Vecuronium, and disconnect the ventilator."

"I guess it wasn't the neurologist's fault that he declared me brain dead. He didn't know about the vecuronium."

"The problem was the vecuronium alone didn't explain your fixed and dilated pupils, and that's when Dr. McConnachie put it all together."

"The eye drops bothered me, because you didn't need them. And Carmen couldn't confirm they were saline. I saw Cynthia's jacket hanging on a hook. On a hunch I checked her pockets, and I found a bottle of Mydriacil."

"She gave me Mydriacil eyedrops?"

"That's how she dilated your pupils. And there was no reason why she needed to carry around a synthetic version of atropine, she's not an ophthamologist. She had no need to dilate anyone's pupils."

"The combination of Mydriacil and Vecuronium mimicked the brain dead state, and that's when Dr. McConnachie ran into the room and found you disconnected from the ventilator." Nikki embraced her, and Carmen pointed to McConnachie. "He deserves the credit. Sherlock ain't got nothing on him."

Nikki released Carmen and reached for McConnachie. They hugged, her eyes teared and Carmen handed her a tissue.

A knock on the door was followed by the arrival of Cogswell, Waddle, Lally, and, Harriet Thayer, the Chief Operating Officer for the hospital.

"There she is. How's our patient?" Waddle asked, not waiting for an answer. "You look no worse for the wear."

Nikki blew her nose.

"We're going to have to talk to our toy manufacturer and have them use you as the model for our next superhero series," George said, and Waddle nodded in agreement.

The nattering heads didn't disguise the true reason for their bedside visit: they were concerned about negative publicity for themselves and the institution, not Nikki's condition. It would've been better for them if she hadn't survived, her death dismissed as a drug overdose, the consequence of depression.

"I guess you heard what happened or else you wouldn't be here," Nikki said.

"We talked to Carmen—unbelieveable," Cogswell said.

"And that's the problem," Thayer added. "The whole story is unbelieveable. We're continuing to gather information, but Cynthia has denied your allegations."

"I wouldn't expect anything else," Nikki said.

Thayer turned to McConnachie. "You should know she intends to file a sexual harassment suit against you with the EEOC. Jinny Shay claims this wasn't the first episode but part of a pattern of abuse."

They all looked at McConnachie for his reaction, expecting outrage and a vehement denial.

"Is that so?" he asked.

"Yes, and this could get ugly," Thayer said.

"Is that so?"

Thayer grew impatient. "Dr. McConnachie, I don't think you're appreciating the full implication of being at the receiving end of a sexual harassment suit. Whether true or not, the media is going to jump on this story with both feet, and I'm afraid your name's going to be dragged through the mud."

The administrator was unfamiliar with the tenets of Trans-ZenCatholicism, and was baffled by McConnachie's lack of concern for his reputation. Recognizing she was not making progress with him, she turned her efforts to Nikki.

"We don't have any proof that Cynthia gave you the drugs, It's all very circumstantial."

Cogswell nodded. "I guess we're saying it may be in the best interest of everyone to work something out. We'll try and get Cynthia and Jinny to drop their charges, but it'll never happen unless you agree to do the same."

"You want us to forget the whole thing?" Nikki asked. She looked over at McConnachie.

"It's a no win situation," Thayer said.

"Just an opportunity for bad publicity," Cogswell agreed, his eyes darting between Nikki and McConnachie.

She waited for McConnachie to speak, knowing the allegations against him would be churned by the media and his reputation destroyed, but he remained silent.

Thayer petitioned further. "We don't want to pressure you for a decision, but Cynthia called a television reporter she knows, and is planning a news conference in thirty minutes. We'd like to formulate our response."

"Why don't we step outside and let you two talk," Waddle suggested. "And Nikki, I'm glad to see you're doing so well."

The covey flocked out of the room.

"I want you guys to know that whatever you decide, I'll be there for you," Carmen said, before she closed the door behind her.

It was a mess, and their course of action was unclear. Fighting it out in public was a no win situation except for Cynthia and Jinny. They enjoyed mudslinging because they were both pigs, and pigs like to roll in the mud.

"It looks like they have us by the short hairs," Nikki said. McConnachie remained calm, hands in labcoat pockets, unconvinced.

"I'm not concerned about their allegations," he said.

"But you don't need your reputation attacked, you worked too hard."

"I know, but when you try and control events, they backfire. I think it's best to just tell the truth."

Capitulating to Thayer's plan protected the institution but prevented justice. Cogswell's lab would continue to function, and continue to hurt patients with experimental drugs like BrobaGen. Before long Cynthia would restart her "injection and rescue" scheme and cause someone's death. McConnachie was right—go with the heart, and everything else would work itself out.

"I have an idea," Nikki said, but before she could share her thoughts with McConnachie there was a knock on the door.

The group filed back into the room. Nikki told them that if they could arrange it, she would speak to the press first. She planned to talk about BrobaGen, and she wouldn't mention the elevator incident. Waddle and Lally were both pleased with her decision, and anticipated an opportunity for free publicity for their breakthrough drug. The brain trust agreed that Cynthia would get the message after Nikki's announcement, and she and Jinny would drop their sexual harrassment allegations against McConnachie.

"You made the right decision. I think it's best for everyone involved," Cogswell said. The others nodded.

"You sure you feel up to a press conference?" Waddle asked, lowering his bifocals to the tip of his nose.

"I feel as ready as a milking cow at 11:00 a.m. that hasn't been milked."

Waddle took that as a "yes" after George gave him a thumbs up sign.

"We knew you were special," Waddle said, and then turned to George. "Let's get our people involved. I want as much media as we can get."

"Mac, why don't we all leave and let Carmen help Nikki get ready," Cogswell said, as he began herding everyone out of the room.

When everyone had left, Carmen walked over to Nikki and jerked out her I.V.

"Ow!"

"I'm sorry, but I can't believe you're letting them get away with this."

Nikki was about to explain, but she decided it was best if she kept everything to herself for now. Carmen helped her swing her legs over the side of the bed. Nikki dangled them before attempting to get up. When she was ready, Carmen assisted her out of the bed and supported her into the bathroom.

"Thanks Carmen, I can take it from here."

Nikki steadied herself with a hand on either side of the sink before looking into the mirror. Her face was pale, but otherwise recognizable. She washed and thought about what she was going to tell the media. It was an opportunity to take control of the situation and separate herself from the insanity before it took control of her. She gargled a generic mouthwash, which soothed her dry throat, and she got dressed. Carmen walked her up and down the hallway to make sure her legs were stable, then handed her over to Cogswell and Waddle, who escorted her to the auditorium. Media representatives of both radio and television cluttered the room, and Nikki was steered to a table distinguished by a gaggle of microphones each lettered with the moniker of their respective stations. Jinny and Cynthia were sitting with George in the first row just behind a wall of technicians shouldering cameras and lighting equipment. Waddle, Cogswell, Thayer and McConnachie mingled offstage to her left. A cardboard sign on the table in front of her indicated she was Nikki Moriarty, M.D., and she blinked when the cameraman turned on the klieg lights in preparation for her statement. One of the crew signaled they would be live on the air in ten seconds, and began the countdown with both hands raised above his head while a CNN reporter readied himself in front of the table with microphone in hand. When it was announced they were on the air, the reporter welcomed the audience to the Manhattan University Medical Center for an important announcement about a new cancer treatment from the Biosense company, and then introduced Dr. Nikki Moriarty.

"We have called this press conference to make the public aware of an experimental drug called BrobaGen, designed to fight cancer," Nikki began, and she could see Waddle and Cogswell, elbow to elbow, riveted to her every word. "This drug was created by Biosense Pharmaceuticals to reverse the debilitating weight loss that often occurs with cancer, and we have found, in a recently completed double blind study, that the patients who had received the drug experienced an increase in muscle mass and significant weight gain. In addition, their immunological parameters improved."

Nikki looked at Jinny and Cynthia. Their eyes were predatory, their heat palpable.

"The weight gain can help patients with cancer tolerate aggressive chemotherapy regimens that previously wouldn't have been possible."

Cogswell appeared pleased as the cameras zoomed in on Nikki for a close-up.

"This drug has other benefits. It can help strengthen the elderly and make them more independent, and in addition, allow our country's athletes to surpass their anticipated potential."

The reporter signaled one more minute, and directed Nikki to wrap it up.

"I've called this press conference not to promote this drug, but to warn the public about its dangers."

Cogswell and Waddle looked at each other as if they had misheard what Nikki had just said, and McConnachie stood behind them, smiling.

Nikki continued. "There's been a coverup by the investigators. They have withheld evidence that shows BrobaGen not only increases muscle growth, but also increases cancer growth, and patients have died prematurely as a direct consequence of this drug."

The reporter became animated at the unexpected announcement of a developing scandal, and sensing the newsworthiness of the story, signaled her to continue. Cynthia looked around like she was trying to find a weapon, a gun, something she could use to silence her. Thayer pushed Waddle and Cogswell towards the table, directing them to interrupt the announcement, but McConnachie grasped each of their arms, holding them back.

"Biosense Pharmaceuticals has supported and condoned unethical research with this drug on unsuspecting twins. The twin who received the drug increased in size, but there were side effects—serious side effects. BrobaGen precipitated a psychotic reaction in the boy that caused him to kill himself."

Questions were shouted from the audience, but Nikki held up her hands, asking for quiet.

"The people who were responsible for these violations are right here in this room: Dr. Cogswell, the Director of Oncology at this institution and the principle investigator of this cancer study; Dr. Waddle, the Medical Director of Biosense; and Jinny Shay, the research nurse, who withheld information and deceived patients in order to get them to agree to participate in the study."

Before Waddle and Cogswell could leave, they were intercepted by the cameramen and reporters, who demanded a statement.

Cogswell spoke into the microphones. "What you're not aware of is that Dr. Moriarty was just fired from our research department for incompetence, and she's a disgruntled employee with an axe to grind. I can assure your listeners that there was neither unauthorized nor unethical research carried out at this institution." Waddle and Thayer nodded in the background, and the reporter returned to Nikki for her response.

"I'm not talking about numbers, I'm talking about people. Documented cases like Mrs. Lamb, who died prematurely because BrobaGen caused her cancer to spread, and a child, Angus Crowe, who received BrobaGen without his knowledge and later committed suicide."

Jinny Shay grabbed the microphone in front of Nikki, and identified herself as the research nurse in charge of the BrobaGen study.

"What she's not telling you is that she's a drug addict who was just hospitalized as a result of an overdose, and you can check that out."

It didn't matter, the media was more interested in the bigger story—a drug that spread cancer instead of curing it, and the cameras were focused on the reporter who capsulized Nikki's announcement, expressing his concern about the effect of the drug on teenagers.

"This experimental drug, BrobaGen, was about to be marketed to unsuspecting youths, capitalizing on both their desire to improve athletic performance and their ignorance of the consequences." The reporter assured the audience there would be detailed follow-up to the story.

A scrum of reporters taunted Waddle, Cogswell, Thayer and Jinny with microphones, waving them in their faces while they shouted questions. Nikki got up from the table and walked towards McConnachie, who shooed away reporters and escorted her out of the building.

"What'd you think?" Nikki asked.

"You did good. Cynthia must've been disappointed that she didn't get mentioned."

"I figured I'd save her for the 19th Precinct."

They left the hospital and walked towards First Avenue, and as they neared the corner, her knees buckled. She grabbed McConnachie's arm in order to maintain her balance.

"Are you okay?" he asked, putting his arm around her waist to support her.

"Just weak."

"You need to lie down. I'll take you to your apartment."

"No, I'm in a hospital building and everyone's going to start asking questions."

"Then it's either my place or a hotel."

He hailed a cab, maneuvered her into the back seat, closed the door, and entered the opposite side. He directed the cab to 110th and Broadway, and as they pulled out, she rested her head on his shoulder and closed her eyes. An all-news radio station droned in the background, and when McConnachie heard the hospital's name mentioned, he asked the driver to turn it up. A spokesperson for the hospital announced that all members of the research team had been suspended pending the completion of a full investigation, and she reassured the public that patient care remained optimal and at no time was any patient's health at risk.

"A patient's health wasn't at risk, just a doctor's," Nikki said with her eyes closed. "The least they could've done was tell us we're suspended before we heard it on the news."

"That's the way institutions work. They protect themselves, not the individual."

"Don't even think about defending those bastards."

"I'm not defending them, just making an observation," he said, as he looked out the window.

"How can you not be pissed?"

"I guess I've come to accept the fact that there's evil in the world, so I'm not surprised when things like this happen."

"I better start meditating, because I can't deal with this shit as calmly as you."

The cab entered the Transverse at 97th Street, and Nikki stared at the passing stone wall.

"Don't worry, it's all going to work itself out," he said, reaching over and squeezing her hand.

"Your mouth to the goddess's ear," she said, and they both laughed, leaning into each other. Nikki smelled the scent of his laundered shirt.

When they arrived in front of his apartment building he got out of the cab, walked to the other side, and opened Nikki's door. She grabbed his outstretched hand, and as he pulled, she butt-hopped to the edge of the seat. With his support around her waist she was able to get up and walk to the apartment building. The doorman was busy talking on the house phone, but he gave McConnachie a nod of recognition. After they entered the elevator, McConnachie pushed the fifth floor button. Nikki wrapped both of her arms around his waist and rested her head on his chest. The elevator stopped at the third floor, and Nikki reflexively looked for the inspection certificate, but a sign said it was in the management office. An elderly woman entered and recognized McConnachie.

"Doctor, how are you?"

"Fine thanks. I'm sorry, but we're going up."

"That's okay, I'll come along for the ride. Is this your friend?" she asked, scanning Nikki, who remained limp.

"Yes," he said, as the elevator resumed its ascent.

"A nice looking girl, a nurse?"

"Not a nurse," he said, relieved they had arrived onto his floor. He traded good-byes, steering Nikki off the elevator, and they listed in the direction of his apartment.

After the elevator doors closed, he could hear the muffled voice of the woman. "The poor thing, that's why I never drink before five."

They weaved their way down the hallway and entered his apartment. He directed her into the bedroom and supported her with his arm while he yanked back the blanket and topsheet. She sat on the edge of the bed until he lifted her legs and directed her into the supine position.

"You want anything to drink?"

"Just sleep," she answered with her eyes closed.

"I'll be in the other room if you need me."

"Luke," she said, wanting to kiss him, but feeling too weak.

"What?"

"Thanks."

A beeper chirped and awakened Nikki the following morning. After she silenced it, she panned the painted walls of McConnachie's bedroom, devoid of adornments, and swung her legs over the side of the bed. When her feet docked with the floor, she pushed off the bed into a standing position. Beeper in hand, she walked into the bathroom, avoided the mirror, and lowered the toilet seat. While urinating, she read the message which requested she report to the Dean's office at 11 a.m. She flushed the toilet, turned on the shower, and adjusted the temperature. When it was hot but tolerable, she climbed into the tub and soaped her body. She looked forward to the meeting. It was an opportunity to set the record straight and have her suspension rescinded. Once the Dean understood the facts, he would apologize and initiate judicial proceedings against those who deserved it. The water drilled her face and streamed suds over her breasts and down her abdomen, the rivulets curling around her legs and into the drain. After she had dried and dressed, she walked into the hallway and found McConnachie sitting in the living room reading the paper. He looked up and smiled.

"How you feeling?"

"Hungover, but a helluva lot better than yesterday."

McConnachie got up, walked into the kitchen, and poured them both a cup of coffee. They sat down together at the dining room table. She told him about the Dean's office summoning her, and he agreed it was an opportunity to get the facts on the table. The chairman of surgery, Dr. Wimpset, was returning from a meeting in Chicago, and McConnachie had scheduled an appointment to discuss the events of the last twenty-four hours. He was confident the chairman would be supportive of them, but Nikki wasn't as convinced. Cogswell wielded influence with the department of surgery, and if the institution was looking for a scapegoat, she was its most likely target.

Her beeper went off again, and she read the message. McConnachie asked her if she wanted to use the phone.

"No, it's my father."

"I guess he's concerned about what he heard on television."

"Not really, he just wants insider information so he can respond to questions posed by his social circle." She checked her watch. "We better get going."

Nikki stopped at the hallway mirror and wiped her face with powdered paper. They agreed to regroup at the 72nd Street entranceway to the park after their respective meetings had ended. She thanked him again for his help and kissed him on his lips, a soft lingering kiss, and before he could decide what to do next she grabbed his hand and pulled him into the elevator.

"We better get a cab," she said.

When they arrived at the hospital, they headed off towards their respective destinations. The Dean's administrative assistant greeted Nikki and directed her into the conference room, where he awaited. Inside she was confronted with the Dean, Harriet Thayer, and Judy Stern, the in-house lawyer for the hospital. All three sat on the same side of the conference table, a tribunal of Supreme Court Justices weighing the evidence. She was directed to sit down opposite them, and the Dean informed her he had called the meeting to gather the facts before making any decision about the individuals involved. They had already interviewed Jinny Shay, Cynthia, Dr. Cogswell and Dr. Waddle.

"The accusations you made on live television were extremely serious, and placed the reputation of this institution in jeopardy," the Dean said, an opening statement that did not augur well.

"I agree going public was not the best way of handling things, but I didn't feel I had a choice."

"We always have choices," he said, and then proceeded to reprimand her for condemning Dr. Cogswell without evidence to support her charges. It was going to be a long morning.

The Dean had reviewed the BrobaGen data, and it was his opinion there wasn't any evidence that BrobaGen increased cancer growth in the patients studied. A multi-centered study that included a much larger number of patients with long term follow-up would have to be completed before any conclusion could be made that would substantiate her charges. At best her accusations were premature, and at worst libelous.

"But Mrs. Lamb had a favorable tumor, and within six months of receiving the drug she died of metastatic disease," Nikki said.

"That happens occasionally, and in addition, she's just one patient. You can't establish a trend with one patient."

Nikki agreed the numbers were small, but she was also concerned that patients who hadn't qualified for the study had been treated with the experimental drug anyway. He responded that he had reviewed the records, and all the patients had signed an informed consent before they were allowed to participate in the study.

There was no point in bringing up Cogswell's suppressed mouse study that proved BrobaGen increased tumor growth, because the Dean would dismiss it as irrelevant. Animal studies predicted what would happen to other animals of the same species, but not necessarily to humans. He wanted incontrovertible evidence BrobaGen was deleterious to humans, but that wasn't possible without a larger study population.

Nikki appealed to his sense of ethics. "Jinny was paid for each patient she signed up. She ignored the study protocols, and recruited patients who didn't qualify. People were deceived so she could make money."

"Capitation fees are an accepted practice in order to expedite research, and again, no patient was entered without an informed consent."

Nikki's tongue kept sticking to the roof of her mouth, and she moved it around, trying to moisten it.

"You should know that Jinny and Cynthia are members of an investment club, and they own shares in Biosense. They have a vested interest in Biosense succeeding."

Her last comment caused the lawyer to signal the Dean that she wanted to respond.

"In this country we all have the right to join clubs, whether they're investment groups or otherwise."

"I agree, but they owned shares in a company that they're working with."

"Isn't it true, Dr. Moriarty, that you owned shares in Biosense?" Thayer asked, undermining Nikki's argument.

Jinny and Cynthia must've told them that she was a shareholder, but she knew they didn't disclose they were the ones who had given her the stock certificates.

"They were purchased by Jinny and Cynthia in my name."

"You're telling us the first week you started in the lab, your co-workers purchased shares in your name and gave them to you as a gift?" Thayer looked over at the other members of the panel, who were shaking their heads.

"I admit it's unusual, but that's what happened. But it's not an issue. I sold the stock the next day."

"At a profit?" Thayer asked.

"Minimal," Nikki said, regretting she had brought up the issue to begin with. "But all the money was returned to them. I didn't keep any of it."

"There's a difference of opinion on that issue."

"A difference of opinion?"

"Members of that investment group—the Lunar Club—they informed us that pooled resources were used to purchase the stock, and 200 shares were obtained at your request. You never returned the money."

Nikki raised her voice. "They're lying."

It wasn't going well. Cynthia's version was more believable, and the Lunar Club members backed her up. Nikki tried to think of other information, facts they couldn't dismiss. Bringing up Mr. Washington's staged arrest would be foolish, because there wasn't proof to support her accusation—Cynthia had trashed his urine sample. It was time to focus on Angus, and Jinny's unauthorized research.

"Are you aware the medical examiner's office documented that the twin boy received BrobaGen, and–"

"Dr. Moriarty, excuse me for interrupting, but we all agree the boy had significant levels of BrobaGen in his blood. The problem is we have no proof he was given the drug by Jinny. In fact, she denies it," the Dean said.

"Then how else did he get it?"

"It's been suggested he obtained it from his mother, who was a participant in the BrobaGen study, which frankly, is a very plausible explanation."

"His father, the coach, told me that Jinny gave him an aerosolized version of BrobaGen and called it a supervitamin."

"Jinny addressed that issue. Biosense does produce an aerosolized vitamin supplement, which she gave to the coach for the benefit of both boys. He wanted to maximize their athletic performance, and, right or wrong, she thought it would help their immune system."

"But I have the cannister used, and it contains BrobaGen."

"Dr. Waddle informed us they are experimenting with an aerosolized version of BrobaGen, but it's confined to the lab. It hasn't been used on people."

"It was used on Angus Crowe."

"Let's assume the cannister you have in your possession contains, as you say, BrobaGen. We still can't prove the boy used that cannister."

The hospital lawyer raised her forefinger, indicating she wanted to make a point. "A court of law could decide in your favor, and you're welcome to seek relief through the judicial system, but this institution can't wait five or six years for all this to be sorted out. We have to make a decision now."

They had an answer for everything, and it was in their interest to support the majority opinion. If they took Nikki's side, the institution would have no choice but to sever their relationship with Biosense and terminate Dr. Cogswell, a renowned oncologist, whose cutting edge studies and experimental drugs attracted patients and filled beds. She had one last chance to convince them before they ended the so-called fact finding session—her Fentanyl overdose.

"Cynthia tried to kill me. She injected me with an overdose of Fentanyl in the elevator. My urine sample will prove I had Fentanyl in my system at the time."

They were silenced by her last point, and the Dean sat back in his chair as he formulated a response.

"One problem, Dr. Moriarty. How do we know you didn't inject yourself?"

She wanted to scream "Because I said so, asshole!" but that would not be an effective response. He was right—there were no witnesses, no one who could corroborate her claim, and obviously Cynthia was not going to admit to what she had done. The needle and syringe found in her pocket had been touched by several people, rendering fingerprints useless.

Harriet Thayer, the Chief Operating Officer, was anxious to deliver the final blow.

"Cynthia stated she wasn't in the building at the time of the overdose; she was with Jinny getting something to eat. Jinny confirmed that."

Big surprise. Cynthia lies and Jinny swears to it.

"Are you suggesting I injected myself with a lethal dose of a narcotic?"

"Your boyfriend thought you had injected yourself," the lawyer said.

"That's one of the reasons why he's my former boyfriend."

It kept getting worse. They believed everything Cynthia and Jinny had told them, seeing what they wanted to see.

"If I was an addict, how could I have functioned at such a high level, I mean such an outstanding level?"

"It's unlikely, but there have been similar case reports, including some very prominent people in their fields," the Dean said, flexing his psychiatric background.

She had exhausted her whole argument and, if anything, she had further incriminated herself. There was no way she was going to salvage her job and, in addition, she could now look forward to a lawsuit by Cogswell, Waddle and their lackeys for impugning their reputations.

"You said I could countersue. Will the institution pay for my legal fees?"

"It's our policy not to pay for either side in a dispute," the Dean said.

"You're saying that someone can hire a lawyer based on a contingency fee and sue me, but I have to pay hundreds of thousands of dollars out of pocket to defend myself."

"That's how our system works," the lawyer said, as if it was a system beyond reproach.

"I'm afraid your suspension still stands. When we conclude our investigation, we'll let you know our final decision," the Dean said.

Nikki had nothing else to say. All her contentions were circumstantial, and the other side had anticipated her allegations and supplied the Dean with a credible defense. She was not going to persuade him she was the victim. But, hopefully, she would have better luck with a jury. The interview was over, and she got up, nodded, and left the office. She pushed the down button and stared at a ceiling-mounted security camera sweeping the hallway while she waited for the elevator doors to open. When she arrived at the first floor, she exited the building and walked with her head bowed towards Central Park. Her career was destroyed, and after surviving Cynthia's murder attempt, she faced the threat of costly litigation and additional debt.

While she was crossing Fifth Avenue she saw McConnachie waving his arm from a park bench to get her attention. He was trying to read her face in order to determine the outcome of her meeting, but she saved him the trouble by giving him a thumbs down sign.

"Not good?" he asked when she sat down next to him.

"Worse than not good. I hope yours was better."

"Not by much. Wimpset was spooked by the sexual harassment charges against me."

"After everything you've done for the department?"

"People are out for themselves, even some chairmen."

"He didn't believe you?"

"He claimed his hands were tied by the Dean. He's too weak to stand up to him."

"I wanted to train here because I respected that prick, one of the first to do minimally invasive surgery. Turns out he's just a spokesman for the hospital lawyers."

"I guess that's why he's lasted so long."

There was no truth, just interpretations of the truth. And everyone's interpretation was based on their self-interest. The Dean didn't want to know what happened; the facts were for the courts to sort out. His goal was to choose the least traumatic course for the institution, something that could be reduced to favorable sound bites, and supplied to the news agencies by the head of public affairs. The chairman of surgery needed the support of both the Dean and the board of trustees to protect his job, and the best way to engender that support was by elimination of controversy. Wimpset would second whatever course the Dean and the Chief Operating Officer decided to take, and Nikki knew the solution with the least repercussions was firing a surgical resident suspected of drug abuse.

"What do we do next?" Nikki asked, knowing she was really asking what should she do next.

"It'll come to us," he said. They walked through the park towards the West Side.

He tried to reassure her that the truth would come out, it always did. But she was concerned it would be too late, and at too great an expense. They walked past a statue of a dog, and Nikki read the inscription out loud: "'Balto, The Heroic Husky Sled Dog.'"

She had no idea why New York City had commemorated an animal associated with the Arctic.

"A Miniature Poodle or a Shih-tzu I could understand, but a Husky?" she asked, managing a smile, looking at McConnachie for insight.

"It must've been one of those bets between mayors–the Mayor of New York bet the Mayor of Juneau that our team would beat their team. We lost, so we had to build a statue to a Husky."

"The only problem is, Alaska doesn't have any professional sports."

"I guess that rules out that theory," he said, and they both laughed, leaning into each other and joining hands.

They passed Sheeps Meadow, a well manicured valley of grass framed in the distance by a sierra of concrete and glass. They continued north along the walkway traversing Strawberry Fields, the memorial to John Lennon. The sinuous path led to the exit at 72nd and Central Park West, and they negotiated their way past a group of tourists who were congregating around a circular stone embedded in the path with the word "Imagine" inscribed. It was a memorial from his wife, Yoko Ono, a tribute to him and his song that imagined a world without conflict. While tourists placed flowers at the site, the tour guide pointed to the Dakota apartment building across the street where Yoko Ono lived, and told the group that Lennon's wife was able to look out her living room window and see the memorial she had built to her husband.

"His grave?" someone asked, pointing to the stone inscription.

"Yes, his grave right here in Central Park."

Nikki and McConnachie looked at each other, wondering if they had heard the same piece of misinformation.

"That tour guide could probably get a job with Biosense. He doesn't let the facts get in the way of a good story," McConnachie said, and Nikki laughed, squeezing his hand.

They continued up Central Park West, past the Museum of Natural History.

"Luke, what do you think'll happen next?"

"I don't know, but whatever it is, we'll deal with it. As long as we're alive, there's always possibilities."

Nikki admired his ability to remain calm, never getting too excited or too upset about anything. It was strange: she'd almost died, lost her job, and now was about to be sued by fellow employees, but yet she'd never felt happier. She stopped walking, and when he turned towards her she kissed him on the lips, his own responding to her overture. They rested their foreheads against each other and took a quiet moment, enjoying the new threshold of their relationship before resuming their journey.

When they arrived at his apartment building, he waved at the doorman and they sauntered to the elevators. The doors opened, and the elderly woman who had seen them the day before stood in the doorway.

"Feeling better, dear?" she asked.

"I'm fine, just a mild overdose," Nikki said, gesturing with her right hand as if she was injecting her left forearm with a needle.

The woman didn't know whether to smile or not, and she walked past them to the lobby without looking back. The elevator door closed and they laughed. When they entered his apartment Nikki removed her hair clasp and shook her head, and her hair unraveled onto the back of her neck, hovering over her shoulders. Luke wrapped his arms around her, and after nosing her hair out of the way, he nuzzled the hollow at the base of her neck. His lips dawdled towards her ear, micromassaging her skin, nipping every centimeter. A shiver of warmth penetrated to her spine and tingled down her back, producing a pleasureable groan. She extended her neck, encouraging him to continue, and after a pause at her earlobe, their lips conjoined, thighs intertwined, and their bodies writhed against each other's. Nikki knew it was time.

They faltered towards the bedroom like contestants in a three-legged race after too much to drink, fumbling with each other's clothes, their molting slowed by cotton impediments secured with buttons and snaps. At the bedside they teetered, then toppled together onto the bed, mindful only of the moment and unconcerned about the future.

Their bodies had responded to each other as if they had been together before, both familiar with each other's desires and preferences. Nikki lay limp, resting her head on Luke's thatch of chest hair, their limbs overlapping in repose.

"How you feel?" Luke asked, looking at the top of her head.

"Better than I ever imagined." She lifted her head towards him, kissing him.

"When was the first time you thought about us being together?" he asked.

"From the beginning, my first meeting with you."

"I got to admit, I thought about it too, but I talked myself out of it. Probably fear of rejection."

"For me it was fear of commitment. I've had a pattern of avoiding relationships with anyone I really cared about. I guess it's a way to avoid compromise."

Luke kissed her on the cheek, got out of bed, and walked into the kitchen, returning with two glasses of water. He gave one to Nikki.

"Its easy to become consumed by medicine, it happened to me," Luke said.

"It happens to a lot of people."

"You see so many relationships fall apart, but surgery, your job, remains a constant. It's always there."

"That's why the job becomes the priority, and either the marriage falls apart, or we end up with facilitators, not partners—people supportive of workaholics."

Luke nodded. "My wife and I, we stopped communicating. It was peaceful, but we weren't happy. And as long as there was peace, I didn't care."

"Same with me and Fred. I told you, I call it celibacy without abstinence. We slept together, but there was no emotional intercourse."

Luke chuckled. "Celibacy without abstinence, I like that. Emotional celibacy."

"It's true. I'm not blaming him, it's just the reality I wanted and created."

"All this stuff that happened, it really puts things in perspective. Everything's impermanent."

"No matter how smart you think you are about planning your life, it doesn't always work out that way," she said.

McConnachie leaned closer, staring at her eyes. "Are you crying?"

She wiped them with the sheet. "No... just happy."

McConnachie hugged her. "Me too."

A letter from the chairman of surgery was waiting for Nikki in the research lab the following morning. It began, "I regret to inform you," and ended, "I wish you every success in your future endeavors." Losing her job wasn't unexpected, but reading the official notification was painful. The institution had punished her for telling the truth, and refused to counter her enemies' portrayal of her as a disgruntled employee with a drug habit. Her eyes and throat burned as she tried to hold back tears, hiding her face from the hallway camera and the passing employees. Her career had always come first, ahead of family and friends, and now she had nothing to show for her sacrifice except a $200,000 debt with more to come. It was her first failure in life, it was huge, and it wasn't justified.

When the elevator doors opened, Luke was about to get off.

"I was just coming to see you," he said, opening up his arms, perceiving she was distraught.

"I just got fired," she said, wrapping her arms around him and resting her head on his shoulder.

"I heard, Wimpset told me."

"That bastard, at least he could've had the guts to tell me to my face. He leave you alone?"

"Sort of."

They left the hospital, removed their white coats and continued westward.

"What did you mean 'sort of'?"

"He gave me a verbal reprimand," Luke said, dismissing it with a wave of his hand as inconsequential.

Dr. Wimpset told Luke he was under pressure from the Dean to resolve things forthwith, and he had no choice but to fire Nikki and reprimand him for not preventing her from giving a public statement.

"I disagreed with his decision, but he wouldn't listen."

"He's too weak," Nikki said. "I keep telling myself that change is good, but I'm having trouble believing it."

"I guess we'd better believe it."

Nikki looked into Luke's eyes. "What's this 'we' shit?"

"I resigned."

"Resigned?"

"I told Wimpset if he didn't reverse his decision, I didn't want to work for him."

"But you know that bastard does whatever the administration says."

"If good people don't speak up, evil will triumph."

"But you spoke up, and evil triumphed anyway."

"Time will tell."

Would she have done the same thing for him—given up a secure position at a prestigious medical center because a resident had been wronged? In the past, the answer was a definite "no," but now was different. She realized there was something empowering about taking a proactive stand, and not capitulating to the decisions of others.

"I'll find a job and so will you," he said, putting his arm around her shoulders. "The guilty will be punished for what they did. It's the Law of Karma—what goes around, comes around."

"That's great if you don't mind waiting around for justice in another lifetime."

"If you can't change the outcome, there's no point in getting upset."

The only way to change the outcome at this point was lengthy and costly litigation, but even that investment of time and money didn't guarantee success. Besides, who wanted to spend five years of their life trying to convince others of the truth? But it wasn't just the lawsuits and losing her job that were upsetting, it was also the thought of Cogswell, Cynthia and Jinny continuing their research under the auspices of Biosense. The Dean had endorsed their investigative methods by his recent decision, and something had to be done now to stop them from damaging others.

"Luke, I don't like the idea of simply meditating on our fate."

"Don't mistake Zen serenity for passivity. You still do what's necessary to neutralize your enemy. You just don't become obsessed with their destruction."

"But right now we're not neutralizing anyone."

Luke didn't disagree. They circled back to the hospital, and an animal rightist greeted them at the entranceway with a flyer protesting the institution's use of animals for research. Nikki scrunched the paper into a ball as she passed through the revolving door and threw it into a garbage can. The hallway camera recorded them as they waited for the elevator, and Nikki digitilized an obscene gesture at the lens. Luke laughed while they walked through the opened doors, and as they were closing, Nikki jumped out, forcing the doors to retract.

"The camera!" Nikki exclaimed, pointing to the hallway security system.

"What about it?"

"That's our proof that Cynthia was lying. It must've documented she was in the hospital at the time of my assault."

Luke kissed her. "You're brilliant. Security should have the videotape."

They left the hospital, crossed the street to another building, and cantered to the headquarters for security located in the basement. After identifying themselves through the intercom, they were buzzed in by a secretary and directed to a room walled with television monitors recording the stream of pedestrian traffic in the hospital hallways. A security officer sat at a desk monitoring the screens. Nikki and Luke introduced themselves, and he shook their hands, staring at McConnachie.

"Dr. McConnachie, Vinny Imperato, firefighter from Ladder 110, Brooklyn. You operated on my brother Frankie, five years ago. A cop, shot in the belly, off-duty?"

"I remember. He was in a diner that was being robbed. He got shot when he identified himself as a cop."

"Right. Thanks to you he's doing great."

"That's good to hear."

"And your father was a brother, a firefighter in Brownsville, 123 Truck."

"You've got a good memory."

They discussed fellow firefighters and mutual friends while Nikki scanned the monitors.

"Luke," she said, pulling on McConnachie's sleeve and interrupting the smoke-eater palaver, "you can identify who's getting on and off the elevators."

Luke looked at the monitor and asked Vinny if he could download the tape of the first and seventh floors the day before yesterday between twelve thirty and twelve forty-five. Vinny nodded. He brought up the requested time sequence on the monitor so they could choose the specific segment they needed him to copy. After a couple of minutes, Nikki identified Harriet Thayer, the COO, animated and talking to someone in front of the first floor elevator. She walked away abruptly, and the other person turned towards the camera. It was Cynthia. The camera panned away from her and onto the empty elevator. It showed Nikki entering. Before the doors had fully closed, Cynthia reappeared and inserted her hand between the doors, forcing them to reopen, and then joined Nikki inside.

"Perfect. That proves she was on the elevator with me, and it also proves Thayer lied in support of Cynthia. She knew Cynthia was in the hospital, not at lunch with Jinny," Nikki said. She placed a hand on Vinny's shoulder. "See if you can catch us on the seventh floor. The elevator was stuck, it took a few minutes to get there."

"No problemo," Vinny said, switching to the seventh floor tape.

The camera showed the closed doors, and when they opened, Nikki staggered out, disheveled and unsteady. Several seconds later Cynthia left the elevator and headed towards the stairwell.

"We got it," Nikki said, squeezing McConnachie's hand in triumph.

The door to the room opened, and a female security officer appeared.

"What's going on, Vinny?"

"Sarge, just helping the docs with something."

"What kind of thing?" she asked glaring at Vinny.

"I think I can explain, I'm Dr. McConnachie and this is Dr. Moriarty, and we're both from the department of surgery," he said, flashing his identification card. "Dr. Moriarty was assaulted on the elevator two days ago, and we wanted to see if the perpetrator was recorded on tape."

"Security is well aware of the alleged assault on Dr. Moriarty, but no one's allowed to review these tapes without authorization."

"But we just want to document who tried to kill me," Nikki said, hoping that the gravity of the crime would cause the sergeant to acquiesce.

"I don't make the rules, I just enforce them."

"We understand," Luke said. Nikki looked at him wide-eyed, while shaking her head out of view of the sergeant.

Luke ignored her head signals, thanked both security officers for their help, and escorted Nikki by the arm out the door. The sergeant walked with them and apologized for not being able to help. Luke smiled and told her they understood her hands were tied. Nikki walked ahead of them, not able to understand why he was being so accommodating. She waited at the exit for him to finish his banter, trying to figure out where she had seen the sergeant's face before. She waved her hand at Luke, but he again acted as if he didn't see it, and the sergeant removed her hat to wipe her brow. Her hair was different, but the face was the same—she had met her at Cynthia's apartment. Nikki's heart palpated while she tried to think of a way to salvage the tape before the sergeant erased it. She signaled him to cut the conversation by skating her index finger across her neck again and again, but although he acknowledged her warning with a nod, he continued the conversation.

"Dr. McConnachie, I need to talk to you," she said, grabbing his elbow.

The sergeant said good-bye and returned to her office, while he walked away with Nikki.

"We got to go back in there," she said, trying to pull him towards the security office, but he resisted. "You don't get it—she's a member of Cynthia's investment club, and she's probably erasing the tape as we speak."

"Calm down," he said, which infuriated her even more.

"Let go of my arm. If you don't want to go with me, I'll go myself," she said, trying to pull away from his grasp.

"It's going to be okay."

"Okay? I thought you believed in neutralizing your enemies, not helping them destroy us."

"I do. We'll have the tape."

"Didn't you hear me? She's destroying it."

"Look, Vinny knew what was going on. Why do you think I walked out with her—to give him time to download a copy for us."

She released his arm. "How can you be so sure he did it?"

"He's a firefighter. He'll do the right thing."

"You gotta give me a better reason than that."

"You heard how grateful he was about his brother. When you were talking to the sergeant, he gave me a wink and a nod."

"And that meant he'd make a copy?"

"That's what it meant."

Luke's patients liked him because he exuded confidence; they felt protected in his hands, and Nikki felt the same way. When he said he would have a copy of the tape, Nikki knew it had to be true. She abandoned any attempt to return to the security office, and they walked outside together to return to the hospital. They crossed the street and heard the screech of rubber, the thwack of body against metal. They diverted to York Avenue to investigate the accident, and when they arrived a few people were surrounding a pedestrian who was lying in the street unconscious, a victim of a hit and run. The paramedics had just arrived, and one was taking her vital signs while the other immobilized her cervical spine. A witness said the woman was crossing the street and a Ford Taurus ran the red light and swerved right at her. She tried to jump back, but the side of the car brushed against her, and she fell, hitting the back of her head on the curb. The paramedic asked if the woman was ever conscious, and she said she was initially awake, and even talking, but then she blacked out.

"Lucid interval," Luke said to Nikki, referring to the classic sign of an epidural hematoma.

Her unconsciousness was caused by the build-up of blood inside her cranium that was compressing the brain. If it wasn't drained soon, it would cause irreversible brain damage. When the paramedics lifted her onto the stretcher, Nikki saw who it was.

"Luke, it's Harriet Thayer, the C.O.O."

They rushed back to the E.R. to alert the team that Thayer had a probable epidural hematoma and advised the triage nurse to notify the neurosurgeon. The patient arrived in the E.R., and after her vital signs were recorded and noted to be stable, she was rushed to the CAT scanner to confirm the diagnosis of epidural hematoma, and to rule out an intra-abdominal injury. The abdominal scan was negative, but the head scan revealed the epidural hematoma along with a predictable fracture of the tempero-parietal bone.

Nikki listened as the the radiologist reviewed the scan with a medical student, using his pointer to outline the fracture site. "You can see the fracture over the middle meningeal vessels. The lacerated artery bleeds between the skull and the dura mater, compressing the brain."

Luke stood with Nikki at the nurses' station, waiting for a response from the neurosurgeon who had been paged "stat" a half hour earlier. While Luke looked at the wall clock, Nikki thought about the videotape. Questions persisted. Why did Thayer cover for Cynthia, and not tell the Dean that Cynthia was in the hospital at the time of the assault? Why was she trying to protect her?

The nurse informed Luke that the O.R. was ready and the neurosurgeon was on his way, but they had been unable to contact the family.

"We can't wait. Let the administrator on call know we're going to the O.R. without a consent from the family. I'll write a note," he said. He walked to the patient's gurney to get her chart.

Nikki looked at the clock, hoping there was enough time to prevent permanent brain damage, and then saw Luke waving at her to join him.

"What did you tell me was the name of their female empowerment group?" he asked, cupping the pendant that hung from Thayer's neck in his hands. It was a five-pointed star that framed a representation of either the sun or the moon, and he showed her the inscription on the back.

"That's their symbol, the moon and the star, and that's the name, the Lunar Club. She's one of them—no wonder I got fired."

The orderly arrived, collected the chart, and wheeled the patient to the elevator. They rode with him and the patient and helped direct the gurney into the waiting O.R. The neurosurgery resident and the nurse slid her onto the operating table while the anesthesiologist began attaching the monitoring devices. The patient's head was positioned on the horseshoe-shaped Mayfield head rest, and the neurosurgical resident shaved her hair and painted her scalp with an iodine solution in preparation for the craniotomy. The attending neurosurgeon arrived and the resident showed him the CAT scan while describing the cause of injury. After reviewing the films they both went to scrub. Luke and Nikki returned to the E.R. to see if any family members had arrived, and they were introduced by a nurse to two detectives from the 19th Precinct, both wanting to talk to the patient's physician. Nikki told them that everyone was in the O.R., but they would try and answer their questions. The first thing they wanted to know was whether Harriet Thayer was going to make it. Luke said he expected her to survive, but the outcome depended on the operative findings and the extent of neurological damage. He explained they would have a better idea about her prognosis at the conclusion of the operation and after she had been examined in the recovery room. The police thanked them, and one of them told Luke that a witness had copied part of the license plate of the Ford Taurus. They were confident it wouldn't be long before they were able to make an arrest. While they talked, a security officer interrupted Luke and handed him a paper bag,

"I think you wanted this," Vinny said.

"Your boss say anything?" Luke asked.

"Not yet, but I'm sure I'll be hearing from her," Vinny said, flashing his Groucho eyebrows at a smiling Nikki.

"You sure you're okay with this?" Luke asked. "When we show this, they'll know where we got it."

"Hey, if they fire me because I gave you a tape of someone attempting murder, then I'm better off outta here."

Nikki and Luke thanked him, and before they left they received word that the patient was in the recovery room, stable, and responding to commands. It wouldn't be long before they had an opportunity to talk with her.

They didn't have an appointment with the Dean, but possession of the security tape trumped all other scheduled commitments. When they walked in two secretaries guarded the Dean's portal, preventing any interruptions of his printed schedule.

"We don't have an appointment, but we have an urgent matter to discuss with the Dean," Nikki said.

"He's in a meeting with Dr. Wimpset, but if you'd like to make an appointment—"

"We wanted to speak with both of them anyway," Nikki said, walking into the office with Luke right behind her. The secretary jumped up from her seat and followed them, apologizing to the Dean for their intrusion.

Nikki spoke before the Dean could ask them to leave. "We have a tape proving that Cynthia lied and was the one who injected me with the Fentanyl," Nikki said.

Luke inserted the recording into the office VHS machine, the Dean nodded to the secretary, and she left the room, closing the door behind her. Nikki narrated the video, identifying Harriet Thayer, who appeared agitated, walking away from Cynthia. In the next sequence Nikki entered the elevator and Cynthia interjected her arm between the doors, causing them to recoil. Cynthia joined Nikki inside and the doors closed.

"I'm sure you received word that Harriet Thayer is recovering from her injury, and maybe she'll share with us why she didn't counter Cynthia's claim of not being in the hospital at the time of my assault," Nikki said to the Dean, who remained silent. "Now you're looking at the tape from the seventh floor camera showing me stumbling out of the elevator after I'd been shot up with the Fentanyl, and a few seconds later Cynthia comes out and disappears down the stairwell."

"I admit the tape raises some questions," the Dean said slowly, and Wimpset nodded.

"It doesn't just raise questions, it gives answers," Luke said, emphasizing the significance of the video documentation to the supervisors.

He asked them how they had procured a copy of the security tape, but Luke wouldn't reveal his source because he didn't want to jeopardize Vinny's job.

The Dean was disturbed, not because the evidence exonerated Nikki and implicated Cynthia, but because it complicated the solution. The firing of Nikki and the reprimand of McConnachie had dispensed with the problem, but now it had been revived by two amateur sleuths.

He announced his decision. "The tape should be turned over to the police involved in the investigation of the case, but our resolution regarding Dr. Moriarty's employment remains."

"I don't understand," she said.

"Cynthia lied about not being in the hospital, but I still don't know what went on in the elevator—unless you have a tape of that also."

"There aren't any cameras inside the elevators," Nikki said.

"That's the problem. We still don't have proof that Cynthia was the one who injected you," the Dean said, and Wimpset nodded.

"But you see me in distress and Cynthia following me out of the elevator before she disappeared into the stairwell," Nikki said, not believing she still had to defend herself.

"Nevertheless, it doesn't prove anything. As we've said before, you people are going to have to resolve this in a court of law, not here," the Dean said, remanding the case to civil court.

"I'll say one thing, and I'm sure the Dean will agree, that tape really strengthens your lawsuit," Wimpset said, as if he expected thanks for his insight.

"We're not interested in suing—I know that sounds unAmerican—but we want justice now, not five years from now," Nikki said.

"I understand your frustration, but we're unable to change our decision," the Dean said.

"It's not that you're unable to change your decision, you just choose not to," Luke said, glaring at the Dean. He grabbed the tape out of the VHS machine and walked out with Nikki.

"What assholes," Nikki said. She had never seen Luke so upset before.

"And Wimpset sitting there, afraid to disagree."

"The Dean wasn't going to let the facts get in the way of his solution."

"I felt like grabbing those little twerps and shaking them," Luke said, as Nikki smiled at his outrage.

"Someone didn't meditate today," she said.

"You're right, and I'd better do it soon before I kill someone."

The tape should've restored Nikki's appointment, and extracted an apology from both the Dean and Wimpset, but instead she remained under suspicion and out of a job. It would take over five years to win the lawsuit, and she needed to acquire a position in another surgical program now. But it was unlikely that a chairman of surgery would want to hire someone who had been dismissed by another institution.

Luke beeper went off. It was the recovery room calling to let him know that Thayer was extubated. She was their last hope for a reversal of the Dean's decision, someone he couldn't ignore. What had she been arguing about with Cynthia, and would she be willing to disclose it? They walked over to the recovery room together, and her nurse told them that Thayer was able to talk. There were also two detectives waiting to question her about possible suspects. Luke reassured the nurse he would only need five minutes. Thayer was sitting up in bed wearing a turban of gauze. A face mask infused oxygen over her mouth and nose. Luke asked her how she felt, and she said she was happy to be alive with a functioning brain.

"It doesn't always work out that way with an epidural hematoma," he said.

"That's what I understand," she said.

Nikki apologized to her for bringing up an important matter while she was still recovering from surgery. Thayer nodded and told her to go ahead. She summarized the findings of the security tape, documenting she was aware that Cynthia was not only in the building at the time of the assault, but also in the elevator.

"We know why you protected Cynthia, we saw your pendant," she said, as if no further details were necessary.

"I thought I was protecting myself," she said, shaking her bandaged head.

The Lunar Club, she explained, was founded by her predecessor, the previous C.O.O., and it had started off as a sisterhood, a group of women who vowed to support each other in improving health care at MUMC. After Thayer became a member, her career advanced, and she climbed up the administrative hierarchy, eventually succeeding the founder as C.O.O. When Cynthia was voted president of the organization, things began to change. The emphasis on improving the health care system changed to investment opportunities, and in particular an obsession with Biosense.

"Cynthia started to make a lot of demands on me—salary increases, office space—that kind of thing. She insisted it was a violation of the tenets of the Lunar Club for people in power not to help advance the careers of their fellow members."

"And you complied," Nikki said.

"Up until I quit the club. I became uncomfortable with the Biosense stuff, and when I heard you requested withdrawal of the BrobaGen abstract, I knew there'd be trouble."

She feared her reputation would be compromised and her career damaged if it was known she was a Lunar Club member, especially when it was discovered she was the administrator who signed off on the increased salaries for Cynthia and Jinny. The raises were not justified; they were disproportionate increases compared to other employees with the same experience.

"What were you discussing with Cynthia in front of the elevator?" McConnachie asked.

"I insisted that the Lunar Club sell their Biosense shares in order to protect the MUMC from conflict of interest charges."

"She didn't agree?" Nikki asked.

"I think 'drop dead' is consistent with not agreeing."

When the Dean decided to suspend everyone pending the investigation, she ignored the opportunity to speak up. She was afraid to counteract Cynthia's claim that she wasn't in the building at the time of Nikki's assault. If Cynthia exposed her as a former member of the Lunar Club, her reputation would be compromised and her career ruined. But now was the time to set the record straight.

"I'm alive," she said, which said it all.

Nikki hoped Thayer's testimony would force the Dean to reconsider, but she wasn't optimistic. He already was aware Cynthia had lied about not being in the building, and that both she and Jinny were members of an investment group owning shares in Biosense. Nothing Thayer had said was additive. Sharing that she had once been a member of the Lunar Club herself would not matter, because the Dean didn't think there was anything wrong with University employees holding a financial interest in Biosense.

"Did you see the driver of the car?" Luke asked.

"I know it was Cynthia."

"You saw her?"

"It happened too fast, but I know it was her."

The car swerved from its lane, obviously with the intent to kill her. She had no enemies, no one to suspect other than Cynthia. Cynthia was angry when she had resigned from the Lunar Club, and in addition, Thayer was the only one who could counter Cynthia's claim that she wasn't in the building at the time of Nikki's assault. It was safer for Cynthia to get rid of her.

The nurse interrupted to draw some blood samples and to check the patient's vital signs. Nikki stepped out of the way and talked with Luke. He thought that Thayer could influence the Dean on Nikki's behalf, but he agreed there was no guarantee. They decided it was best to let the detectives get a statement and document what she had just told them. When the nurse finished, they thanked Harriet for her help and told her to concentrate on getting better.

"Dr. Moriarty," Thayer said, holding onto her hand, "I'm sorry— I should've spoken up."

"At least you've spoken up now, and hopefully it'll make a difference. Feel better," Nikki said, and she walked out with Luke.

They sat down in the waiting room, debating whether the Dean would respond in their favor after he heard Thayer's statement, but their discussion was cutoff by his arrival. He had come to visit his colleague in the ICU, and the Dean detoured into the waiting area when he saw the two of them sitting there.

"I thought you'd be interested to know the police identified the owner of the Taurus—it was Cynthia," he said, as if he had suspected it all the time.

Nikki waited for him to say that his previous decision about her employment status still remained, offering some lame explanation such as the car was owned by Cynthia, but it didn't mean that she was driving it at the time. It could've been stolen, unbeknownst to her. But this time there was no vacillation.

According to the Dean, Cynthia had been arrested for attempted vehicular homicide and was plea bargaining for a reduced charge in exchange for cooperation with the police. Cynthia told her lawyer she had evidence that Dr. Cogswell, in accordance with Biosense, had shrouded data that proved BrobaGen increased the spread of cancer. In addition, her friend Jinny had conducted an unauthorized study on a minor with the full knowledge of Dr. Waddle, resulting in the child's death.

"She also claims Waddle contracted her to kill you. I'm not sure what to believe." Luke smiled at Nikki, both of them gratified that the truth was going to finally come out. "In any case, Dr. Moriarty, I've reinstated your position."

She had been exonerated, but she was unsure whether she wanted to accept his offer. Cynthia would no longer be at the hospital, but Cogswell and Biosense would resume their collaboration while their legal team responded to the allegations. Luke understood her hesitation, and she knew he would support her either way.

"I appreciate your offer, but I don't feel comfortable working under Dr. Wimpset," she said, "and I certainly don't want to associate with Cogswell and Jinny." Nikki looked over at Luke who gave her a nod of support.

"I know where you're coming from, but it won't be an issue—they've all resigned."

Biosense had a contingency plan, and it was initiated when Nikki requested withdrawal of the BrobaGen abstract. Negotiations were begun with a Medical Center in one of the outer boroughs, and Biosense had offered to finance a research lab under the auspices of Dr. Cogswell, and a new cancer institute with Wimpset as the director.

"They're going to be allowed to continue where they left off?" Luke asked.

"We hold no authority over the decisions of other hospitals. I hope you'll reconsider," the Dean said, and he walked over to a nearby sink, washing his hands before he entered the ICU.

Nikki walked out with Luke, thinking to herself that corrupt academicians like Cogswell never get punished, they just take their support group with them to another institution. They went to a coffee bar to talk, and Luke asked the counterman for a small cup of coffee.

"No 'small,'" he said flicking his head in the direction of the wall display of cup samples and their titled sizes.

"He meant a 'tall,' and make that two," Nikki said. She held Luke's face between her hands. "Don't you know there's no such thing as 'small' in this country?"

"First comes the corruption of man, and then comes the corruption of language," he said, lifting the two cups of coffee from the counter and walking to a table. Nikki picked up sugar, spoons, and napkins before sitting down next to him.

"Plea bargain or no plea bargain, Cynthia is going away for a long time, you agree?" Nikki asked.

"I agree."

"I'm concerned about the others. They're going to discredit her and claim she lied about them in order to get a reduced sentence. Waddle will deny everything."

"That's a given."

"I guess they think I won't say anything. Too interested in protecting my career and all that."

"Not just your career. The last thing they'd expect would be for you to corroborate Cynthia's story after she tried to kill you."

The copies of the BrobaGen mouse study that documented the spread of cancer was safe in Nikki's apartment, along with the pilot study in which Cogswell had discontinued a college student from the experiment because of auditory hallucinations. Jinny probably destroyed the original paperwork, but they were unaware Nikki had her own copy. Dr. Green would verify the cover-up, especially since he was no longer going to be working for them.

"Think the D.A. would be interested in knowing about the aerosol cannister of BrobaGen that Jinny gave Angus?" Nikki asked.

"I think he'd be very interested."

"The coach spoke about the benefits of the drug Jinny had given him for his adopted son, and I'm sure we can get him to identify the aerosol cannister of BrobaGen as the 'super vitamin.' Once Jinny feels pressure, she'll finger Waddle and Cogswell as her silent partners in the experiment. And that'll put an end to Biosense, at least in this institution."

They drank their coffee content that everything was going to work out, a feeling she enjoyed whenever she was with Luke. He kissed her on the cheek.

"Nikki, there aren't too many people who'd have done what you did—risking career for a principle."

"You did."

"I guess we both did."

"It feels good."

On the way out they dumped their cups into a garbage can with "thank you" inscribed on its lid, and walked towards the park holding hands. Nikki had a feeling they would be spending a lot of time together, and that felt good too.

Check out these other fine titles by Durban House
online or at your local book store.

EXCEPTIONAL BOOKS
BY
EXCEPTIONAL WRITERS

A DREAM ACROSS TIME	Annie Rogers
AFTER LIFE LIFE	Don Goldman
an-eye-for-an-eye.com	Dennis Powell
BASHA	John Hamilton Lewis
THE CORMORANT DOCUMENTS	Robert Middlemiss
CRISIS PENDING	Stephen Cornell
DANGER WITHIN	Mark Danielson
DEADLY ILLUMINATION	Serena Stier
DEATH OF A HEALER	Paul Henry Young
HANDS OF VENGEANCE	Richard Sand
HOUR OF THE WOLVES	Stephane Daimlen-Völs
A HOUSTON WEEKEND	Orville Palmer
JOHNNIE RAY & MISS KILGALLEN	Bonnie Hearn Hill & Larry Hill
THE LATERAL LINE	Robert Middlemiss
LEGACY OF A STAR	Peter Longley
LETHAL CURE	Kurt Popke
THE MEDUSA STRAIN	Chris Holmes
MR. IRRELEVANT	Jerry Marshall
OPAL EYE DEVIL	John Hamilton Lewis
PRIVATE JUSTICE	Richard Sand
ROADHOUSE BLUES	Baron Birtcher
RUBY TUESDAY	Baron Birtcher
SAMSARA	John Hamilton Lewis
SECRET OF THE SCROLL	Chester D. Campbell
SECRETS ARE ANONYMOUS	Fredrick L. Cullen
THE SERIAL KILLER'S DIET BOOK	Kevin Mark Postupack
THE STREET OF FOUR WINDS	Andrew Lazarus
TUNNEL RUNNER	Richard Sand
WHAT GOES AROUND	Don Goldman

NONFICTION

BEHIND THE MOUNTAIN	Nick Williams
FISH HEADS, RICE, RICE WINE & WAR: A VIETNAM PARADOX	Lt. Col. Thomas G. Smith, Ret.
JIMMY CARTER AND THE RISE OF MILITANT ISLAM	Philip Pilevsky
MIDDLE ESSENCE— WOMEN OF WONDER YEARS	Landy Reed
SPORES, PLAGUES, AND HISTORY: THE STORY OF ANTHRAX	Chris Holmes
WHITE WITCH DOCTOR	Dr. John A. Hunt
PROTOCOL	Mary Jane McCaffree, Pauline Innis, and Richard Sand.

For 25 years, the bible for public relations firms, corporations, embassies, foreign governments, and individuals seeking to do business with the Federal Government.

DURBAN HOUSE FICTION

A DREAM ACROSS TIME   Annie Rogers

Jamie Elliott arrives from New York onto the lush Caribbean island of St. Lucia, and finds herself caught up in Island forces, powerful across the centuries, which find deep echoes in her recurring dreams.

AFTER LIFE LIFE   Don Goldman

A hilarious murder mystery taking place in the afterlife. Andrew Law, Chief Justice of the Texas Supreme Court, is the Picture of robust health when he suddenly dies. Upon arriving in The afterlife, Andy discovers he was murdered, and his untimely has some unexpected, and far-reaching consequences—a worldwide depression, among others. Many diabolical plots are woven in this funny, fast-paced whodunit, with a surprising double-cross ending.

an-eye-for-an-eye.com   Dennis Powell

Jed Warren, Vietnam Peacenik, and Jeff Porter, ex-Airborne, were close friends and executives at Megafirst Bank. So when CEO McAlister crashes the company, creams off millions in bonuses, and wipes out Jed and Jeff, things began to happen.

If you wonder about corporate greed recorded in today's newspapers, read what one man did about it in this intricate, devious, and surprise-ending thriller.

BASHA
John Hamilton Lewis

LA reviewer, Jeff Krieder's pick as "Easily my best read of the year." Set in the world of elite professional tennis, and rooted in ancient Middle East hatreds of identity and blood loyalties, Basha is charged with the fiercely competitive nature of professional sports, and the dangers of terrorism. An already simmering Middle East begins to boil, and CIA Station Chief Grant Corbet must track down the highly successful terrorist, Basha, In a deadly race against time Grant hunts the illusive killer only to see his worst nightmare realized.

THE CORMORANT DOCUMENTS
Robert Middlemiss

Who is Cormorant, and why is his coded letter on Hitler's stationary found on a WWII Nazi bomber preserved in the Arctic? And why is the plane loaded with Goering's plundered are treasures? Mallory must find out or die. On the run from the British Secret Service and CIA, he finds himself caught in a secret that dates back to 1945.

CRISIS PENDING
Stephen Cornell

When U.S. oil refineries blow up, the White House and the Feds move fast, but not fast enough. Sherman Nassar Ramsey, terrorist for hire, a loner, brilliant, multilingual, and skilled with knives, pistols, and bare hands, moves around the country with contempt, ease and cunning.

As America's fuel system starts grinding to a halt, rioting breaks out for gasoline, and food becomes scarce, events draw Lee Hamilton's wife, Mary, into the crisis. And when Ramsey kidnaps her, the battle becomes very personal.

DANGER WITHIN
Mark Danielson

Over 100 feet down in cold ocean waters lies the wreck of pilot Kevin Hamilton's DC-10. In it are secrets which someone is desperate to keep. When the Navy sends a team of divers from the Explosives Ordinance Division, a mysterious explosion from the wreck almost destroys the salvage ship. The FBI steps in with Special Agent Mike Pentaglia. Track the life and death of Global Express Flight 3217 inside the gritty world of aviation, and discover the shocking cargo that was hidden on its last flight.

DEADLY ILLUMINATION
Serena Stier

It's summer 1890 in New York City. A ebullient young woman, Florence Tod, must challenge financier, John Pierpont Morgan, to solve a possible murder. J.P.'s librarian has ingested poison embedded in an illumination of a unique Hildegard van Bingen manuscript. Florence and her cousin, Isabella Stewart Gardner, discover the corpse. When Isabella secretly removes a gold tablet from the scene of the crime, she sets off a chain of events that will involve Florence and her in a dangerous conspiracy.

HANDS OF VENGEANCE
Richard Sand

Private detective Lucas Rook returns still haunted by the murder of his twin brother. What seems like an easy case involving workplace violations, the former homicide detective finds himself locked in a life and death struggle with the deadly domestic terrorist group, The Brothers of the Half Moon. A must-read for lovers of dark mysteries.

HOUR OF THE WOLVES   Stephane Daimlen-Völs

After more than three centuries, the *Poisons Affair* remains one of history's great, unsolved mysteries. The worst impulses of human nature—sordid sexual perversion, murderous intrigues, witchcraft, Satanic cults—thrive within the shadows of the Sun King's absolutism and will culminate in the darkest secret of his reign; the infamous *Poisons Affair*, a remarkably complex web of horror, masked by Baroque splendor, luxury and refinement.

A HOUSTON WEEKEND   Orville Palmer

Professor Edward Randall, not-yet-forty, divorced and separated from his daughters, is leading a solitary, cheerless existence in a university town. At a conference in Houston, he runs into his childhood sweetheart. Then she was poverty-stricken, American Indian. Now she's elegantly attired, driving an expensive Italian car and lives in a millionaires' enclave. Will their fortuitous encounter grow into anything meaningful?

JOHNNIE RAY AND MISS KILGALLEN   Bonnie Hearn Hill
                                        and Larry Hill

Based on the real-life love affair between 1950's singer Johnnie Ray and columnist Dorothy Kilgallen. They had everything—wealth, fame, celebrity. The last thing they needed was love. *Johnnie Ray and Miss Kilgallen* is a love story that travels at a dangerous, roaring speed. Driven close to death from their excesses, both try to regain their lives and careers in a novel that goes beyond the bounds of mere biography.

THE LATERAL LINE   Robert Middlemiss

Kelly Travert was ready. She had the Israeli assassination pistol, she had coated the bullets with garlic, and tonight she would kill the woman agent who tortured and killed her father. When a negotiator for the CIA warns her, suddenly her father's death is not so simple anymore.

LEGACY OF A STAR   Peter Longley

Greed and murder run rampant—the prize: desert commerce of untold wealth, and the saving of the Jews. From the high temples to Roman barracks; from bat filled caves to magnificent villas on a sun-drenched sea; to the chamber of Salome, and the barren brothels where Esther rules, the Star moves across the heavens and men die—while a child is born.

LETHAL CURE   Kurt Popke

Dr. Jake Prescott is a resident on duty in the emergency room when medics rush in with a double trauma involving patients sustaining injuries during a home invasion. Jake learns that one patient is the intruder, the other, his wife, Sara. He also learns that his four-year-old daughter, Kelly, is missing, and his patient may hold the key to her recovery.

THE MEDUSA STRAIN   Chris Holmes
Finalist for *ForeWord Magazine's* 'Book of the Year'. A gripping tale of bio-terrorism that stunningly portrays the dangers of chemical warfare. Mohammed Ali Ossman, a bitter Iraqi scientist who hates America, breeds a deadly form of anthrax, and develops a diabolical means to initiate an epidemic. It is a story of personal courage in the face of terror, and of lost love found.

MR. IRRELEVANT   Jerry Marshall
Booklist Star Review. Chesty Hake, the last man chosen in the NFL draft, has been dubbed Mr. Irrelevant. By every yardstick, he should not be playing pro football, but because of his heart and high threshold for pain, he endures. Then during his eighth and final season, he slides into paranoia, and football will never be the same.

OPAL EYE DEVIL   John Hamilton Lewis
"Best historical thriller in decades." *Good Books.* In the age of the Robber Baron, *Opal Eye Devil* weaves an extraordinary tale about the brave men and women who risk everything as the discovery of oil rocks the world. The richness and pageantry of two great cultures, Great Britain and China, are brought together in a thrilling tale of adventure and human relationships.

PRIVATE JUSTICE   Richard Sand
Ben Franklin Award 'Best Mystery of the Year'. After taking brutal revenge for the murder of his twin brother, Lucas Rooks leaves the NYPD to become a private eye. A father turns to Rook to investigate the murder of his daughter. Rook's dark journey finds him racing to find the killer, who kills again and again as *Private Justice* careens toward a startling end.

ROADHOUSE BLUES   Baron R. Birtcher
From the sun-drenched sands of Santa Catalina Island to the smoky night clubs and back alleys of West Hollywood, Roadhouse Blues is a taut noir thriller. Newly retired Homicide detective Mike Travis is torn from the comfort of his chartered yacht business into the dark, bizarre underbelly of Los Angeles's music scene by a grisly string of murders.

RUBY TUESDAY   Baron R. Birtcher
When Mike Travis sails into the tropical harbor of Kona, Hawaii, he expects to put LA Homicide behind him. Instead, he finds the sometimes seamy back streets and dark underbelly of a tropical paradise and the world of music and high finance, where wealth and greed are steeped in sex, vengeance, and murder.

SAMSARA
John Hamilton Lewis

A thrilling tale of love and violence set in post-World War II Hong Kong. Nick Ridley, a captain in the RAF, is captured and sent to the infamous Japanese prisoner-of-war camp, Changi, in Singapore. He survives brutal treatment at the hands of the camp commandant, Colonel Tetsuro Matashima. Nick moves to Hong Kong, where he re-unites with the love of his life, Courtney, and builds a world-class airline. On the eve of having his company recognized at the Crown Colony's official carrier, Courtney is kid-napped, and people begin to die. Nick is pulled into the quagmire, and must once again face the demon of Changi.

SECRET OF THE SCROLL
Chester D. Campbell

Finalist '*Deadly Dagger*' award, and *ForeWord Magazine's* 'Book of the Year' award. Deadly groups of Palestinians and Israelis struggle to gain possession of an ancient parch-ment that was unknowingly smuggled from Israel to the U.S. by a retired Air Force investigator. Col. Greg McKenzie finds himself mired in the duplicitous world of Middle East politics when his wife is taken hostage in an effort to force the return of the first-century Hebrew scroll.

SECRETS ARE ANONYMOUS
Frederick L. Cullen

A comic mystery with a cast of characters who weave multiple plots, puzzles, twists, and turns. A remarkable series of events unfold in the lives of a dozen residents of Bexley, Ohio. The journalism career of the principle character is derailed when her father shows up for her college graduation with his boyfriend on his way to a new life in California.

THE SERIAL KILLER'S DIET BOOK
Kevin Postupack

Finalist *ForeWord Magazine's* Book of the Year' award. Fred Orbis is fat, but he dreams of being Frederico Orbisini, internationally known novelist, existential philoso-pher, raconteur, and lover of women. Both a satire and a reflection on morals, God and the Devil, beauty, literature, and the best-seller-list, *The Serial Killer's Diet Book* is a delightful look at the universal human longing to become someone else.

THE STREET OF FOUR WINDS
Andrew Lazarus

Paris, just after World War II. A time for love, but also a time of political ferment. In the Left Bank section of the city, Tom Cortell, a tough, intellectual journalist, finally learns the meaning of love. Along with him is a gallery of fascinating characters who lead a merry and sometimes desperate chase between Paris, Switzerland, and Spain in search of themselves.

TUNNEL RUNNER
Richard Sand

A fast, deadly espionage thriller peopled with quirky and sometimes vicious charac-ters, *Tunnel Runner* tells of a dark world where murder is committed and no one is brought to account, where loyalties exist side by side with lies and extreme violence.

WHAT GOES AROUND
Don Goldman

Finalist *ForeWord Magazine's* 'Book of the Year' award. Ray Banno, a medical researcher, was wrongfully incarcerated for bank fraud. *What Goes Around* is a dazzling tale of deception, treachery, revenge, and nonstop action that resolves around money, sex, and power. The book's sharp insight and hard-hitting style builds a high level of suspense as Banno strives for redemption.

DURBAN HOUSE NONFICTION

BEHIND THE MOUNTAIN: A CORPORATE SURVIVAL BOOK
Nick Williams

A harrowing true story of courage and survival. Nick Williams is alone, and cut off in a blizzard behind the mountain. In order to survive, Nick called upon his training and experience that made him a highly-successful business executive. In *Behind the Mountain: A Corporate Survival Book*, you will fine d the finest practical advice on how to handle yourself in tough spots, be they life threatening to you, or threatening to your job performance or the company itself. Read and learn.

FISH HEADS, RICE, RICE WINE & WAR
LTC. Thomas G. Smith (Ret.)

A human, yet humorous, look at the strangest and most misunderstood war ever, in which American soldiers were committed. Readers are offered an insiders view of American life in the midst of highly deplorable conditions, which often lead to laughter.

JIMMY CARTER AND THE RISE OF MILITANT ISLAM
Philip Pilevsky

One of America's foremost authorities on the Middle East, Philip Pilevsky argues that President Jimmy Carter's failure to support the Shah of Iran led to the 1979 revolution. That revolution legitimized and provided a base of operations for militant Islamists across the Middle East. A most thought provoking book.

MIDDLE ESSENCE... WOMEN OF WONDER YEARS
Landy Reed

A wonderful book by renowned speaker, Landy Reed that shows how real women in real circumstances have confronted and conquered the obstacles of midlife. This is a must have guide and companion to what can be the most significant and richest years of a woman's life.

PROTOCOL
(25th Anniversary Edition)

Mary Jane McCaffree,
Pauline Innis, and
Richard Sand

Protocol is a comprehensive guide to proper diplomatic, official and social usage. The Bible for foreign governments, embassies, corporations, public relations firms, and individuals wishing to do business with the Federal Government. "A wealth of detail on every conceivable question, from titles and forms of address to ceremonies and flag etiquette." Department of State Newsletter.

SPORES, PLAGUES, HISTORY: Chris Holmes
THE STORY OF ANTHRAX
    "Much more than the story of a microbe. It is the tale of history and prophecy woven into a fabric of what was, what might have been and what might yet be. What you are about to read is real—your are not in the Twilight Zone—adjusting your TV set will not change the picture. However, it is not hopeless, and we are not helpless. The same technology used to create biological weapons can protect us with better vaccines and treatments." CDR Ted J. Robinson, *U.S. Navy Epidemiologist.*

WHITE WITCH DOCTOR   John A. Hunt
    A true story of life and death, hope and despair in apartheid-ruled South Africa. White Witch Doctor details, white surgeon, John Hunt's fight to save his beloved country in a time of social unrest and political upheaval, drawing readers into the world of South African culture, mores and folkways, superstitions, and race relations.